החומדה

The ArtScroll History Series®

Rabbi Nosson Scherman / Rabbi Meir Zlotowitz
General Editors

FLIGHT

A Jewish family's valiant struggle to escape Nazi occupation

by Renee Worch

Published by
Mesorah Publications, ltd

FIRST EDITION
First Impression . . . June, 1988

Published and Distributed by
MESORAH PUBLICATIONS, Ltd.
Brooklyn, New York 11223

Distributed in Israel by
MESORAH MAFITZIM / J. GROSSMAN
Rechov Harav Uziel 117
Jerusalem, Israel

Distributed in Europe by
J. LEHMANN HEBREW BOOKSELLERS
20 Cambridge Terrace
Gateshead, Tyne and Wear
England NE8 1RP

THE ARTSCROLL HISTORY SERIES®
"FLIGHT"
© Copyright 1988, by MESORAH PUBLICATIONS, Ltd.
1969 Coney Island Avenue / Brooklyn, N.Y. 11223 / (718) 339-1700

No part of this book may be reproduced
in any form *without* **written** *permission from the copyright holder,*
except by a reviewer who wishes to quote brief passages in connection with a review
written for inclusion in magazines or newspapers.

THE RIGHTS OF THE COPYRIGHT HOLDER WILL BE STRICTLY ENFORCED.

ISBN
0-89906-490-6 (hard cover)
0-89906-491-4 (paperback)

Typography by CompuScribe at ArtScroll Studios, Ltd., Brooklyn, NY
1969 Coney Island Avenue / Brooklyn, N.Y. 11223 / (718) 339-1700

Printed in the United States of America by Noble Book Press Corp.
Bound by Sefercraft, Quality Bookbinders, Ltd. Brooklyn, N.Y.

This book is dedicated to the

memory of our beloved parents ע״ה

and

our treasured son

יחזקאל שרגא ז״ל

who gave me so much encouragement

to record these events.

Preface

At a recent bar-mitzvah party for my great-nephew Sholem Marcovits, his great-uncle was asked to say a few words. He rose to his feet and looked around, his gaze affectionately taking in the family assembled on this happy occasion. They had gathered in London from as far away as Australia, Israel, and North and South America.

Instead of giving the usual learned discourse, as expected, he surprised all present with these words:

"It is now forty-six years since Sholem's *Zeyde* (grandfather) celebrated his bar-mitzvah in Antwerp.

"The darkening clouds of the Holocaust were already gathering over the country; Jews in our town had heard first-hand accounts of what was happening from the many German and Austrian refugees who had come to settle in our community. Soon afterwards, we too had to flee." He paused for a moment, then continued. "I feel the time has come to tell our children and grandchildren about the truly amazing miracles we have lived through, and the *hashgachah pratis* which helped us to survive.

"There are not many of us left who remember, and in another thirty years there will be no one left of whom to ask." He then related a few remarkable incidents to the eager listeners.

❈   ❈   ❈

Well, dear reader, I have decided to follow his example and recount the miracles of which I have immediate knowledge. These are the *nissim* performed for members of my family and some acquaintances, as I remember them today and as related to me by several relatives and friends, all teenagers growing up in Europe during those fateful years.

Acknowledgments

Much time elapses between the writing of a first draft and the book in its final form. During that time many other people become involved; old friendships grow even stronger while many new ones develop.

I am grateful to:

My dear brother and my dear sister-in-law for patiently bearing the considerable demands I have made on their time;

Mrs. Anne James for her help whenever called upon;

Rabbi Meir Zlotowitz and Rabbi Nosson Scherman, general editors of ArtScroll Mesorah Publications, whose initial warmth and encouragement only increased as this project came into fruition;

Mrs. Nina Ackerman Indig who meticulously and devotedly edited the entire manuscript;

Rabbi Sheah Brander for his excellence in graphic design, and his associate Michael Horen for the beautiful color illustration on the dust jacket;

Rabbi Avie Gold, Shimon Golding, Sheila Tennenbaum, Mrs. Faygie Weinbaum, Mrs. Menucha Silver, Zissi Glatzer and Chavi Gluck of the ArtScroll team for their efficiency in handling details, each in his own field of expertise;

And, above all, to my dear husband for the help and loving support he has shown during these very difficult times.

R. N.
June 16, 1988
2 Rosh Chodesh Tammuz 5748

Prologue

May 10th, 1940
3:25 A.M.

The faint light of early dawn was breaking over the horizon. Looking up, one would not have noticed the ominous dark shapes gliding silently across the morning sky, coming ever closer to their targets. They had left their air base somewhere near Cologne on a mission of destruction, without benefit of a formal declaration of war. This was the culmination of six months of intensive training. Excitement and bravado made these crack German airborne troops heady with anticipation, but they were far too disciplined to allow it to affect their performance. They knew that the success of the invasion of Belgium and Holland depended on achieving their objective, which was to capture the four bridges with the minimum of damage. These bridges spanning the Albert Canal at Maastricht, on the border with Holland, would be the conquerors' gateway into Belgium.

Twenty miles from their targets, the gliders dropped dummy parachutists with firecrackers attached, to confuse the defenders, while the glider-borne shock troops, towed by Junkers-52 transport planes, closed in on their unsuspecting targets. Not only did they aim to capture the bridges, but simultaneously to destroy the Eben-Emael fortification, deemed to be the most formidable defense system then in existence.

When dawn gave way to sunrise, the full horror of the treachery became apparent. Over three thousand five hundred planes were unleashed on a sleeping, peace-loving nation. The Luftwaffe's fighters and Stuka dive bombers flew overhead to protect the Panzer divisions as they seized the four vital bridges over the canals. The Belgian troops, fighting heroically against overwhelming odds, managed to destroy one of the bridges.

Choosing their targets with great precision, the German warplanes fanned out simultaneously over Holland and Belgium, destroying most of the planes on the airfields and blowing up the ammunition dumps. So total was the surprise that they had hardly any anti-aircraft flak to contend with.

One of the great ammunition dumps to be destroyed was in Berchem, just a twenty minute stroll from the heart of the Jewish quarter in Antwerp.

The district rocked and shook with each successive explosion, sending shock waves through every part of the city.

The attack put an end not only to our sleep, but also to our safety. And thus began a terrifying adventure which most participants did not survive . . .

Chapter One

I was awakened by a strange rattling noise coming from the windows in my bedroom. I had never been disturbed by rattling windows before. I lay still and listened for a moment. All was quiet. Then the noise started again. Not only did the windows vibrate, but our bedroom rocked on its foundation. Jumping out of bed, I almost collided with my sister, who had also chosen that precise moment to race to the window and investigate. Panic rising within us, we flung the windows open and watched in horrified fascination as two aircraft engaged in a dogfight, machine guns blazing. A lone Belgian fighter was belatedly trying to lure the German plane away from the ammunition depot.

So began our introduction to a new era that brought in its wake death, destruction, hunger, and untold misery to millions of people — most particularly, to Jewish people.

Our bedroom window overlooked the courtyard of the thriving wholesale fruit market. Small groups of people were gathered in earnest discussion, frequently peering anxiously up into the sky. I was not to know, nor would I have believed, that our days in the apartment, which had always been home to me, would soon be no more than a fond memory. To leave one's home, one's belongings, a lifetime of accumulations — be they priceless treasures, or humble but lovingly-cared-for possessions — is an incomprehensible experience to anyone brought up in the comparative peace and safety of our present-day existence.

But that was still to come. Meanwhile, we stood there in silence, realization creeping into our minds and adding to our bewilderment. The dreaded war with Germany had begun!

"Esti," I ventured, as we both absent-mindedly watched the men moving about in the courtyard below, "tell me, does this mean that we too will have the Gestapo coming and arresting Jews, as they are doing in Germany and Austria?" She shrugged her shoulders, not wanting to dwell on this horrifying subject. We were only too familiar with the stories of unspeakable torture and deprivation being inflicted on innocent humans just because they were Jews. But little did we know then that man's inhumanity to man was to result in the most savage brutalities in the annals of our Jewish history.

A welcome diversion from our gloomy thoughts came when Pappa and the boys arrived home from the synagogue. We hastily dressed and joined the rest of the family in the dining room. This room also served as a temporary bedroom for our grandmother, Oma, and our cousin Edith, who had arrived the previous year from Austria, and were waiting for the rest of the family to join them — a reunion that, sadly, never took place.

In spite of the gravity of the occasion, we were filled with an ever-growing sense of excitement as we waited for the three grownups who, quite oblivious of us, were now engaged in earnest conversation.

The anxious looks on their solemn faces told us that, unfortunately, our fears were well founded. Pappa's troubled but caring gaze held each of us in turn: Esti, less than two years my senior, and the eldest at sixteen, petite, with jet black hair which she constantly brushed until it resembled a shimmering silk curtain. My own blond curls, in contrast, never stayed in place, so I kept them under control in two bunches. I envied Esti's immaculate coiffure, as I did everything else about her. Then there were the three boys: Yehuda, thirteen, whom we all called Brudi, small and studious, always mindful of his parents' wishes; Ziggy, ten, and Shmuli, eight, perpetually engaged in trying to beat each other at a game of marbles. Lastly, Pappa's eyes rested on our lovable four-year-old cousin whom we all called "little Edith." Well, she wasn't very big.

In those precious moments there was a closeness that needed no conversation, borne out of a sense of imminent danger and frustration, and we drew comfort from each other's nearness. Pappa decided that it would be best for all concerned if we went to school as usual, so we ate breakfast and left the house at our regular time. We went quite happily, in anticipation of being able to exchange news with the other students.

Before leaving the apartment I went to little Edith. She was standing in her favorite place, by the open window, looking out. I bent to kiss her, but she hardly noticed. Not wishing to disturb her, I hurried out, reflecting as I walked how this child would stand for hours staring silently into the distance, never complaining and never crying, looking as far as her mind's eye would take her, to another place and another time. Perhaps she was looking into the home she had left behind, searching for the mother she longed to see...

What monster of a nation is this, I wondered, that can deprive little children of their parents?

Chapter Two

In my class were a number of refugee girls, a few from Germany and one from Austria. They seemed to draw comfort from telling us hair-raising tales. Just to hear them mention the SS would fill us with terror. We heard of fathers and uncles and even older brothers being brutally beaten and deprived of their livelihood. Atrocities against innocent women and children, however, were not yet common. These were still to come.

"Renée, Renée!" It was my friend calling me, making me snap out of my reverie. Grateful to be distracted, I turned toward her. Feeling very important, I said, "Oh, Anneke, you should have heard the explosions this morning! They made the windows rattle, and we watched two planes fighting. It was so exciting!"

"Bah!" said my friend. "You just heard it, but we live in Berchem and we could actually see the ammunition exploding, sending up a sheet of flames! It lit up the whole area, as if giant spotlights had been focused onto the whole place."

Of course! Anneke lived opposite the ammunition depot. I looked at her in wonder. So that was the cause of the terrific noise and rattling that had woken us so early! Anneke was still panting from running to catch up with me. "Are you all right?" I asked. "I mean, you live so near, did your house get damaged?" Anneke's parents were well-to-do and had a beautiful home in Berchem.

"It is truly amazing, but there seems to be no damage to the house," she replied. Nevertheless, her mother had been badly shaken, and had been persuaded to go back to bed and rest.

As we approached our school, we met several other girls and, still exchanging stories, we walked into the school playground, which was now rapidly filling up with girls all talking excitedly.

"Did you hear the machine guns?" asked one.

"Yes, and the thunder!" said another.

"Don't be silly, that was an explosion, not thunder!"

"My father said that in another day the Germans will walk into Antwerp."

"Oh, how could you say such a thing?" exclaimed a horrified girl.

"My brother was called up to the army this morning," the first one explained. "He assured me that we can fight off the Germans as long as we have control of the bridges, and he said that no one was going to take those away from us. And he should know!" she concluded, with unashamed pride in her soldier brother. So it went on . . .

We did not even notice that the headmistress, followed by all the teachers, had entered the playground, and were walking towards the raised platform near the entrance to the sewing room. Immediately the playground fell silent. The look on their faces was strange and unfamiliar. They didn't look strict and critical — they were solemn and vulnerable, just like other people! The headmistress surveyed the playground with a practiced eye. Did I just imagine that her gaze lingered sadly on the few Jewish girls in the predominantly Christian state school?

I came out of my reverie just in time to catch the last sentence of her address, ". . . So under the circumstances, I have decided to close the school for the present. We will notify you as soon as possible as to when classes are to be resumed."

None of us spoke as we slowly made our way towards the exit.

"Oh, and girls," she called, after a hurried consultation with the teachers, "please go straight home. And remember, if you hear any shooting, explosions, or any other disturbances, you are to lie down in the gutter as fast as you can. You must not worry about soiling your clothes."

We all nodded our heads. As we passed through the school gates I glanced at my friend Anneke, admiring her beautiful navy blue suit and white blouse with its crisp white collar. The image of her lying in the gutter seemed quite droll!

It was a beautiful spring morning. We enjoyed the unexpected vacation and did not hurry, standing outside *Bon-Marché* to admire the attractive window display. "How long do you think it will be before we have to go back to school?" Anneke mused. (We could not know then that neither of us was ever to set eyes on our school again!) As we crossed the square, which had recently been renamed the "Queen Astrid," in memory of our beloved queen who had been killed so tragically in a car accident, we stopped to watch a convoy of armored trucks and marching soldiers. Here was ample evidence of a country preparing for battle.

"Anneke, come, I'll walk you to the bus stop." We walked past the magnificent entrance of the Central Station. Suddenly, we both wished to be home. With a quick wave of the hand she boarded her bus and was gone. (How strange to reflect that the next time we met, quite by chance, was years later — in Manchester, England ...) I hurried along the busy main road, hardly noticing the loud clanging of the tram cars as they drew slowly away from the stop, the driver impatiently pressing his foot on the bell in a vain effort to disperse the small circles of men who were clustered halfway across the tram lines, absorbed in earnest conversation. When he finally succeeded in getting the people off the tracks, an army dispatch rider stopped his motorbike just ahead at the intersection, dismounted, and held up his hand to halt traffic. Almost immediately, a military convoy sped through.

Standing at the corner of our street were my three brothers. They too had been sent home, with Mijnheer Kleerkopper, the headmaster, assuring them that school would be resumed in a few days' time. (He was to survive the war, and resume the headmastership, although, to his deep sorrow, hundreds of his pupils would perish.)

※ ※ ※

How very resilient *Hashem* had made us Jews. In a town with over sixty thousand Jewish souls, there was no panic — just a sad, silent hive of activity. Families were making their own preparations to leave homes and comfortable lives, putting aside their hopes and aims. The young and the old, the weak and the strong — all were getting ready to go. The exile of the Jews from Europe, which had begun with Hitler's rise to power in 1933, was taking place on a scale unparalleled since the Exodus from Egypt. For the last few years, Antwerp had become a haven for thousands of Jews who had considered themselves fortunate to settle and rebuild their shattered lives in a free country. The memories of the inhuman treatment they had received at the hands of the sadistic, self-styled *Herrenvolk* ("master race") made them the forerunners of the masses who were now trying to escape to safety. But sixty thousand people cannot leave in one day. There was no Moses to lead them, no heavenly cloud to protect them. This was not an Exodus into a Promised Land, just a confused exile to the unknown by the unwanted. In those early days of the war people believed, erroneously, that as long as they could get to the coast they would be safe; that in a matter of weeks everything would return to normal. Few had any plans beyond the wish to flee as far as they could from the advancing enemy troops. How sadly different events turned out to be . . .

※ ※ ※

(The British Expeditionary Force [B.E.F.] was gathering along the river Dyle between Louvain and Wavre and behind the river Scheldt skirting Antwerp. Major General Bernard Montgomery with his men reached Louvain the following day: May 11, 1940.)

※ ※ ※

From my window I watched with fascination as endless streams of people passed by on their way to the Central Station, rucksacks on their backs, sadness and bewilderment etched on their faces. It was early Sunday morning, May 12, the third day of the attack on Belgium.

As my gaze swept over the crowd, I began to pick out individual faces. How pathetic Mr. Hershkowic looked! Although his daughter Sori was in my class, I knew her parents only slightly. Her younger brother went to school with our boys and the two older brothers were away at yeshivah. The old lady leaning heavily on Mrs. Hershkowic must be their grandmother, I assumed. I did not know that Sori had a grandmother living with them; perhaps they had just fetched her so they might travel together. I followed their arduous progress as they slowed down and kept stopping to allow the old lady to keep up with them.

As I watched, a horse and cart drew up outside the grocery store facing our apartment building. Mr. Stern and his two teenage daughters began to load their bags and rucksacks onto the cart, while the horse contentedly munched hay from the feedbag knotted securely on top of his reddish mane. (Belgian shire horses are famous for pulling heavy loads — their great strength and patience make them ideal cart horses.) Well, at least the grandmother Stern would be spared the strenuous trek to the station. The bags were obviously sewn from bedspreads and packed full of clothing. Mrs. Stern arranged them neatly inside the cart: these would have to serve as their seats.

While the family was thus absorbed, a small crowd of gentiles had spilled out of the tavern next to the entrance of the fruit market. Seeing the crowd of laughing and joking spectators, the cart driver began to entertain them by making hilarious faces and grimaces as he pointed at the dignified figure of Mr. Stern. The driver, encouraged by his audience, stroked his imaginary beard, but Mr. Stern ignored the jeers of the crowd. There was more cruel hilarity as the ailing grandmother was helped with great difficulty into the cart, which had two rather high steps. Finally she sank onto a candlewick bag. The driver then demanded that one of the Stern daughters sit next to him, but Mr. Stern was adamant in his refusal. "No," he said, "*I* will sit next to you."

Pappa had been watching this spectacle from a distance. He approached Mr. Stern, who was greatly respected in the neighborhood for his dignity, good nature, and Talmudic scholarship.

"Do not leave with the gentile," Pappa told him quietly. Mr. Stern looked at Pappa, and then at his family sitting expectantly, squashed into the rickety old cart.

"Reb Yoel," he pleaded, his voice breaking, "what shall I do? I gave this driver a lot of money in return for taking us to the French border. I have known him for years. He used to make deliveries for me, and I have never had cause for concern until now. I have an old mother," he concluded, "who has not been out of the house for many years, except to sit in the doorway of the shop. Shall I make her walk now?"

He shook his head, and with a last lingering look at his well-stocked shop, the result of a lifetime's work, he mounted the cart and took his place on the narrow seat next to the driver. With a final abusive remark for all to hear, the driver pulled at the reins and the horse clip-clopped away, into the unknown and out of our lives.

What makes some gentiles suddenly turn into raving Jew-haters?

Chapter Three

King Leopold III of Belgium, too, feared for the lives of his children, motherless since the death of Queen Astrid. As soon as hostilities became imminent, he sent them in the care of their governess to France for safety. Not far from Mons they passed British and French troops and were caught in an air raid as German planes flew overhead. They were taken to a shelter while bombs fell all around them. Eventually they arrived at a remote chateau, where they remained until the collapse of France in June.

No one prayed for the king's safety with more fervor than did his loyal Jewish subjects, yet blatant hatred was evident wherever they went. The Belgian populace did not share their sovereign's tolerance of the Jews. Ordinary people no longer felt the need to observe the niceties when dealing with their Jewish compatriots.

※ ※ ※

A soldier marched up the street in the middle of the road, rifle slung over one shoulder, spiked boots causing his footsteps to echo on the uneven cobblestones. He studied the list in his hand, entered the hallway at number Fifty-seven and scanned the names printed on the long row of letter boxes. Having found the name he was looking for, his footsteps were audible outside as he ascended the sweeping marble staircase.

Meanwhile Mrs. Ginsberg, an attractive middle-aged widow, was surveying her neat dining room. With a duster in her hand, *she nervously began to move around the large table, picking up the spotless ornaments, then setting them down again. She picked up a gleaming silver candlestick and walked towards the high-domed, ornately carved, mahogany-cased radio, resting on a corner table. She adjusted the volume and listened to the latest bulletin, her pale drawn face softening as she gazed at the framed photograph of a handsome young man in uniform.*

A knock on the door startled her; the duster fell onto the polished floor. A few moments later, through the open windows of the second-floor apartment, came the heart-rending screams of a mother who had just been informed that her beloved son had died in active service. (Yes, in those early days of war they sent soldiers to inform the next of kin.)

The soldier stepped out into the sunlight, consulted his list, and continued on to his next assignment.

What a paradox. Jewish boys were dying in defense of their homeland, while many of their fellow countrymen ridiculed their co-religionists...

※ ※ ※

The muffled sound of heavy artillery fire could be heard in the distance. Evidently the fierce fighting was not far from Antwerp. The need to flee was taking on a new urgency. At first many were lulled into a false sense of security upon seeing the large numbers of British personnel driving through the streets. But once the news trickled through regarding the advance of the victorious German divisions, no one felt safe any longer.

※ ※ ※

On the second floor, in the most prestigious apartment in our building, overlooking the busy street, lived the Lederman family. They owned the popular delicatessen shop adjoining the entrance to the house. In their mid-thirties with three young children, they had confided to Mamma only a few weeks earlier that Mrs. Lederman was expecting another baby. Mamma was her best friend and, therefore, the first to be told.

A very hardworking couple, they had devoted their energy to making a success of the dilapidated shop they had taken over from the previous owners, elderly people, some years earlier. At first their living quarters had been the two dark and damp rooms at the back of the shop, separated by a wall from the courtyard of the fruit market. There they lived while they ploughed back every centime to build the shop into the showpiece it eventually became. People from all parts of Antwerp would come to buy their attractively displayed delicatessen and enjoy their infectious good humor. Never complaining of their own hardships, they were also careful not to neglect their children — the baby's playpen was a familiar feature of their shop.

At last the wonderful day arrived when they could improve their living conditions. The apartment on the second floor, both comfortable and convenient, had become vacant. They were delighted to be able to move upstairs, and to gain for themselves the additional storage space which the thriving shop now needed. How short lived their joy was to be. Only two months ago Esti and I had been allowed to help Mrs. Lederman prepare the tables for the *chanukas habayis* party. Mamma had been busy for the previous two weeks making mouth-watering delicacies for the housewarming. How exciting it had all been.

Now they were standing mournfully in front of the shop. Mr. Lederman was holding a ring of keys in his hand and talking earnestly to Pappa.

"Take the keys," he said. "The shop is yours. I have been able to buy tickets for our passage to South America. There is a ship leaving from Le Havre. We should be able to get there in good time."

Pappa took the keys, both men close to tears. There was no need to say any more since it was obvious that Pappa, too, was preparing to leave. Mr. Lederman was doing no more than easing the pain of abandoning the business into which he had put so much effort over so many years.

The couple was ready to leave, she with a baby stroller in which their youngest was sharing his seat with some essential provisions — his bottles, and cans of powdered milk. The child's little feet rested awkwardly on a very large tin of assorted biscuits. With her practical mind, Mrs. Lederman had chosen edibles which would not spoil and were easy to carry. So much food to choose from, so much left behind! She sighed. Most of their baggage contained clothing for the children, and diapers. She did not forget the string-drawn oilskin bag which the oldest boy used for his swimsuit. Mrs. Lederman had decided it would be very useful for storing soiled diapers until a place could be found in which to launder them.

(Such were the treasures that accompanied the Jews into exile. Items not taken for practical reasons were often taken for sentimental ones. Many families, for example, could not bear to be parted from their silver candlesticks which had, in many instances, been handed down over several generations. There was always another *Shabbos* to look forward to...)

Rucksacks securely fastened on their backs, Mr. and Mrs. Lederman took the two oldest children by the hands and became just another family heading for the station. They were never to know that giving Pappa the shop would be such a tremendous help to him in the unhappy months ahead. Years later, after the war, Pappa tried, unsuccessfully, to trace them.

❧ ❧ ❧

(Tuesday, May 14: The broadcast of military surrender by General Winkelman, the Dutch Commander in Chief, increased the fear felt by the Jewish community. Any hope that the enemy would be driven back by the combined strength of the French, the Belgians, and the British Expeditionary Force had proven vain.)

❧ ❧ ❧

What was the commotion coming from the direction of the park at the end of Lange Kievitstraat, our street? We listened, puzzled, and watched as a mass of humanity emerged from the park, wending its way towards us.

Moving slowly, men, women and children approached, pushing carriages, wheel chairs, carts filled with babies and the frail, with a few belongings. Several asked for water, and eager volunteers ran to bring some in large pails. The travelers were Dutch people from the border, who had been forced to flee before the intensive attack and heavy bombing. They had walked a long way. They were heading for the Town Hall; their arrival was expected and a hastily prepared meal awaited them.

I will never forget the sight of a young boy, maybe twelve years old, in short trousers and on roller skates. A heavy rope over his shoulder was attached to his grandmother's wheel chair behind him; he skated and pulled her along. The old lady was dressed in a traditional black dress, her feet barely visible beneath the heavy pleated skirt, her black bonnet tied in a neat little bow under the chin. Thus they had traveled the thirty-odd miles over the border into Belgium until they reached Antwerp. Why they chose to come this way I do not know, but it was a touching sight. The strong took turns pushing the makeshift carriages of the young and the infirm. These Dutch people had left no one behind.

Preparations to flee — somewhere, anywhere — became more urgent...

※　※　※

Into our apartment came Mrs. Weiss with her only son, an arm draped lovingly around his shoulders. Her tears flowed as she looked from Pappa to Mamma.

"I have brought you your son Artur," she said with difficulty. "We are leaving, Yankel and I, but Artur belongs with you," she continued, still holding the child. "He will be better off with you and your children." The tears flowed once again, uncontrollably.

> *About seven years earlier Pappa was approached by Mr. Weiss, then a total stranger, in the shul which they both attended. One evening after maariv, he asked if Pappa would spare him a few moments, as he had an earnest request. They sat down in the beis hamedrash and Mr. Weiss began to explain that he had a very sick child, an only son, in the hospital. The man was obviously deeply distressed and Pappa at first wrongly assumed that the unhappy father wished Pappa to help him raise money for hospital expenses. But no, that was not the case. Incredulously, Pappa listened to the facts.*
>
> *Mr. Weiss explained that they were hard-working people; his wife sewed neckties and they used to travel all week selling them at markets in various parts of the country, but always returned home for Shabbos. Since the boy had become eligible for school, Mr. Weiss' family no longer accompanied him on his travels, in order to ensure that their son would have the benefit of a good Jewish education. The new arrangement worked quite well. They had been so proud of the progress their son was making in chedder, and of how easily he had settled into the new disciplined routine of the Jewish school.*
>
> *One day, however, the father returned home to find his wife*

greatly distressed. Artur had developed a high temperature and she could not get him to eat.

"Really, Bayla, you must be sensible. All children get ill sometimes," he said. "We must be grateful that our son has always enjoyed good health, and with Hashem's help, in a few days' time he will be his old self once again." His son was dozing on a makeshift bed in their living room, which also served as a kitchen and workroom. Near the window was a sewing machine piled high with the week's quota of ties, only half finished.

Concern turned to alarm as the weeks passed and Artur's health deteriorated. Their own doctor had referred them to a specialist after treating the child unsuccessfully with various medicines. The months dragged on, the doctors being unable to find the cause of his constantly recurring fever. Meanwhile his frail little body wasted away. My father listened to all this with great sympathy.

"So," said Mr. Weiss, looking at Pappa, "my wife and I have decided that maybe the Almighty does not want us to have the privilege of bringing up our son, and we reasoned that perhaps if we were to give him away to a more deserving couple —" he hesitated, then whispered, "— we could still shep nachas and watch him recover and regain his strength."

Pappa looked at him incredulously. "Why me?" was all he could say.

"You have an open house and many poor people eat at your table. I have heard about your gemilus chassadim; your name is known even amongst the market men. So whom else should I turn to?"

"But," Pappa repeated, "why me? There are so many others!"

Before he could say any more the man interrupted, taking hold of Pappa's arm, and pleading tearfully, "Please do not refuse me; we have thought about it for a long time. We want our son to be cared for by you and your wife. Talk it over with your wife and I will contact you tomorrow."

My father related the story to Mamma, and they discussed it late into the night. Never had they heard anything so strange — the enormity of the responsibility overwhelmed them. They eventually fell into a fitful, uneasy sleep.

The next few days were difficult ones. Mr. Weiss came daily to plead with my parents, who were visibly affected. One evening he brought his wife along. A lengthy discussion followed, as kind-hearted Mamma enquired about various aspects of the case. This was indeed a most unusual request; never had they heard of anything so strange.

But how could they refuse the urgent pleading of the frantic parents? As Pappa explained to Mamma, "One reads about such things, old customs and traditions. What if we refuse and the boy should, Heaven forbid, not survive? We would never forgive ourselves."

It was finally agreed that Pappa should go to the foremost rabbi of our community for advice. What exactly transpired I will never know — strange that, during all the years which followed, we never asked our parents.

Eventually my parents informed us that we had a new brother, who was very ill in the hospital, and we should all pray for Artur's speedy recovery.

Thus we were involved and awaited every new development with great concern and excitement. That first day Mamma patiently tried to explain this turn of events, and we did feel a great sense of pride that it was our dear parents who were chosen. From then on, Mamma's days were divided between tending to us, and the time-consuming duty of seeing doctors and specialists, and of course spending much time at Artur's bedside, urging him to eat some of the nourishing food which she would bring him daily. It was not easy at first.

Mamma had to overcome the child's natural reluctance to accept her as his new mother. Once he felt secure in the knowledge that his natural mother had not deserted him, and he had merely acquired an additional mamma, he tolerated the new arrangement. Full acceptance came only after his recovery.

Almost from the start his condition slowly improved. We children shared the concern of the adults over his progress. Finally the day came when he was well enough to leave the hospital. After a convalescence in the Ardennes with a kind Jewish family, he came to meet his new brothers and sisters. What excitement prevailed, as we waited to welcome our new brother! How traumatic an event it must have been for Artur!

He entered the room with his mother, a tall lanky boy, his

face still pale and thin from the long illness, but with bright, penetrating eyes. He was the same age as Shmuli.

His mother accompanied him and had obviously prepared him. He knew our names, as she introduced him to each of us. By this time, strange as it might seem, we felt as if we knew each other, and to the great relief of the two mothers, it was not long before Artur joined us in our games.

The first afternoon passed very quickly. Artur and his mother stayed for supper and then went home. We were sorry to see him go; there was undoubtedly an affinity between us right from the start. We accepted him with open arms and he loved coming, spending many a Shabbos and Yom Tov with us.

And now, today, his mother was bringing him to share in our exile.

Mamma comforted Mrs. Weiss, and said, "Artur has been in your care, and has grown into a normal healthy boy. You continue to look after Artur for me, and *HaKadosh Baruch Hu* should grant us all a speedy deliverance from the threat hanging over us. Go in peace with all my blessings." She kissed them both and held them tight. We said good-bye and watched them leave, Mrs. Weiss still with her arm around Artur's shoulder.

(Sadly, to the best of our knowledge, they did not survive the Holocaust. Despite Pappa's extensive inquiries after the war, we were never able to locate their names on any of the lists of survivors. However, they were never far from our thoughts, where they remained an integral part of our family.

Shortly before my mother died, she confided to me that she and Pappa deeply regretted the decision they made on that fateful day. "We did not want to take him away from his parents," Mamma said. "They too left Antwerp. How were we to know then that only we would be spared?")

Chapter Four

Everyone anxiously awaited each newsflash and debated with growing concern as each bulletin was read over the radio. By May 15, Antwerp itself was threatened. The railway station was packed solid with people waiting uneasily for the next batch of trains to take them out of Antwerp, and news also came trickling back of the unbelievable devastation of the main roads leading towards the coast to the west, and south into France. Truckloads of troops mingled with thousands of fleeing civilians. The Stuka bombers dropped their deadly cargoes, unhindered, on the southbound masses, who were without any help or guidance. Yet they continued their exodus, for what else could the people do?

On this fateful day, Wednesday the 15th of May, we bade farewell to our home. Pappa kissed the *mezuzah* on the doorpost, his lips moving in silent prayer. How many generations of Jews throughout the ages have fled from their homes? It is part of our tradition to kiss the *mezuzah* as an act of faith, even as we follow our forefathers into an exile which began almost two thousand years ago. People and places change, but the reasons and causes for our eternal need to flee are always the same. One last longing look around the familiar and comforting room, before the door would close forever...

※ ※ ※

We trooped past a young woman sitting on the black marble stairs, leaning on the solid, ornate railings and cradling her two children. She had been sitting there since early that morning, sadly watching the last few remaining families leave. All had tried to persuade her to join in the flight, but she remained steadfast in her belief that her husband, a French-Algerian Jew, would somehow rejoin them.

Since the outbreak of the war, Judy had felt the isolation of her situation. She prayed for her husband Gilbert to return, so that they too could flee with their children. As each day passed, her fears for his safety grew. He was a commercial traveler and she knew that he and his colleague, Raoul, were in a town called Sedan, inside the French border. (The Namur-Sedan line was an important part of the Allied defenses, turning the region into a fortress.)

As Raoul was to tell Judy later, Gilbert was apprehended and conscripted as they tried to cross back into Belgium. Raoul managed to slip over the border and undertook the arduous journey back to Antwerp, in the hope of collecting his own family as well as assisting his friend's wife and children. Arriving on Tuesday, he lost no time in speaking to Judy and pleading with her to leave.

"No, Monsieur," she replied, adamant. "I will be here when my husband comes to fetch us."

That had been yesterday. Her faith in her husband's ultimate return remained unshaken.

Theirs had been an idyllic marriage. She was a cultured and highly educated girl from a respected Polish family. Having lost her parents under tragic circumstances at the age of nineteen, she had been grateful to be offered the post of governess to the children of a business acquaintance of her late father, and so the years had passed with not much chance of her marrying. Then one day Raoul and his wife, who were friends of Judy's employers, arranged for her to meet Gilbert, a young man whom Raul had befriended. He was a handsome and solemn foreigner, who hoped to settle in Antwerp although he would continue to travel to sell his wares. His reason for wishing to settle in Antwerp was typical: he wanted the chance to marry and raise a family in a secure Jewish environment.

Their liking for each other was instantaneous. The differences between their cultures troubled them not at all. Judy was an Ashkenazic Jewess, while Gilbert followed the Sephardic tradition. Predictably, their friends and neighbors feared that differences in their cultural backgrounds might be too great, but the couple proved them all wrong.

Gilbert proudly continued to wear his fez and to serve his Maker in the ancient tradition of the middle-eastern Sephardic Jew, with Judy at his side, eagerly learning his customs and adapting herself to her husband's way of life.

As they descended the stairs, Pappa and Mamma tried to persuade her. "Judy, for the sake of your children, you must come with us!" they pleaded. "Or you will be caught by the Germans — Heaven forbid!"

The muffled sounds of heavy gunfire coming from just outside the town could be heard, making the building vibrate.

"I will not leave without my husband!" was all she said, cradling the children closer. How long would she sit there on the stairs in the now-deserted building? How strange it must have felt to be alone in a six-story apartment house that used to be a hive of activity. Gone was the laughter of children echoing down the long corridors, teenagers giggling and an old man coughing as he rested on the landing. No one remained but a heartbroken mother and two frightened little children huddled together against the cold iron railings of the staircase. Reluctantly my parents turned, and with a final parting plea ushered us through the heavy swinging door and out into the bright sunshine where we mingled with the ever-growing mass of humanity, heading mainly for the railway station.

The few who had cars, together with some driving horse-drawn carts and others pushing overloaded baby carriages, headed west for the coast. How many actually made it to their destination is not recorded. *How did so many people manage to acquire rucksacks?* I wondered, looking around me as we were carried along with the flow of people. Some rucksacks were masterpieces of ingenuity, made up of the most mundane to the most exotic materials, with every conceivable type of shoulder strap — from ornate leather to sturdy rough twine. There was not a suitcase to be seen anywhere.

It was a long trek to the Central Station, and no one talked much.

"Will any trains still be running by the time we get there?" was a major concern. *Bad enough for us, brought up in Antwerp,* I thought, *but what of those poor people, the refugees who had come to escape hostilities, hoping to find peace and security?*

Was it only last week that we thanked Hashem because we were Antwerpener and therefore safe?

Looking at Oma, I noticed how weary she appeared, but she did not complain, being concerned for little Edith, who was holding my brother Shmuli's hand. When Edith tired of clutching her favorite doll, Shmuli placed it in his large pocket. He loved his little cousin, and considered it a privilege to take care of her. They had an affinity which was to endure, even though destiny would lead them oceans apart.

Our tortuous progress took us past the world-famous diamond Bourse, usually a throbbing hive of activity with millions of francs being exchanged daily for the most sought-after baubles in the world. Usually every seat at the little table by the window overlooking the street was occupied by the diamond merchants displaying their merchandise.

Now the place was deserted.

As I passed daily on my way to school and back home again, I never tired of admiring the pure white brilliance of the diamonds as they nestled on the specially prepared white paper. Just a few stones were in each tiny packet which fit easily into the dealer's pocket. (There is an art in folding these packets to ensure that the diamonds are not lost.) The tiny packets would acquire a life of their own as the merchant unfolded the sheet to display the precious stones.

Sometimes I used to stop outside the Bourse and help search for these little diamonds. Business was not confined to within the ancient building — small groups of men would stand on the pavement outside, discussing the finer details of some stones glittering in the sunlight as they were displayed, resting on the white squares cradled in the palm of a hand. It needed only the slightest involuntary movement of the elbow and they would take off into the air, landing on the pavement. Where else except in Antwerp would you find grown-up men on hands and knees looking for diamonds? My friend Anneke would join me in helping to look for these tiny elusive pieces of glitter, although she did not share my love for them.

My father was a diamond cutter and often brought home uncut stones. At this stage the little diamonds are a dull dark brownish color, but even so they already possess the magical ability to 'jump' out of their little tin containers. One slight wrong movement of the elbow would cause them to sail up and away, usually to land in the most inaccessible place, many of which abounded in the well-worn linoleum-covered floor. Now, as all experts in these matters know, the art in finding them is not to look for them, but to get down on all fours and patiently and methodically feel for them. One slides one's hands along the floor, mindful not to miss any parts near the baseboards, and taking extra care around the legs of the workbench. In this way the hands would eventually make contact with what would seem like just bits of grit to the uninitiated, but in fact would most probably be the raw diamonds which had been lost.

"Renée, what is the matter with you? You are trailing behind!" Pappa called. "Daydreaming as usual!" We had reached the imposing facade of the Central Station. In front was the pleasantly laid out Queen Astrid Square. On the right was the entrance to the zoo, the largest in Europe, a fact which added to the prestige of the city. To visit it at least once a year was a must for every child, and we had eagerly looked forward to these outings.

Soldiers with rifles at the ready stood guard at the entrance to the vast station hall which now resembled a packed stadium. It was almost impossible to move. The only thing to do was to allow the masses to move you slowly forward, and up the wide curving staircase. Bayonet-holding soldiers stood rock-like, feet apart, at eight-foot intervals along the stairs, acting as a barrier against the surging human tide intent on reaching the platform where the trains were being filled to capacity.

The magnificent glass-domed roof of the Central Station reflected myriads of glinting sunbeams onto the crowd below. There was hardly room to move as we reached the top and were swept slowly towards the lines of waiting cars stretching as far as we could see along the rows of platforms. Hardly anyone spoke as the crowd progressed, surging forward, a resigned weariness etched on the faces of harassed parents intent on keeping their families together. At last it was our turn to board a waiting train. Although most were filled to overflowing, none had as yet left, for unknown to us, soldiers had for several hours been clearing debris from the railway tracks leading out of Antwerp. This obstruction had been caused by the latest bombardment of the air-force squadron which had moved to

Grimbergen and Hemiksem just outside Antwerp in a vain attempt to regroup.

We were to spend another three hours in the train before the guard walked alongside the length of the cars, presumably to make sure that every available place was taken. Then he blew his whistle, waved his flag, and we glided out of the station. There was no one to say good-bye to, just anxious faces slowly fading into the background. Thus we left our home, not to return for forty years ...

A collective sigh went up, and relief showed on everyone's face. People had not moved from their allotted places in all the hours the train had remained stationary, but a feeling of suppressed excitement now gripped the weary occupants. To walk about was difficult, as every available space was being used.

Our seating accommodations consisted of two benches, one on either side of the car. Normally, a bench would seat two adults. Now Oma, Mamma, little Edith and Shmuli sat on one side; Pappa, Esti and Ziggy on the other; while Brudi and I took turns sitting on the floor. No matter — once we were moving it should not be long before we would all be enjoying the thrill of being at the seaside! Thus we embarked on a journey we had often made in peacetime, a journey normally taking only two and a half hours.

No one could have guessed that we would all spend the next two days on that train! Pappa told us that it was not certain whether the train was headed for the Belgian coast or over the border to Paris. It soon became clear that it was indeed proceeding towards the coast. Other trains, also packed to capacity, fared much worse as they tried to reach Paris. Whether they ever made it through some of the most congested lines into France is not clear. We were undoubtedly among the lucky ones, having left while there was still time, and were thus spared the agony of witnessing the triumphant entry of the German Wehrmacht into our home town.

The proud and ancient city of Antwerp fell into their hands on the following day. Later we heard that hardly a soul appeared on the streets. Only an occasional stray cat wandered through the ghost town. Even the merry landlord of the beer house who, with his cronies, had derived such pleasure from watching the Jewish population depart, had closed his inn. No one likes the bitter taste of defeat.

The breeze blowing through the open windows helped to cool the cars as the train gathered speed. Gone were the railway arches, and as we passed the perimeter of the zoo, we had a fleeting glimpse of a tiger sunning himself, his powerful paws resting against the jagged boulder of the newly extended simulated jungle enclosure. Away we went, the rhythmic clanging of the wheels soothing young and old, lulling some to sleep.

But not for long. With much screeching of brakes and hissing of steam the train came to a sudden halt, then started moving slowly forward again. Silence reigned as everyone gazed out the window in stunned disbelief, not quite able to grasp the full horror of what was happening. We were almost alongside a train going in the same direction, and there was another one a little further on. They had both been hit by low-flying Stuka bombers. Some of the carriages were burning and we could just make out the khaki-uniformed figures scrambling out of broken windows as we passed them. The second train was full of fleeing civilians. We knew we had had a miraculous escape as we listened to the bombers climbing, still clearly visible to those now leaning out of the open windows. Many a fervent prayer of *Tehillim* was said in silent thankfulness for being spared, and sadness for those who had not been as lucky.

As dusk settled over the charred and scarred countryside, our train was shunted into a deserted railway station, no doubt so that we should have some protection for the night. We had scarcely covered half the distance...

The night air was mercifully cool and brought some measure of relief from our intense thirst. Very few had brought drinks for the journey, and what little there was had long since been used up. To explain to little children that there was no drinking water was not easy, to toddlers impossible. Soothing their babies into fitful sleep would provide the only respite for the harassed mothers.

A guard made his way down the length of the train, reassuring the anxious passengers and explaining that the night would be spent in the comparative safety of the station, with the journey being resumed early the next morning. He urged everyone to settle down and get some sleep. He was constantly waylaid by people throughout the car requiring assurance and information. He patiently listened to the same questions, and repeated the same answers over and over again. All the lights had been switched off, but there was sufficient light shining through the large windows from a bright moon in a cloudless sky.

Pappa surveyed his sleeping family. His brow furrowed as his gaze rested on the dozing figure of Oma, her head sunk into her shoulders, one arm around little Edith.

Pappa fondly recalled Mamma's delight when he had finally managed to obtain the necessary documents for Mamma's mother to join us in Antwerp.

He remembered how, within days of the German troops' marching into Austria, news had come through of Jewish husbands and fathers being forcibly abducted in the middle of the night by the dreaded SS troops.

Barely a year had passed since he had collected Oma and little Edith from the border town of Aachen. They came with nothing but the clothes on their backs, Edith clutching her favorite doll in her tiny hands, bewildered and desperately tired, to a foreign land where they understood not a word spoken. It did not matter, they were safe. Oma and little Edith both spoke German. It did not take long for the child to learn Flemish. But Oma would good-naturedly insist on us children speaking German to her, which resulted in much hilarity as we attempted to use the odd words we had picked up.

Yes, Pappa reflected with a deep sigh, *Antwerp had always been a safe place for Jews*; he had assured Oma of this as they had welcomed her into their home. Now they were all refugees. Pappa turned his head and looked at Mamma; he wondered how long she had been watching him. She smiled at him reassuringly. Soon Pappa too was finding some peace in fitful slumber.

The hissing of steam released from the engines diverted attention from the airborne attacks which went on through the night. The sound camouflaged the panic-provoking sounds of dive bombers unloading their deadly cargoes, and helped muffle the penetrating whistles which even the little children could scarcely ignore. Nothing, however, could prevent the shock waves rocking and shaking the train as bombs fell around us.

It was late into the night. Once again a violent shudder jolted the sleeping travelers. We had become accustomed to try and pretend to go on sleeping as we eased ourselves into more comfortable positions. I tried to lull myself into a semblance of comfort by imagining I was back home in my soft feather quilt . . .

> *The kitchen was filled with a delicious smell of hot coffee mixed with chicory, bubbling on the large gleaming kitchen range. It was a popular meeting place for a circle of Mamma's*

and Oma's landsleit, grateful to be able to spend a few hours reminiscing about the "good old days" back in the land of the Blue Danube and Carlsbad. Ah! Carlsbad! Oma and her friends would recount endless stories about the times they took the baths in this resort. I developed a great fascination for the place, and the people, who seemed to spend their lives sipping spring water and watching spectacular sunsets. Oma would look her most radiant as she entertained her old-world cronies. At these times she could forget that in Antwerp they were called Fluchtlingen, refugees, a word she hated. It sounded offensive to her ears.

Dorika, a young girl with blue eyes, a thin blond fringe framing her pale face, would accompany her elderly parents (perhaps they only seemed elderly to me), and we soon found common interests. I looked forward to her coming on Wednesday afternoons, as it was half-day and we had no school. Her clothes were exquisitely tailored, and she was painfully shy. It puzzled me why she preferred my company to that of my equally shy and earnest sister. Perhaps it was the attraction of opposites, as I was a total extrovert.

Once, Dorika said to me, "When all this trouble is over, and we can return to our home in Vienna, I would like you to come back with me. Austria is so beautiful and I could show you all the wonderful places, and take you skiing at our winter chalet.

"Mamma," she called, "when we go back home, I would like Renée to come with me. Could we adopt her? It would be so nice."

"Well, ahem." I cleared my throat.

"Let me tell you," she continued, sensing my hesitation, "we will buy you a gorgeous Himmelbed like I have."

"A what bed?" I enquired.

"Don't you know what a Himmelbed is?"

I shook my ignorant head. There was no stopping her now; she was doing what she excelled at — getting her own way.

"Why, it's a large, luxurious, four-poster bed with heavy silk embroidered drapes, and a velvet canopy with a beautiful blue lining, so when you lie in your bed and look up it resembles the sky, and it also has figures of cherubs painted on it, floating in the clouds."

Dorika's father gently rebuked her. "Don't you think you should ask Renée if she would agree?"

For once it was my turn to be shy! All this and a Himmelbed too! How could I refuse? At this moment I felt my mother's pained look. Avoiding her eyes, I studied my shoes with great concentration. What was she to make of her frivolous, happy-go-lucky daughter? Dorika was bubbling excitedly to her parents...

The train rocked and shuddered violently to and fro. Anxious, worried faces emerged from makeshift covers. That one had been dangerously close! It was probably the reenforced structure of the station roof which saved us from a direct hit. (How vexing to be reminded so rudely of the uncomfortable present!)

Glancing at Mamma as she tried to comfort Oma, I longed even now to explain that I did not really prefer to go with Dorika. Oh, no. I just wished to see what a *Himmelbed* was all about!

Chapter Five

My thoughts were once again interrupted by a most horrific bang, followed by violent shock waves which threw everyone into confusion and made it difficult for us to hear each other above the noise of the hissing steam. We had long since discovered that whenever enemy planes flew overhead on one of their frequent bombing raids, the engineers would release a deafening, hissing burst of steam, so we would not hear the air raid. But we certainly felt the cars shudder as the bombs exploded nearby.

The success of the engineers' maneuver was borne out by the absence of panic, though fear and anxiety were clearly visible on most faces.

If this continues much longer, we will all end up in a "Himmel" bed, I observed to myself. What a joke! The pun pleased me no end — I longed to tell it to my friend Anneke. I wondered where she was. *Had her family remained in Antwerp? Anyway, I must remember to tell her.*

"How can you enjoy yourself while we are being bombed?" my sister Esti admonished me.

"I was not enjoying myself!" I replied indignantly.

"So why were you laughing?"

"I was not laughing!" I pretended to fall asleep, since an explanation might have invited ridicule.

Thus the night dragged on, the incessant hissing of steam only adding to the irritability of children and adults alike.

When I awoke the sun was already streaming into the train. Getting up from my seat, I looked out the window. To my surprise, we were no longer in the station. How long or how far we had traveled, I had no way of knowing. A cloudless blue sky, with the soothing flat fields of Flanders below, stretched as far as I could see. I leaned out of the window to take a closer look. The train had come to rest in a field. At first sight there seemed to be nothing but the trees and grass, but looking more intently, I could make out a cluster of buildings in the far distance. I reflected on the contrast between our congested car and the space outside. How lovely it would have been to leave the stifling train and run through the open meadow!

Thirst, the need for water, became most pressing. As we anxiously scanned the countryside around us, someone noticed two figures in the distance, and we all strained our eyes in that direction. Then, as if with one voice, a loud cry broke from the train.

"Allo! Water, we want water, s'il vous plaît!"

The soldiers, for those were the figures we had seen, responded at once. As they approached, we were pleased to see that they wore the familiar uniform of the Belgian army.

In a flurry of activity they lost no time rounding up buckets to be filled at the cottage in the slope just beyond our horizon. They came running towards us, as fast as they could through the long grass, spilling some of the precious liquid on the way. Supplying hundreds of thirsty souls with delicious cold water was a slow process. There were four soldiers. One started at each end of the train, while the other two went to refill their large metal buckets. Dozens of times they made the journey to and fro, in heavy battle uniforms, guns slung over their shoulders, tin helmets on their heads, perspiration pouring down their faces. In gratitude we showered them with cigarettes, which they stuffed into their pockets and around the brims of their helmets, while everyone in turn received a large cupful of water. In awe I watched Pappa quietly decline his turn. It was Thursday today, and ever since the first pogroms that had shattered the lives of so many in Germany, our dear Pappa fasted every Monday and Thursday. Mamma looked at him apprehensively. Surely these were mitigating circumstances? Then, shrugging her shoulders, she looked away; experience had taught her the futility of trying to change his mind. Oma, having watched this little wordless scene, took her cue from Mamma and remained silent.

Twenty-four hours had elapsed since we first boarded the train, and a marked change in attitudes had taken place. No longer did everyone stay strictly within his or her own self-imposed little area. A common bond united us, born out of the prolonged proximity and uncertainty about the future.

A little water, and life was sweet again.

There was a natural curiosity to know one's neighbor, and we discovered that a surprising percentage of non-Jews also wished to avoid the advancing German army. Of course there were those who were simply caught up in the crush while on a business trip or some other innocent pursuit. In our car there was a party of youths with dual nationality, Belgian and British, on their way to England. In the course of conversation they declared that not a single one among them could speak English. But that did not deter them from their flight!

❦ ❦ ❦

I could think of one young boy who would have done well to flee, and I wondered whether his parents had exercised sufficient prudence to send their only son away to a place where his parentage was unknown, or whether his father had relied on his own high rank to protect him. The scene on a crowded pavement on a cold wet autumn afternoon the previous year rose vividly in my mind...

> Thousands of excited children were jumping up and down, impatiently awaiting the arrival of the popular Carnival floats with dragons, clowns and fairies. No child would want to miss that sight! Their parents watched good-humoredly just behind them.
>
> Keyserlei — the tree-lined main road linking the Central Station with the most prestigious department stores — a street normally so sedate and elegant, erupted in a salvo of beating drums and the blaring of a Gramophone. Suddenly, above the din, the indignant shout of a boy was heard. He was probably no more than eight years of age.
>
> "Mamma, Mamma, look! A Jew-boy is touching me!" Fortunately the outburst was heard only by those in the immediate proximity. In his excitement, since he was in danger of being pushed over, my brother Shmuli had gripped the boy's heavy coat. We stared at this offensive child in stunned silence. All our light-heartedness evaporated. He looked at us with unconcealed disdain, and edged closer to his mother.
>
> The eyes of the two mothers met, expecting to exchange a

hostile gaze. But the hostility in Mamma's face changed to incredulity.

"Breindle, it can't be you!" she cried. The other woman tried to cover her embarrassment by fussing over her son, who by now was totally carried away by the sight of the wonderful creatures prancing on the moving floats, accompanied by a noisy brass band. Finally, she reluctantly straightened and faced Mamma once again; a tall, elegantly dressed woman, not particularly beautiful, but very striking.

There was a tinge of sadness in her voice as she replied, "Yes, it is. Please, my name is Babette — don't call me Breindle," and she cast a fearful glance at her son.

"But what happened to you?" demanded Mamma.

It was not until much later that I was to learn the full story, since at that moment my attention was diverted to the spectacular floats receiving rapturous applause from the crowd.

Mamma remembered Breindle as a vivacious young girl who had briefly joined the Jewish community in Antwerp some ten years earlier. After she was orphaned in Czechoslovakia, her aunt and uncle had brought her to Belgium and taken her into their care. This kindly couple, who lived close by, were acquaintances of my parents. They did their best to protect their wayward niece against the many temptations of the big city, coming as she did from the sheltered environment of a small town in Slovakia. As she was intelligent, she soon learned the new language and enrolled in evening classes for shorthand typing. It was not long before she walked off with a coveted job as the new assistant to a prominent businessman. He was not known for his partiality to Jews, but nonetheless was strongly attracted to this young, refreshingly different girl with the attractive lilting accent. She, in turn, became totally captivated by all he represented: wealth, influence, and the unusual power he seemed to have over people with whom he came into contact.

It was only after she had been married to him a short time that she stumbled onto the secret of his power. He held a high position in the Belgian fascist party named the *Rex* party — the very name evoking almost the same feeling of dread in the hearts of Jews in Belgium as did the SS in Germany. By this time, enjoying the protection of a loving husband, she did not have the strength of character to relinquish her new-found pampered existence. When she was no longer seen at her uncle's house, it was assumed that she had returned to her home country, and no more was said about her.

Now, here she was, her eyes searching Mamma's face for some sign of sympathy.
"Surely, taking all circumstances into consideration, you must understand?"
"No," Mamma answered. "I do not understand." Pointing to the little Jew-hater, she asked, "Does he know that you are a Jewess?"
"No, no!" she cried, covering her mouth. "He must not find out! No one in our circle even suspects the truth. My husband made sure of that."
"Why don't you leave him and take your son with you?" suggested Mamma. Breindle hesitated before she answered.
"How can I? He is so good to me! Besides," she continued, almost in a whisper, "I dread to think what would happen if my son were to find out that he is a Jew!"

※ ※ ※

Someone shouting "Bravo!" brought me back from my reverie.

The train had suddenly started moving. With the clanging of the brake pads and a shudder, it started moving slowly away from the water-supplying soldiers. With a last wave and our shouts of thanks they were soon out of sight. The fields and hedges passing the windows, the sound of wheels grinding over the rails cheered us. Every minute increased the distance between us and the enemy.

At last we steamed into Ostend. This bustling, noisy and prosperous port, Belgium's most popular summer retreat, was now strangely quiet.

Chapter Six

It was a bedraggled, travel-weary crowd that slowly emerged from its marathon journey of approximately forty-eight hours, a journey which would normally have taken two to three hours.

Where to from there? The relief we all felt upon arriving safely was tinged with uncertainty. Few of the travelers had a clear plan of action. Apart from military personnel — French, Belgian and English, who seemed to have taken charge of the town as well as the station — the place was strangely deserted, without even stray dogs. There was only the now-familiar sight of army lorries and heavy military vehicles.

An aura of foreboding hung over everyone, with the soldiers looking as exhausted as the newly arrived travelers.

"Look," called Pappa, trying to inspire his tired brood, "these soldiers are English. Together with our army, they will soon drive the horrible Germans out of Belgium. Perhaps the war is nearly over!"

"Perhaps," we ventured. How many of those making up the crowd wending its way to the harbor would survive the war? How many would never make it out of Ostend?

Darkness was falling. Weary children could be heard crying all around us; the elderly and sick suffered in silence. There had been some talk earlier that the Ostend Municipality would provide the weary travelers with some kind of shelter, but these hopes had evaporated when no one appeared at the station. There was no alternative but to make for the harbor.

"Halt!" Soldiers with fixed bayonets guarded the road leading to the harbor, with its quay and ships alongside.

I took a deep breath and filled my lungs with sea air, watching the rhythmic lapping of the waves against the wharf. In the not far distance I could see ships bobbing gently up and down. I loved the smell of the sea, the screeching of the sea gulls as they swooped to catch a morsel from the waves and climb skyward again with hardly a pause. It brought back fond memories from previous years in Knokke-Zoute, some twenty miles to the north of Ostend.

"The harbor is closed to civilians for the present," an officer explained patiently. "But," he added, unconvincingly, "it may reopen tomorrow."

What to do now? Little groups of families contemplated their predicament. To retrace their steps would lead them nowhere. Many preferred to settle down on the spot, so that they would be ready at a moment's notice should people be allowed on the ships. Rucksacks and traveling bags were opened to find a few belongings to provide a little comfort, as most prepared to spend the night sleeping on the road.

The area soon resembled a tentless campsite. Some had had the foresight to pack blankets or an odd rug, which were now spread over the cobbled stones.

Pappa deliberated on the best course to take.

"Are you prepared to walk a little longer?" he asked. "I know a couple who have a boardinghouse nearby." He thought for a moment. "Of course they may not be there, but if you like, we could go and find out." He looked at my grandmother, concern showing in his face. He did not want to raise her hopes unduly, so he pointed out that even if it were open, he could not be sure of finding room for us.

Oma sighed. "It would be nice to have a bed for tonight. It does not matter if we only get a few beds. The little ones can all come and share one with me!"

All this was too much for little Edith, who had been watching a small girl being tucked in for the night with her head resting against her rag doll. The sight made her feel even more tired and the tears rolled down her cheeks.

"Oh, why don't we stay here?" she pleaded. However, she was consoled when Brudi offered to give her a piggyback ride. Off we went, Brudi good-naturedly pretending to be a horse galloping ahead of us, and the tears were magically replaced by squeals of laughter.

It was not difficult to distinguish the house we were seeking from the surrounding ones, since it was the only one with a *mezuzah*. Tired and weary, we mounted the stairs leading to the front entrance. Mamma remained with us in the entrance hall while Pappa went in search of the owners. Mr. and Mrs. Feldman would normally only arrive in Ostend at the end of May to prepare for their summer guests. This well-established boardinghouse would then stay open until September. Pappa knew the couple from Antwerp. They owned a café near the diamond Bourse. Mr. Feldman, a natty dresser, had a gift for making everyone who entered feel like someone special. The café had become a popular meeting place; many a business transaction was concluded over scalding hot cups of coffee served with the ever-popular salted bagels.

Mrs. Feldman, a shy middle-aged woman, her thick auburn hair pinned into an unfashionable bun, always preferred to stay in the kitchen. And in the basement kitchen of their Ostend boardinghouse was where Pappa found her. She was sorting through the provisions they had brought with them from Antwerp. They were so few. How was she to provide a hot meal for all her unexpected guests? She wiped her brow with the corner of her apron as she greeted Pappa. Her eyebrows were arched in perpetual surprise, accentuating the roundness of her face.

"I know," she interrupted Pappa, as he started to apologize for imposing without prior warning. "Make no apologies, we too left everything behind. We pray it will not be long." She sighed. "You and our other guests are welcome. We brought what food we could. The bakery was closed, so we could only bring the bread we still had in the café."

Pappa thanked her, and went in search of her husband. Mr. Feldman and his two teenage sons, Yankel and Chaim, were busy preparing the bedrooms. Never had they expected so many people seeking shelter. To turn someone away, as long as there was still room, was unthinkable.

Chaim and Yankel brought all the spare folding beds down from the attic. Mr. Feldman organized the placement of the additional beds in the bedrooms, and the lounge, too, was turned into sleeping quarters. Together they prepared the beds with clean linen. Once this was accomplished, Mr. Feldman took charge of each family in turn, making sure all had somewhere to sleep.

Finally, helped by his sons, Mr. Feldman pushed the last of the camp beds against the dining room wall. He straightened up and looked at his two children, allowing himself a moment to relax, with his back leaning against the sideboard.

"We did very well," he said, "to accommodate so many unexpected guests — thirty-two, if you include the children and babies! Now let us go down to the basement and see if we can help Mamma. It will take a miracle to feed so many."

Mrs. Feldman was busy cleaning vegetables. In normal times they would have brought a van loaded with a variety of foods. The larder and refrigerator were always filled to capacity days before their first guest was due. Now, trying to make the most of what she had, Mrs. Feldman was throwing the washed vegetables into a large pot on the stove.

"Chaim!" she called. "You stay here to help me, and Yankel can help Father prepare the dining room table for the Sabbath meal. Make sure our guests are aware that it will be *Shabbos* in an hour's time."

Mr. Feldman went to inform all his guests of the exact time for lighting the *Shabbos* candles. Then, helped by Yankel, he spread the crisp white tablecloth over the large, fully extended table. Soon many of the guests came and offered to pool the little food they had, eager to help. One lady offered her two home-baked *challahs*. Someone brought a piece of pickled meat, a jar of Matjes herring, some cake.

One by one, the women came to light the candles. In the center of the table was a beautiful silver candelabra belonging to the Feldmans. Along either side were the candlesticks brought by each couple. The *challahs* had been placed at the head of the table and covered with a beautiful, white satin, lace-edged *challah* cloth.

The women and children sat down around the table, while the men finished the evening prayers welcoming the Sabbath.

The flickering candle lights spread a warm glow and a feeling of intimacy. Soon the conversation flowed as if the women had known each other for a long time.

The young children had been fed and were asleep. We all waited patiently for the men to conclude the service. Mrs. Feldman, too, was sitting with her guests. I wondered what she had prepared for the meal. I was ravenously hungry.

At last the men joined us, and we all grouped around the table and waited for the host to allocate the seating. Once that was done, the traditional songs were sung, transforming a house full of strangers into a home filled with Jews sharing a common bond.

Could I ever forget that wonderful hot meal on that fateful Friday night? We were each given a slice of *challah* — could anything ever taste as delicious? Then followed the highlight of the meal.

Yankel and Chaim carried in an enormous pan filled to near overflowing with steaming hot *lokshen*, and a huge pot of soup. It was all Mrs. Feldman could muster to feed her unexpected company, but how she managed to make soup for so many will remain a mystery. Followed at a safe distance by her two sons holding the boiling pots, she carefully filled each plate with the noodles until they formed a peak, and then added the soup. I took my plate of steaming delight. Never has soup tasted anything like it, and forty years later I can still conjure up the taste, the table and the people around it, just by looking at a plate of *lokshen* soup. Little did we know that this was to be the last meal we were to share as a family for three long years.

Mr. Feldman led the *zemiros* in his clear melodious voice, his sons joining in the singing along with most of the male guests.

"Where are you planning to go from here?" asked one guest, sitting opposite Pappa. This released a flood of ideas, suggestions and advice, which in turn led the conversation onto politics and strategy. All options were examined and discussed — not that there were all that many options available. Some were pure conjecture, as events proved.

"If we cannot get on a ship to France, then we will try to get on one going to England," volunteered the elderly Mr. Furst, sitting next to his wife, who nodded in agreement.

"Why do you prefer to go to France?" It was a jovial little man with a pretty blond wife and four young children who asked.

"Well, we think France is quite safe and well defended. The Germans will never breach the Maginot Line, even if they manage to hold Belgium, which is doubtful. Furthermore," Mr. Furst added, having given it some thought, "the French language poses no problem for us, as would English."

"Besides," his wife continued, "we have relatives in Lyons where we could stay for the duration of the war."

And so the discussions continued until late into the night. All were desperately tired, yet reluctant to break the cozy intimacy even long after the last candle had stopped flickering, and only the pungent smell of melted wax was left. With how much nostalgia would the people lingering there recall those precious few hours during the turbulent years ahead! Not all were destined to survive...

"From where do you originate?" asked Pappa of the young man who sat facing him.

"From Berlin," he answered. "I arrived in Antwerp almost six months ago. We had arranged for my parents to follow as soon as possible. I had everything ready, even an apartment overlooking the park. They were due to come and join me within days. Now, I don't know what will happen," he concluded, almost in a whisper.

He looked at Pappa, and then towards their host. Soon, no doubt encouraged by a feeling of sympathy, he remarked, "These are troubled times we live in. We Jews have to be careful not to be conspicuous." He paused, as if expecting an answer, then he explained. "Please do not misunderstand me. I know that a religious Jew should have a beard and wear a black hat, but since we live in difficult times and the lives of Jews are threatened, I do think it is only prudent to try and blend into the background."

There followed an embarrassed silence.

"You foolish boy!" Pappa retorted. "To Hitler and his henchmen it makes no difference how you are dressed or if you sport a beard and *payos*. They have a pathological hatred of us Jews. They are not deceived by the outward trappings of the Jew in fashionable clothing. If all their hatred would be towards the traditional Jew, then surely you would not have to flee?" Pappa looked enquiringly at the troubled face of Arnold, the young man so full of confidence until a few moments ago.

"Arnold shares a popular misconception," said Mr. Furst, joining in the debate. "But the Nazis want to eradicate the Jew, no matter what his level of religious adherence. Hitler has made that clear in his rabble-rousing speeches."

"And since shaving my beard will not save me, who knows? Maybe my determination to retain my beard will one day stand me in good stead," added Pappa prophetically.

At last, even the most reluctant had bedded down for what was left of the night.

❦ ❦ ❦

A tremendous crash shook the house, an uneasy silence followed, then a whistling sound followed by an explosion! Instantly everyone was awake. Hurriedly the children were dressed; evidently we had been caught in the cross fire as the Allies were desperately trying to hold their latest positions. In grim silence, rucksacks, rolled-up blankets and the children were hastily assembled.

We gathered for a quick frugal breakfast of bread, some biscuits, and, for a few lucky ones, fruit. Yawning, stretching, and totally bewildered, most of the little ones were in no mood to eat, and were unable to comprehend the tiresome adults who would not leave them alone. It only took one leader with healthy lungs, and in a short time the place reverberated with wailing children.

"Oma, why don't we go back home?" was little Edith's logical suggestion, as she looked disdainfully at the howling mob around her. "I don't like it here, and I don't like the noise," she declared, leaving us to speculate whether she was referring to the noise inside or out. Once more there followed an uneasy stillness. How long would it last? It was *Shabbos* morning on the 18th of May.

Small groups of families stepped out of the house to join the swelling masses heading in the direction of the harbor. Evidence of the turbulence of the previous night was scattered everywhere along the way; glass from shattered windows littered the pavement, and smoking debris highlighted the nearness of the battle.

"We do not know how long this lull will last," remarked Pappa, as we quickened our steps. Oma had not slept more than an hour, and fatigue showed on her face, but she resolutely stayed abreast of the rest of us; while little Edith kept skipping ahead, for Pappa had produced a bar of chocolate and told her to keep it until we were safely on a boat! We laughed, taking it as a joke. It had worked wonders, for tears and temper were dispelled and the chocolate was held aloft in a brown paper bag. We looked forward to boarding that ship, never for a moment doubting Pappa's words.

Rows of ships were tied up along the jetty. I counted five rows deep, ships of every size and many different countries of origin. The focus of attention were two gleaming white French ocean-going liners. Refugees were streaming up their gangplanks, swelling the crowds of passengers already on the decks. Those people who had spent the night sleeping on the harbor approach had been among the first on board. There were no soldiers guarding the harbor any more. Orders must have gone out to get people into the boats and out to sea as soon as possible.

Suddenly out of the cloudless blue sky emerged two or three Stuka dive bombers, strafing the defenseless crowd with machine-gun fire, climbing, then reappearing seconds later to dive again and spray the ships and boats with their deadly bullets. Too late, the gunfire was returned from the anti-aircraft battery lodged on one of the British warships tied alongside, and this only added to the panic and confusion.

How long it took to regain one's senses and take stock of the situation is difficult to gauge. I found myself alone, looking for the others. I finally spotted Pappa and Brudi — they had been thrown against some bales — and, dazed, I walked towards them. How long we then continued searching for the others, wondering whether we would find them among the wounded, I am not clear.

Meanwhile Mamma, Oma, Esti, Ziggy, Shmuli and little Edith had been caught up in the last surge of the crowd, being literally pushed onto the nearest ocean liner. The other ship was already gliding silently away from the quay, heading for the open seaways and safety. Suddenly Mamma noticed Pappa, Brudi and me standing in the harbor as she scanned the shore from the ship's railing. Realizing that the ship was preparing to depart without us, she let out a piercing scream. The captain, who was standing directly above on the bridge, demanded to know what the commotion was about. A sailor informed him that we had been split up and Mamma wanted the rest of her family.

"Of course," he answered, "get the other members of the family."

The captain watched the sailor approach us while the ship prepared to sail. As Mamma was to tell me later, when the captain saw to whom his sailor was talking, he roared, "*Ils sont des Juifs!*" ("These people are Jews!")

"*Oui,*" answered a sailor.

"Well, get them off my ship!" he shouted. Mamma was sobbing and pleading for him to have pity, gazing up towards the bridge. Oma, weeping, was supporting Mamma. In a flash, orders were given and they were surrounded by sailors who proceeded to lift them one by one and deposit them onto an English cargo ship wedged alongside.

Terrified and humiliated, Esti and the two boys tried to comfort Mamma who was by then in a state of collapse and had to be held up. The captain of the cargo ship and his crew had been watching this shocking scene. He sent a personal message to Mamma, assuring her that they were all welcome aboard his ship, then signaled for us three to be brought aboard.

Wherever one looked there were frantic efforts being made by some desperately trying to get off the ships and by others pushing to get on, as many families had been separated during the recent air attack. At the very moment that a sailor lifted me up and handed me into the outstretched arms of a sailor on board, we heard the ominous sound of dive bombers coming straight at us, swooping, then climbing and discharging their deadly cargoes.

It was evident that this attack was carried out with greater accuracy than the previous one. Loud bangs rippled through the air as the merchants of death scored a direct hit on the fuel tanks of a British naval vessel, sending columns of smoke and fire into the air, with burning debris landing on the adjoining ship's deck. Both ships were burning fiercely. Now the British ship was listing crazily to one side of us. The sailors frantically climbed onto the other ship, which was also beginning to list, but it was the only way they had of reaching the quayside.

The quayside! Suddenly, as if coming out of a trance, I saw the figures of Pappa and Brudi receding into the distance. During the ensuing havoc, all ships still seaworthy had slipped their moorings and were now heading for the comparative safety of the open sea. I stood alone, watching the two forlorn figures blurring into the distance while tears ran uncontrollably down my face. Unable to tear myself away, I strained my eyes to see them until they were no more than imaginary specks on the horizon.

Thus were the fortunate ones saved from the advancing enemy.

It was time for me to find out if any of the other members of our family were possibly on this particular ship. There had been so many vessels in the harbor.

Was it days or hours that had gone by? It did not matter. Suddenly, loneliness overwhelmed me as I turned to search the crowded ship. It appeared as if everyone on board was intent on looking for some loved one. Now and again a familiar face would pass by, someone we had shared a car with on the long train journey to Ostend, or an acquaintance from Antwerp.

"Have you seen any of my family?" I would ask hopefully.

"No," they would answer, gravely shaking their heads.

"If you meet my family, please tell them I'm here."

I leaned over the railings as a feeling of seasickness overwhelmed me, but nothing happened. Of course not, we had had nothing to eat that day and very little the day before. I watched its wake as the ship zigzagged across the English Channel. It was to continue in this manner a whole day and through the night until we reached Folkstone.

"Renée! Renée!" It was Ziggy's joyous voice calling me! I ran to where the rest of my family who were on the ship were crowded together, sharing three sturdy-framed deck chairs. Mamma asked what had happened to Pappa and Brudi, and I told her. She must have known, but wanted to be wrong. How comforting it was to see the delight little Edith displayed upon seeing me! She was still clutching her battered doll.

I settled down on the only place available: the floorboards of the deck next to the deck chairs.

Later, while Oma and Mamma dozed, we children ventured about exploring our ship with its English-speaking crew, and made friends with a couple from Antwerp, whom we later introduced to Mamma. Mr. and Mrs. Shindler were to remain close friends and a great comfort to Mamma in the difficult times ahead. Oma especially would remain the lady's lifelong confidante. We watched for hours as the foaming wake trailed in a zigzag pattern behind us, its color changing from ice-cold green to a lovely blue. Then, with darkness falling, we huddled together on deck to try and sleep. A kindly sailor provided us with two warm blankets, which somehow we managed to share between us. In the morning it was rumored, later confirmed, that both of the beautiful French liners had been attacked the previous day, and had sunk. All aboard had drowned. How could we ever have deluded ourselves into believing that a gleaming ship would be safe, its white splendor etched against the blue horizon? Those two liners were sitting ducks for the roving bombers and U-boats on the lookout, whose mission was to seek and destroy.

The news was greeted with horror and the fervent prayer that we should be spared. There was hardly a family aboard who did not have some member missing as a result of the haste in which the harbor had been evacuated the previous day.

The white cliffs of Dover loomed excitingly ahead of us, but all the while we did not know if a loved one might have been on one of the doomed French liners or on another of the ships now heading towards an unknown destination. Weary from lack of sleep, sadness, and trepidation about the future, the shivering refugees huddled on the heaving deck.

Excitement gripped us youngsters as we leaned far over the railings to catch a glimpse of the beckoning land which was to be our future home. We would experience three glorious summer months getting to know the resilient good-humored British at their best, before the London blitz would wipe out our newly acquired dwelling and force us to move once again, to settle in the damp, fog-shrouded town of Manchester with its warm, vibrant Orthodox community.

Chapter Seven

et us retrace our steps to find out what happened to those less fortunate than we were.

❋ ❋ ❋

Devastation was everywhere as Pappa and Brudi searched for someone to direct them. It was futile to linger, Pappa reasoned, as they watched the listing ships still burning fiercely in the debris-littered waters of the once-prosperous Flemish harbor. The town now showed all the signs of defeat. On that same day the Belgian government went into exile, first to La Panne, and on the following day, Sunday, May 19, to Le Havre, which is approximately two hundred miles to the south.

Pappa took Brudi by the hand. "We are going to walk to France," he said simply.

"But, Pappa, do you know the way?"

"Just look around you," Pappa answered gently. "We are not alone. See how many people are joining us on this road! If we follow the coastline southwards, we will surely reach the French border, and safety."

Would so many people have made this arduous journey on foot, with the merciless sun beating down from a cloudless sky, if they had known that the enemy was only a matter of days behind them? But there was nowhere else to go.

Pappa and Brudi walked for many hours, sometimes resting by the roadside and watching the multitude of people all heading south.

(It amazed Brudi how very few familiar faces there were, he told me years later. He felt so lonely out on the crowded dusty highway.

"What did you eat?" I asked.

"We had no food.")

As dusk was falling, they stopped outside what appeared to be a large guest house, with people sitting or leaning on the iron fence surrounding the building.

"Perhaps we could get a drink here," said Brudi, his eyes pleading eloquently. Pappa's troubled eyes softened. He really should have taken into account that a young boy would suffer more from thirst. Pappa hesitated for a moment as he looked up at the darkening sky. The day had passed in comparative peace, with just the occasional enemy aircraft swooping down on a prominent landmark, but now that night was falling, Pappa thought they should be prepared for another air attack.

Events were to prove him right; but for the moment, they entered the crowded hallway and pushed their way into what would normally have been the dining room. A perspiring landlord approached them and explained that for a reasonably small fee they could stay the night, sleeping on the floor in this room since all other rooms were fully occupied. Pappa thanked him but declined.

"Could we please have some bread and coffee if you have any? Then we will go on our way."

"As you please, monsieur," said the landlord. "I can find you some bread, not much — the baker will deliver a fresh load in the morning — but I have no more coffee left. Again, we are getting a fresh delivery in the morning. We did not expect to be so busy," he explained unnecessarily.

They sat on a bench, ate the bread, and drank from a large mug of fresh cold water. How delicious it was! Brudi listened to Pappa as he explained to the people around him why he considered it unwise to spend the night in a crowded building. "The bombing is sure to start again, and a building such as this is an easy target."

"Well," concluded an elderly man, as Pappa started for the entrance, "I would sooner spend the night in the safety of a solid building like this, than in an open field, huddled against the damp air."

Pappa's step did not falter as he walked past the gate, while Brudi dragged his feet beside him. He would have liked to spend the night in this place where the water had been refreshing, and the bread not enough. The thought of fresh bread being served in the morning was tantalizing, but Brudi could not question his father's decision.

They had walked but a short distance when they suddenly heard the sound of approaching aircraft. It was not possible to see what they were, too late even to find shelter, as a tremendous explosion ripped through the air, followed by smaller bangs. Pappa and Brudi watched from afar as the guest house crumbled. Flames shot out of the roofless building.

Sadly they walked on. This was only the first of several times that they would be saved from danger thanks to Pappa's uncanny gift of premonition.

That night they slept in a field, as did thousands of others, and were awakened by the sweet sound of birds proclaiming another warm and sunny day. Everywhere military vehicles, crammed with soldiers, roared along the roads. No one took notice of the weary, dirty, hungry wanderers, all seeking safety.

After passing through Middelkerke and the picturesque fishing town of Nieuwport, they arrived at La Panne, late in the evening of the second day. This small town nestling on the border with France was to become a magnet for tens of thousands of refugees. It had been abandoned by its own householders. Where did they all go? The now peaceful streets showed plainly the signs of recent bombings. A ghost town — but on they went, past the deserted houses.

Pappa was intent on reaching the border without further delay, taking the forsaken town of La Panne as proof that safety depended on crossing the border into France. On they trekked, with hunger, thirst and fatigue their constant companions. The nearer they drew to the border, the more congested the roads became. The stream of refugees became a flood. It consisted of exhausted, footsore pedestrians intermingled with every conceivable type of transport. There were even a few valiant walkers supported on crutches.

Pappa and Brudi were still approximately half a mile from the border when they were caught up in a solid mass of humanity. Pappa soon decided that crossing at this particular point would be difficult, so after patiently extricating themselves, he and Brudi passed through some wooded terrain and over a ploughed field. They stood ankle-deep in mud, sometimes sinking further into the soft, churned-up soil, as they surveyed the dismal sight that greeted them.

A dense mass of people formed a solid wall as far as the eye could see. Dusk was falling; crying children could be heard. Perhaps they would soon find relief and oblivion in merciful sleep. Pappa reflected, as he lay down in a furrow of the ploughed field, that they had not eaten all day. He prayed that Mamma, Oma and the children had fared better and had reached safety by now. Weariness overtook them both, and they were immediately enveloped in sleep.

Pappa woke abruptly as the deadly Stuka dive bombers screeched down over the defenseless sleeping masses. Perhaps they were mistaken for columns of troops in the bright moonlight. The bombers caused untold misery and havoc before returning to their bases. No aircraft or anti-aircraft guns were heard challenging them. Brudi still slept, although fighting could be heard in the distance. As the morning sun rose over the horizon, Pappa considered their hopeless situation.

"Come, Brudi, we will try and force our way into France."

Eagerly, Brudi jumped up. "Food! Maybe we'll get some food! No use staying here," he agreed.

With much pushing and shoving through the crowd they made it to the border, only to be confronted by a menacing line of French gendarmes with fixed bayonets, looking as if they meant to use them. Some people managed to produce the necessary papers which magically allowed them through. Rumors abounded that the Germans had invaded France, but few who heard them were prepared to believe this unwelcome fact. Pappa deliberated on what would be the best move; he was not a man to tarry when a situation seemed hopeless. He did not want to spend another night in that field!

He and Brudi began to retrace their steps towards La Panne, as did many others. They passed a young couple, each with a toddler strapped securely on top of a rucksack, the father with an additional bag containing essential provisions strapped across his chest. The mother also held a little boy by the hand, her soft soothing voice urging him to walk just a little bit more. But mainly they walked against the stream of bedraggled travelers.

A farmhouse lay in the distance to their left, and Brudi offered to go and see if he could beg for some food, while Pappa slowly walked on. An old farmer was drawing water from the well with great difficulty — clearly a task he was no longer used to doing. Brudi offered to help and grudgingly the farmer agreed. They both drank, then after looking around for signs of discarded food, Brudi plucked up courage and asked for bread. The farmer looked at the mournful eyes of the hungry boy. Without saying a word, he went inside and returned with a bulging brown paper bag in one hand and a tin can in the other. He filled the can from the freshly drawn water and silently handed both over. Brudi tried to thank him, but he grunted and went indoors, so Brudi ran as fast as he could back to Pappa.

The brown paper bag contained a few boiled potatoes, which they ate gratefully.

La Panne beckoned the weary travelers. It was indeed a town deserted by its inhabitants. The many unlocked houses bore silent witness to an unexpected and hasty departure. Pappa and Brudi walked along a street which branched off from the center of town, with solid terraced houses on either side of the road, abandoned by their owners, but filling with an influx of refugees in search of food and shelter.

Food, there was none. Did the fleeing owners take all the edibles with them, or were they taken by the first wave of refugees who had arrived during the previous days? Pappa wondered about this as he looked around the deserted kitchen of the house which they had entered.

They retraced their steps and went back into the hall, with its dark brown parquet floor and neat bright rugs spread in front of each door leading off it. Pappa hesitated for a moment.

"Come, Brudi, we will take a look at the second-floor apartment. Perhaps we will find something to eat, and maybe rest awhile."

Brudi eagerly mounted the stairs, a spring returning to his footsteps at the thought of a comfortable bed.

They knocked on the door at the top of the stairs, then tried the door handle, but no one answered. The door opened. This apartment seemed to be more spacious than the one on the ground floor, an illusion created by the large windows. Here too, there was no food in the kitchen. Pappa opened the door leading from the sitting room and entered the master bedroom.

The large double bed was draped with a pink satin cover. A dressing table with a sunken ceramic washbowl decorated with a delicate rosebud pattern, and a water urn to match, struck a note of luxury in the midst of desolation.

How peaceful it seemed! Brudi looked longingly at the bed. Lace curtains flapped gently in the evening breeze. Pappa instinctively moved across the room to close the window which overlooked a courtyard at the back of the house. Hearing voices from below, he paused, then opened the window a little wider and leaned out. Someone looked up and called, "It is not advisable to spend the night upstairs!"

"Mr. Frank!" Pappa exclaimed, delighted to find an acquaintance. "Where are you staying?"

"Come down and I will show you," Mr. Frank replied.

Brudi looked longingly at the bed, "Could I ... No, never mind," he said to himself, following Pappa.

"Are you here with your family?" asked Mr. Frank, as they emerged from the building.

"No," sighed Pappa, "just the two of us."

"Not many families have managed to stay together," remarked their friend. "Come, let us go down into the cellars. There is hardly room to lie down, but at least we should be safe. Rumor has it that we can expect heavy air raids tonight. These cellars seem to be the safest place to spend the night." He spoke with the air of one who knew about such things.

He proved to be right.

They crossed the courtyard to the entrance of the cellars, where someone was filling large vessels with water from a tap. Pappa and Brudi drank from the clear water before they joined the others.

The rumble of distant fighting could be heard as they wound their way down the badly lit stairs. An overwhelming tiredness gripped them as they surveyed the crowded scene.

There were two cellar rooms, lit by a single naked bulb hanging from the center of the archway dividing them. Gratefully they accepted space on the floor, just enough to stretch their tired legs. Ignoring his pangs of hunger, Brudi put his head in Pappa's lap and fell asleep. Pappa sighed, then joined in the general conversation. This was to be their home while the fierce battle of Flanders was fought over the next few days.

The Germans had succeeded in driving a wedge between the Allied forces in an astonishing lightning operation, thereby setting in motion Operation Dynamo, which would go down in the annals of history simply as Dunkirk. But that was still to come.

For that moment, even the din caused by the renewed bombings raging through the night could not disturb the blissful slumber enjoyed by a few in the cramped quarters of this cellar. But Pappa could not sleep. *Where might his wife and children be? Were they safely together?*

His thoughts were jerked back to the present by the insistent whimpering of a small child suffering from the early symptoms of measles. Next to him was his younger brother, delirious, his frail little body burning with the tiny red spots. Their mother was trying to soothe the children by dabbing them with a handkerchief dipped in cold water. Across the room was another young couple with three children; no doubt they too would develop measles in the weeks to come. In the far corner, barely visible in the uncertain light, Pappa recognized the couple whom he had passed earlier that day on the road back from the border. He noted, with a sigh of relief, that they all seemed to be peacefully asleep.

The bombs whistled all around them, each explosion followed by an intense, brief silence before the next.

Chapter Eight

Not everyone had found shelter before darkness fell and the bombings began. Many refugees were caught in the open, trying to find shelter, and causing serious concern to the Allied troops whose movements they hampered. My friend Anneke and her brother were among those refugees.

❦ ❦ ❦

At about the same time that we had left Antwerp by train, Anneke's parents, Mr. and Mrs. Wolf, were preparing to make the journey to the coast in comparative luxury. Anneke's eldest brother, Yankel, a successful clothing manufacturer, had arrived to collect his parents, along with Shloime and Anneke, and drive them all to the seaside, or perhaps over the border into France. This trip, he reckoned, would take them at most three hours in his high-powered American Buick — it was a journey he had made many times — so their discomfort in an overcrowded car would last only a short time. Yankel's wife Raisy and their two young children were already seated in the vehicle. The trunk was filled with stock from his warehouse which he hoped to be able to sell when the need arose, so food and all other essentials had to share the space inside the car with the passengers. They took with them as much as could be squeezed inside, which was just as well, for this car was to be their 'home' and the provisions their only food for the next eventful week.

It took them no less than two arduous days to reach the outskirts of Ostend, during which time they were caught up among the hordes of refugees and experienced all the rigors of the bombardments.

Wisely, they decided there would be no point to stopping in Ostend, so without wasting time they headed in the direction of La Panne, just one more car joining the endless stream of refugees. Cars, taxis, donkeycarts, wheelbarrows, baby carriages, carts, strollers — all could be found on the trek towards the magical frontier. Though rumors abounded that the enemy had raced ahead, there were few who were willing to believe them.

It was Friday, May 17. The heat was intense, the children were leaning their heads out the windows as the car crawled towards the town of La Panne. Just ahead, in the slow-moving, heaving crowd, Yankel spotted the familiar figure of Rabbi Shmuel Yosef Rabinow, one of the most respected rabbis of Antwerp. Beside him walked his frail elderly wife, barely able to keep up as they mechanically followed the crowd. How had they made the journey so far? There was no time to ask questions. The *rav's* face creased into relieved recognition as Yankel stopped the car alongside him, jumped out of the driver's seat and called to Anneke and Shloime to give up their places. They were already out, however, offering their seats as a matter of course. It was done as graciously as if they all had met while strolling on a sunny afternoon. No, no! The *rav* and his wife would not accept, not wanting to be a burden. Only after Anneke and Shloime had assured them that they would indeed prefer to walk, rather than spend any more time squeezed in the car, did they accept. With immense gratitude and relief at being able to rest their feet, they climbed into the automobile.

That night was spent at the roadside, the family huddling close together for warmth, making it possible for Mr. and Mrs. Wolf, along with the *rav* and his *rebbetzin*, to enjoy a small measure of comfort within the car; but it was not a night for sleeping. They fared even worse than those who had remained in Ostend. The world seemed to explode around them, as waves of enemy planes swooped overhead, releasing their deadly cargoes. Shortly before sunrise, the bombing stopped and the planes headed back to their bases, giving the multitudes a welcome respite and a chance to fall asleep. The people remained strangely detached, and an uneasy quiet hovered all around them, as the morning sun rose majestically on the horizon.

Everyone was slowly awakening. Raisy was thoughtfully slicing a large honey cake she had brought with her — obviously it would have to last longer than she had anticipated. She wondered whether she dared offer everyone two slices apiece, but decided it would be wiser to save the second portions for later. Children can be very trying when hungry. She had brought a large flask of water, which no one drank, preferring to reserve it for the children's needs. By mutual agreement it was decided to delay no longer, but to attempt to cross into France.

Rabbi Rabinow became the accepted leader of this little group. "We must try to cross as soon as we can. Dunkirk is not far from here," he said. "Once there, head straight for the harbor, and we will try for a boat to take us to England."

"To England?" Yankel enquired, astonished, as they piled back into the car, leaving Anneke and Shloime once again to walk beside it. England had never been part of their plan. Yankel had intended to make for Portugal, though he had to admit, if only to himself, that what he would do once he got there was not clear.

By sheer patient perseverance they reached the border some hours later, and encountered the same solid wall of humanity as did Pappa and Brudi. By a freak unwritten rule, room was made to allow a constant stream of cars to pass through. As the car inched slowly forward, the family was horrified to see the truncheon-wielding gendarmes hitting out indiscriminately. They halted alongside a gendarme who asked to see their 'green cards', the Belgian identity cards which were issued only to those born in Belgium. All others made do with a yellow card. Out of approximately sixty thousand Jews who lived in Antwerp, only a very small percentage enjoyed the distinction of possessing this magical green card. To be denied the chance to escape the enemy because of the color of one's card! The frustration of the masses was understandable. The brutality of the French border guards could in a small measure be forgiven in the light of their strict orders and the well-nigh impossible task of implementing them. If only the crowds could have known that within a few days all barriers and guards would vanish!

Tension was building up inside the Buick. Although Yankel and his family did possess green identity cards, he knew that the *rav* and his wife did not. They had come from Germany at the onset of Hitler's rise to power. As they neared the checkpoint, the *rav* broke the uneasy silence. "Yankel, just show them your cards through the window." It worked! They were waved on, and followed the narrow convoy edging its way into France.

Tension eased. The children felt it too, and once more dared to complain, demanding noisily to be allowed to romp along the roadside. This was an impossible request, as they were caught up in a moving column of trucks, cars, carts, army lorries, and even menacing-looking gun carriages with enormous wheels. The French soldiers in full battle gear were almost unable to keep the never-ending traffic flowing, and the sweat poured down their faces.

As Yankel drove the car into Dunkirk, site of the largest assembly of military might, he consciously looked for a place to park, finally coming to rest outside an unfinished concrete air-raid shelter. A short way back, he had suddenly realized that his brother and sister were no longer walking alongside the car. To turn back was impossible. A constant stream of traffic was flowing into France. Yankel wondered whether the other occupants of the car had also noticed the absence of the two teenagers. A glance around — gloomy faces — he had no need to ask. Mrs. Wolf's eyes were filled with tears which trickled down her tired and dusty face.

Yankel was the first to break the silence. "We will stay here until Anneke and Shloime catch up with us."

A quick consultation confirmed his decision to stay where they were, to the delight of his two children, who lost no time in taking advantage of the situation to cavort through the muddy field, chased by Raisy, who was also glad of a chance to exercise her stiff legs. Everybody pretended not to be overly concerned, and went about making preparations for the night.

Leaving the car where it could be seen from the road, they surveyed the interior of the dark, dank shelter. Raisy busied herself improvising makeshift beds for the tired children. Supper was a simple meal consisting of a slice of honey cake and a piece of precious cheese, which she gave to everyone, followed by the remainder of the water. Soon the children were blissfully asleep.

The adults left the children in the comparative safety of the shelter and went to walk back and forth in front of the entrance, since they all felt the need to exercise. It was decided that Raisy and Yankel would venture a little further along the road in search of water. They did so, and soon found that were not alone. It was not possible to avoid the constantly moving vehicles, military personnel, and other refugees. Yankel asked someone if he knew where to obtain fresh drinking water, and was told of a water pump in a deserted farmhouse a short walk up an incline. They hurried in an attempt to get the water and be back before dark, but once there, found they had to patiently await their turn to pump water into the containers they had brought along. Then, it was back down the hill to rejoin their parents and traveling companions, and watch the sun dip behind the row of tanks silhouetted against the yellow and crimson skyline. In the distance bombs thudded dully. Reluctantly they decided to join the sleeping children inside.

Little did they know how lucky they were to have found shelter; the night was to prove one of the most horrific in the annals of modern warfare. No one who was there could ever forget it, or describe it accurately without being suspected of exaggeration.

※ ※ ※

Anneke looked in bewilderment around her. She and Shloime had been separated from the car and their family by truncheon-wielding gendarmes, who waved the flow of cars onwards, while herding the lucky green-card holders who had come on foot into the barbed wire enclosure. So this was France! She tried to understand the situation that had put her behind barbed wire. How could she, forcibly separated from her family, consider herself better off than the free masses on the Belgian side fighting to be admitted? She looked at her brother; he shrugged his shoulders.

People all around them were relaxing, ignoring the appalling conditions — hundreds herded together without provision for food or bodily needs — relishing the feeling of having reached safety. There was even a rumor that they would soon be provided with food and drinks. In anticipation of this pleasant event, everyone settled down to wait.

Surveying the vastness of the night sky, Anneke reflected that she had never seen so many twinkling stars. How starkly the moon illuminated the trees and buildings and cottages against the skyline, throwing menacing, long shadows all around her! She tried to ignore the rumbling sounds of the fighting that was raging all around them, and that would continue for the next few days. A shiver ran through her as she watched the arrival of the first wave of bombers which were to hammer away at the area throughout the long night.

A moment later Anneke and Shloime were both sprawled on the ground, as an ear-splitting explosion ripped through the air. A direct hit had landed on the outbuilding of a nearby farmhouse, sending hundreds of chickens flying through the air, most of them dead; the complaints of those that survived were loud and clear against this violent interruption of their sleep. Did the Germans think the barn was full of soldiers? Perhaps it looked like a tank from the sky. Anneke felt strangely detached from the battles raging around them.

The enemy was successfully cutting off large detachments of troops while advancing towards the coast in a bid to stop the retreating units from escaping across the sea. All this was taking place in the fields of Flanders. Caught in the midst of the action, the two teenagers made a great effort to suppress their rising fear and panic, each mindful of the other. Faith and the resilience of youth would keep them going, that and the companionship of others in similar circumstances.

Anneke and Shloime searched in vain among the hundreds of groups for their own people, until at last, overcome by fatigue, they found a spot where they could spend the night. Anneke reflected on how lucky she was to have her brother with her; it made her shudder to think of the possibility that she might have been alone. The thought of their parents' anxiety distressed both youngsters, but finally, exhausted and hungry, they fell asleep.

※ ※ ※

Tremors shook the earth, sending shock waves in all directions.

"My bed is shaking!" called Anneke. The next instant she was fully awake as the blast of falling bombs ripped through the air. There was no time to think as they jumped up and ran to be nearer to their fellow-prisoners. Screaming children were everywhere, with anxious parents trying to comfort them. Engines whined overhead as the enemy's planes dived towards their targets in yet another surprise attack. Some bullets struck a row of fuel tanks, producing an instant inferno and making the use of flares unnecessary. The night sky lit up as the flames shot heavenwards. Hundreds were killed. The compound was sprayed with tracer bullets from low-flying planes, but was mercifully spared a direct hit by one of the bombs which fell nearby and sent everyone diving for the safety of the shuddering earth.

(There was no panic. The way people react when faced with overwhelming terror is truly remarkable. A numbness creeps into the bones. One sees the destruction all around — hears it — smells it — but does not feel it, not yet . . .)

The battle continued unabated. The cry of a woman in labor could be heard occasionally above the din. Anneke watched in horror as the tremendous column of flames reached skywards, sometimes obscured by clouds of smoke that would continue to pollute the area for days. At this point the baby chose to make his entrance into the world. *Would he grow up to light the world with wisdom? Would he grow up at all?* A group of women were clustered around the young mother as they helped deliver her of a healthy lusty baby boy. She even managed a weak smile when told that her husband had fainted. Two distinct groups evolved — one of men reviving the father, and another of women attending to the mother. One generous lady brought an exquisite silk shawl in which to wrap the baby. There was a great deal of kindness and consideration within the confines of the barbed wire.

Finally stillness prevailed, except for the odd enemy plane and guns firing in the distance. The main fighting appeared to have moved further afield, or it could just have been that armies locked in combat take some time to rest. Little groups of people in disarray were sleeping. Some wounded were being tended as well as was possible in the difficult circumstances. The luckier ones among the wounded would later be moved to the hospital near La Panne, where the Queen Mother (Queen Elizabeth of Belgium), ignoring the risk to her own life, greatly boosted the morale of the unfortunate refugees who had become trapped and wounded in the fierce battles raging around them. She walked among them with a kind word for everyone, helping to alleviate the shortage of medical care and lighten the discomfort to which they were subjected. She had been persuaded to leave the palace in Brussels and take up residence in the royal family's summer villa near La Panne. No one who was in that hospital would ever forget the deep concern the Queen Mother showed for her subjects, and the high esteem in which she was held.

❦ ❦ ❦

Anneke gently shook her brother awake. She was not sure how long they had been sleeping, but the sun was high in a cloudless sky. All around them families were preparing to move on, leaving through the gaping openings which the blasts had made in the barbed wire, as everyone realized that any hope of an organized distribution of food was futile, and all were left to find their own. The shortage of food was becoming an ever-increasing problem. Many had set out with ample food provisions, but had lost some or all on the roads when suddenly having to run for shelter. Anneke wondered about the newborn baby as they shook clumps of earth and grass from their clothing and prepared to go on. The instinct for survival renders one indifferent to the larger historic events unfolding all around, and causes one to focus, instead, on the smaller, personal details.

Will life ever be the same again? Anneke wondered, sighing, as she recalled her cozy bedroom with its bright fashionable wallpaper and crisp starched curtains, her very own dressing table where she would sit every morning, brushing her hair the required fifty strokes that would make it shine as she moved in the sunlight. Then, down to breakfast ...

Hunger pangs jolted her back into the cruel present. Were there still people left having breakfast in their homes this morning?

Shloime was busy plucking sorrel growing along the roadside.

"Do you remember," he asked, straightening up, "how we used to pick these in the fields in Knokke and eat them?"

Of course she remembered.

"Well, they never harmed us then, so let's eat a few now."

Anneke marveled at the resourcefulness of her brother, as they munched the edible sorrel leaves with their slightly sour taste. It quite refreshed her for the moment — at least her stomach juices had something to work on.

The devastation before them was beyond belief, as they trudged along the muddy road towards Dunkirk. People searched for food; military lorries, cars, artillery converged from all directions. Even the two youngsters could see that all was disorder and confusion. They reached Dunkirk unhindered. The scene that met their eyes on all sides was so incredible as to seem unreal.

They walked along the deserted streets, abandoned by their rightful inhabitants. Evidence of a panic flight lay all around them: the deserted houses, the closed shops, the smokeless chimneys, the absence of domestic animals — and yet, the streets were far from empty. They were teeming with hordes of refugees walking in all directions and seeking food.

The many valuables strewn along the streets, spilling out of burst rucksacks and torn traveling bags, did not even merit a second glance! Anneke almost tripped over a tattered bag lying on the pavement; irritated, she kicked it aside and out spilled a heavy silver candlestick. Anneke judged it to be of an old Russian design. To have been carried all this way as a treasured possession, a symbol of faith, and then abandoned in panic! Would it ever grace a *Shabbos* table again?

※ ※ ※

"Shloime! Anneke! Over here!" It was Yankel, shouting and gesticulating in the distance. With cries of delight, the three ran towards each other.

"What happened?" asked Yankel. "Where have you been?"

"Where are Mamma and Pappa? Is everyone safe?"

The questions came tumbling out, releasing in Anneke a flood of tears. It felt so good to be walking with Yankel again! He pointed towards the Buick, parked a short distance away. "Did you not see it?" he asked. "You must have passed it as you entered the town!" The next moment they were embraced by loving arms from all sides.

"Where are your rucksacks?" their father asked, once the joyful reunion was over.

"Rucksacks?" Shloime repeated. No, they had no idea what had happened to them, or even when they had last carried them. "But then you must be very hungry!" exclaimed Raisy, always the practical one, as she hurried to bring them some food.

They ate hungrily as they talked about their experiences. It was truly amazing that they had escaped physical injury while caught in the center of some of the most brutal fighting at the commencement of the Battle of Flanders. But the strain and shock were clearly etched on their tired faces.

Anneke walked to the entrance of the partly constructed air-raid shelter. She marveled that they had all survived, unharmed. She slowly descended, stepping on the loose boulders used as stairs, picked up a piece of shrapnel with its razor-sharp edges, and marveled again. She found another piece embedded in the wooden beam supporting the corrugated roof. Directly below was the blanket where one of the children had slept, oblivious to the destruction all around.

The *rav* suggested to Yankel that they try to find a boat which would take them to England, so Yankel drove to the harbor.

Total destruction lay before him, as far as his eyes could see. There were several smoldering vessels, abandoned by their owners. The acrid smell of smoke from the burnt-out tanks and other military equipment filled the air. Yankel shuddered as he passed, relieved to see that there were other refugees also walking towards the harbor or aimlessly searching for food. No, there was not a single seafaring vessel around. He walked back to his car which was, by then, dirty and mud splattered. Only last week it had been his most pampered possession, polished and gleaming and constantly inspected. He switched on the engine. "I suppose it looks no worse than we do," he consoled himself as he drove back to the bunker.

Shloime came towards him. "Well?"

"Nothing doing. The harbor is deserted," Yankel told him. They were joined by the rest of the adults, and once again everyone looked to the *rav* for guidance.

"Let us not waste any more time," he said. "We will go to Calais, and let's hope that we will find a ship there to take us to England."

Raisy quickly packed their few meager possessions into the car. The two older ladies and Mr. Wolf climbed in, and when they were comfortably installed, Raisy sat inside with the two children. Lastly, Rabbi Rabinow took his place in the front next to Yankel, insisting that one of the children share his seat. Some last-minute advice was called out to Shloime and Anneke, who were once again setting off on foot, and the small convoy was on its way. It soon merged with the hordes of displaced persons blocking the roads. It was not difficult for the two youngsters to keep up with the Buick. The roads were strewn with debris and clogged with humanity. (No one could know that the German Seventh Army, commanded by the brilliant General Rommel, had raced ahead of them, cutting off the Allied forces from the French Army, thereby throwing them both into disarray.)

Leaderless and dispirited soldiers roamed the streets, mingling with the multitude. Some lay asleep under the shelter of an old chestnut tree. Anneke wished that rain would wash away the dust on the roads and relieve the heat of the sun, which beat down relentlessly. How delightful it would be to sit in the shade of the chestnut tree in their garden back in Berchem, sharing a bottle of lemonade with her school friends! Better not dwell on such things! It only made her even thirstier.

They reached Calais, another town abandoned by its inhabitants, but teeming with the unending stream of war-weary refugees. Yankel braked to a halt near the harbor approach where he observed two old-timers with weather-beaten faces peacefully smoking their clay pipes, seemingly oblivious to the strange happenings around them.

Yankel walked towards them. "Could you tell me, please, when the next boat is due?"

One of them, his sea-stained and weather-bleached beret pulled over his left ear, eyed Yankel. He took a deep long suck on his pipe, then spat with practiced precision at Yankel's feet before he answered. "Monsieur, there are no boats left in Calais." He pulled hard at his pipe, and once again blew the obnoxious brown liquid through the gap in his blackened front teeth, straight at the same spot, indicating that he had said all there was to say on the matter.

Yankel chose to ignore the man's rudeness. "Surely there must be some fishing craft out at sea that are due in with their catch?" he pressed, smartly stepping sideways to avoid a direct hit.

"Out fishing?" It was the old-timer's hitherto passive friend who answered Yankel's question. "Fishing? We have no boats left for fishing, nor the men to sail them. They have all been commandeered to transport the soldiers to England these last few days." Then having decided as abruptly as he began that he had said enough, he turned back towards the sea. Yankel returned to the car, where eager faces turned towards him. His heart went out to his dear parents, to the *rav* and *rebbetzin*, and to his restless children, all cooped up in the cramped interior.

Rabbi Rabinow urged Yankel to proceed further south to the next harbor, Boulogne, and he readily agreed. It was comforting to have someone assume the role of leader. With an encouraging nod towards his brother and sister, he took the wheel and once again they were traveling along the dusty road.

Evidence of recent bombings could be seen all around them as they passed the now-familiar sight of twisted metal, which only the previous day would have been a well-maintained army lorry. A gasoline tanker had been blown apart. Here and there a soldier lay asleep, tin helmet shielding his face, rifle left carelessly at his feet, for a few brief moments oblivious of the surrounding chaos.

Dusk and tiredness overtook them, still some miles out of Boulogne. The need to find shelter for the night was now most urgent. With a boldness born of desperation, they decided to beg for shelter at the nearest farmhouse, which lay at the end of a narrow dirt track. Raisy knocked on the door and waited apprehensively as the muffled boom of the air raid and ground attack gathered momentum. The door creaked open, exposing a narrow strip of interior, then her view was blocked by the solid frame of the farmer, who was eyeing her suspiciously. He listened sullenly to her plea for herself, two small children and two elderly couples. She was afraid to mention the others. The farmer, obviously unused to making quick decisions, scratched his head while contemplating this intrusion into his life. He would surely have refused, but a bomb exploding sent the chickens racing in all directions in the courtyard. This jolted him into agreeing to give them shelter. She thanked him profusely and hurried to relay the good news. The relief of the adults was surpassed by the joy of the children at being allowed to leave the confined space of the car. Their excitement mounted as they skipped down the winding path and suddenly found themselves surrounded by the frightened chickens which the farmer was collecting and returning to the henhouse. This was a welcome diversion for the two children.

The farmer, having settled his chickens, now beckoned the travelers to follow him. They went around the back of the building, past the pigsty where a contented sow was blissfully rolling in her mud bath. The children squealed with delight at the sight of this pink mass wallowing in the dirt.

"Look!" shouted little Betty. "Now I know why they are called pigs! Because they are so dirty!"

The joke was lost on the farmer since he did not understand Flemish. The family allowed themselves a little smile. Reaching the entrance of the barn, the farmer gestured to them to enter. He pointed to a fresh bale of straw, and allowed them to make use of it.

Yankel and Shloime hurriedly prepared the sleeping arrangements, while Raisy busied herself sorting out whatever food was left, wondering if she dared give the children a second piece of bread. She was glad that she had wrapped the bread so carefully in grease-proof paper, for it had kept remarkably fresh. Or did it taste so good because they had not eaten all day? The last of the water had been drunk. The flasks must be filled next morning from the pump in the yard. How fortunate they were, Raisy reflected, as she watched the two young men spreading the last heap of straw against the opposite wall and lovingly shaping it into a 'bed'. Not all beds were prepared so luxuriously, only those for the elderly couples. She was relieved that the children did not complain, and were soon fast asleep.

Raisy went to the entrance and watched the other two ladies slowly walking up and down in an effort to relieve their stiff limbs. It reminded her, ironically, of a peacetime *Shabbos* afternoon walk — but gunfire soon brought it to an end.

Everyone prepared for the night. Anneke had been the first to curl up and soon drifted into sleep. The *rav* surveyed his sleeping charges in the dim light. On one side of the large barn lay the sleeping children and the women, at the other end were the men. He prayed for guidance as he listened to the rhythmic breathing of the sleepers. They were his responsibility.

❈ ❈ ❈

The following morning they were back on the road, reaching Boulogne in the afternoon.

"You want to go to England?" repeated one of the old fishermen. "You are too late. All the ships have gone."

"When will they return?"

"They won't!" he answered with a shrug. At least this one did not spit!

"Let's just sit down by the roadside," someone suggested.

"No," said the *rav*, firmly. "We shall go back to Calais. Our best plan will be to reach the farm where we spent the night, before it gets too dark."

Once more they waited while Raisy knocked on the farmer's door. To say he was pleased to see them again would be incorrect. However, he did allow them the use of his barn.

Raisy was desperately short of food and felt she had nothing to lose by asking the farmer if he would sell her some, so once more she knocked on his door. "I will pay you well for food," she offered. To her surprise, he agreed, and asked what she would pay for a freshly killed chicken. He would wring its neck and pluck it in front of her so that she could be sure of its freshness.

"No, no!" she said. "We are all vegetarians!" she added hastily, glad that she had thought of the excuse so quickly. He would never have understood about kosher food. "Can you sell me some eggs and potatoes?"

They finally settled on a dozen eggs and a bag of potatoes. She was delighted when the farmer agreed to let her cook the eggs on his kitchen range, using the pan which she had brought with her. The potatoes were put directly into the fire, and she watched them to make sure they did not burn. What a feast she produced! This was their first cooked meal since leaving Antwerp.

After eating, the children fell asleep quite contentedly on the same straw bed they had shared the previous night, but all were beginning to feel the need for a wash and a change of clothes. Neither the *rav* nor Anneke's father managed to sleep that night, for the hopelessness of their present situation worried them both. While the others were sleeping, they discussed the problem. Yankel tried to stay awake and join in the discussion, but was soon dozing off. They were no longer disturbed by the noise of the guns.

❊ ❊ ❊

Next morning, the sun shone down on billows of black smoke. Anneke watched the children chasing the chickens as they searched for food among the pebbles. They cried when it was time to pile into the car once again, and would happily have remained on the farm with its beds of straw.

It was not yet noon when the Buick inched its way into Calais harbor. What had still remained two days earlier of this once peaceful old seaport was now in ruins. Wisps of smoke curled upwards from the shattered jetty, and there, like some desert mirage, a cargo ship bobbed up and down, tied to a leaning capstan. Sailors were feverishly loading crates into the hold.

Fathers with young children in their arms, women huddled in small groups with their children, all were begging the sailors to take them on board. Everyone knew that this was their only way of escaping the monster that was rapidly swallowing a continent. In an instant, Yankel grasped the situation. He walked up to one of the sweating sailors and demanded to know the name of the ship's owner. The sailor pointed to a dapper dark-skinned man watching from the bridge, who was trying to ignore the panic gripping the refugees as he watched the sailors working. He had been well paid to deliver the crates safely to England, and was well aware of the dangers of the crossing. He only half listened as Yankel explained to him that he was offering his Buick with its load of sample gowns in return for passage on board the ship, but the sense of what he was saying fired the Frenchman's imagination. He hesitated. He had always wanted a new Buick, and he knew many chic ladies who would be only too eager to buy the dresses.

"Well, where is your car?" he asked.

Yankel breathed a sigh of relief. "Come, *mon capitaine!*" he said, as he led the man to the car which was parked nearby. He opened the trunk and displayed the contents. "This is my Buick. As you can see, it is in perfect condition."

The captain hesitated. "Food and drink are expensive."

Yankel hastened to assure him that they would not need food or cabin accommodations. All they asked for was to be allowed on deck.

It seemed a reasonable enough request. The Frenchman's eyes lingered on the elegant lines of the mud-splattered Buick. It could soon be polished, to rival even his friend the Lord Mayor's official car. He turned towards Yankel. "But only on the deck," he said grudgingly, and strode back towards his ship.

Yankel could hardly believe his good fortune. The next instant he sprang into action — he must not waste even a second! He moved with lightning speed, for he realized that the vessel's owner did not know the exact number of his family. The sailors were busy hauling in the gangway as he shepherded his confused family towards the laden boat.

While Yankel had been engaged in bartering for a place on board, his parents, the *rav*, his wife and the others of his group had joined Shloime and Anneke on the quayside. Many others had gathered there too, longingly watching the ship as it prepared for departure. Racing towards the ship, Yankel begged the sailors to stop a moment as he lifted his children, handing them over the railing to a sailor. He called in Yiddish to those families nearest him that they, too, should jump onto the ship. Instantly there began a clamor for space on the plank. "It's worked!" Yankel thought excitedly, as he and Shloime helped his frail parents onto the elevated gangway. Although the sailors were willing to help the children on board, they refused to help the old people. Rabbi Rabinow refused to move unless his wife, who was near collapse, was assisted. They had come so far together — somehow they had to help the *rebbetzin*. With the two men lifting her, and Raisy with Anneke pulling her gently, they made it, as the sailors impatiently continued to raise the gangplank.

Suddenly, to their horror, they saw someone fall into the water: he had lost his balance as the gangplank had begun to rise. No one could help him — the quay was too high. The people watched helplessly while the ship slowly began to move away. The victim's heart-broken young wife and children watched in shock as he drowned. Kind arms soon led the bereaved woman to a deck chair and tried to comfort her.

Was it only a week since they had left Antwerp, a close-knit happy family, seeking refuge? Yankel surveyed the crowded deck. Only a short while ago, he had successfully bartered all his worldly possessions for a place there for his own family and the many others who had managed to come on board. However, his heart ached for the family from whom such a greater toll had been exacted.

❊ ❊ ❊

Nobody cared that there was no food on board. They arrived in England after a crossing which could only be described as a nightmare, with nothing but the dirty clothes they were wearing.

Chapter Nine

ow let us see what had happened to those who had found shelter in the crowded cellar of a house in La Panne.

❧ ❧ ❧

Morning dawned, bringing a welcome stillness in its wake. In the cellar people were waking up. The need for food was desperate. Pappa had prayed most of the night for the safety of his family; now he readily agreed to help search for food. Brudi eagerly joined the others as they cautiously climbed the stairs. The door leading to the forecourt was swinging to and fro on one broken hinge. Wherever they turned, their eyes met nothing but devastation. In stunned disbelief they looked up at the house to see that the bedrooms, which had been so tempting only the night before, existed no more. The east wall had completely disappeared, exposing the interior of the rooms. The wallpaper hung in strips; wardrobes were smashed, exposing rows of neatly folded linen. A sewing machine was hanging precariously over a girder above gaping floorboards, near a bed with two legs missing. Yet there on the wall was a clock, unscathed! The minute hand moved silently, proclaiming, "Time stops for no one!"

They had been inches away from a direct hit. Where had the house's inhabitants gone?

❧ ❧ ❧

Obtaining food was the first priority. Thousands of refugees roamed the streets, desperately hungry. They searched houses long since stripped of anything edible.

Pappa and Brudi followed the crowd along a road that was to take them towards the beach, which was crowded with remnants of the British Army, massing to await evacuation. Military vehicles were parked bumper to bumper as far as the eye could see.

Brudi watched a group of soldiers, squatting in a circle and eating. Impulsively, he approached them. How could he show them he wanted food? Begging has a universal symbol; he stretched out his hand, palm up. Good-naturedly, they offered him a small bar of chocolate. Hungrily he stuffed most of it into his mouth, remembering at the last bite that Pappa was waiting. Guilt overwhelmed him. Pointing to the one remaining square of chocolate in his hand, he pleaded, gesticulating, and they understood. One English Tommy handed him a bag of army biscuits and a few bars of chocolate. Greatly pleased, Brudi hastened to Pappa, who ate a little chocolate, and saved the rest to share with their friends. Perhaps if the soldiers had known about the critical shortage of food, they might have given more to be distributed.

Eager to share their good fortune with the others, they hurried back to the shelter. Brudi ran down the stairs and handed the bag of food to one of the delighted women for distribution among the children.

As he re-emerged from the cellar, Brudi found Pappa engaged in conversation with a neighbor from Antwerp, Mr. Rappaport, who was telling Pappa, "I heard a rumor that the Town Hall has organized the baking of bread and is about to distribute some!" Could this really be happening?

"How do you know?" Pappa asked.

"It is just a rumor, maybe, but let us go and find out."

"Let's go towards the Town Square." There, sure enough, they found that a large crowd had gathered. There was even a policeman on the scene, patiently trying to coax the crowd to form an orderly line outside the bakery.

"Yes, monsieur," he was repeating, "as soon as we get it, the bread will be distributed. Just stand in line, please, and everyone will get a share."

Within a short time the line had grown to form a file four deep, right round the square. Brudi noticed a school friend of his standing in line, and they greeted each other with delight — Brudi would have loved to join Leibel. It was the first time since being separated from the rest of the family that he had come across someone his own age who was not a stranger. But patiently they stood waiting in their places, glancing idly upwards at the sound of planes engaged in a dogfight, a Spitfire and a Messerschmitt. It was no longer remarkable. Suddenly Pappa grasped Brudi's arm. "Let's go. Now is not the time to be caught in large gatherings!"

"But Pappa," Brudi pleaded, "they will soon open up the bakery and we will miss the bread!"

Pappa was adamant. "Now is not the time."

Brudi could not control the tears spilling down his cheeks as he obeyed his father. Hardly had they reached the next corner, when a German plane swooped down on the hapless refugees, machine guns blazing. It was all over within seconds, and the plane was gone, climbing behind the Town Hall spire. Cries and screams reverberated throughout the square. Pappa and Brudi raced back to find wounded, dead and dying sprawled across the cobblestones and on the pavement. Others were too stunned to do more than stare, bewildered.

Brudi looked for his friend Leibel. The hideously injured boy was lying in the gutter, his lifeblood spilling into the road. They had been at school together, played games together, had had friendly fights and passed secret signs during exams, and now he was no more.

A short while later, the bakery doors opened. The delicious smell of freshly baked loaves helped, if only in a small measure, to restore a sense of hope. The supply was soon exhausted, however, and promising a new batch as soon as he could obtain a fresh supply of flour, the baker regretfully closed the doors.

Pappa and Brudi wended their way back, in the late afternoon, with a single loaf of bread. One man had found a small bag of the lump sugar so favored by the French when drinking coffee, and a handful of seed potatoes donated by a kindhearted farmer. They washed the potatoes at the tap in the courtyard. They would have to be eaten raw. (It is amazing how tasty and satisfying sliced raw potatoes can be, when there is no other choice!) Everyone put the food they had collected on a little table, and when all had arrived, the allocating of the food began. There might have been a little lighthearted merriment, but the thought of the ones who did not return saddened everyone. Pappa's and Brudi's bread was greatly appreciated, and one gentleman produced the "prize trophy" — a bottle of oil! He held it up in a gesture of triumph, bringing a welcome relief of tension. Next, he set about slicing the bread into the exact number of slices required. Pouring some oil into a small pan, he ceremoniously dipped the first slice into the golden liquid, inviting others to do the same, and when sprinkled with a few grains of sugar, it was quite delicious. All were so engrossed that they could almost ignore the explosions of guns and mortar attacks raging a short distance away.

Earlier, one of the men had brought water from the pipe in the yard, and the elderly refugees longed for a hot drink. How can one heat water with neither gas nor electricity available? Someone produced a packet of candles and Brudi offered to try to boil the water by holding a small pan over a lighted candle. A more tedious job would be hard to find! Time dragged; the water first started wafting minute puffs of steam, much later produced the first magical bubble, then another and another. The second pan was more successful, because Brudi discovered that if he used a piece of paper as a lid, the water heated up much more quickly. By then his arm and shoulder were aching and he was immensely relieved when someone else offered to take over. A few grains of tea leaves added to the water, along with a good imagination, made a most welcome drink.

They could not ignore the severity of the fighting taking place throughout the night. For a while the comforting murmur of the menfolk reciting *Tehillim* could be heard, then suddenly, all was quiet. The silence was stunning in its abruptness. No one spoke, but fear showed clearly on their tired faces. Sick children whimpered as they stirred restlessly on the makeshift beds.

Dawn crept over the horizon, forcing its damp grey fingers through the night sky, making way for the golden rays of sun spreading across the horizon. Alas! This day, the 25th of May, 1940, was destined to strike terror into the hearts of thousands of Jewish refugees.

❈ ❈ ❈

The stillness was shattered by the sound of marching jackboots, echoing as their wearers strutted along the cobbled roads, passing quite close to the cellar windows. The stamping of heavy boots could be heard coming down the narrow stairs. Before them stood an officer of the Wehrmacht with his adjutant, who carried a fixed bayonet.

"*Gut Morgen*," he greeted them, with Teutonic politeness. "We are pleased to inform you that we have successfully driven the enemy out of the country. The French Army has surrendered, so now you have nothing to fear. You may safely come out into the streets." As he was about to leave, he added, "You should all return to your homes as soon as possible. We want everyone to resume his or her normal life. You have nothing to fear. The terrible British have mostly been captured and the rest driven into the sea."

Abruptly turning and clicking their heels, both men climbed the wooden stairs and went out into the street. Only then did those present relax and allow a sigh of anxiety to escape from their throats. Their worst fears had become reality.

For some time no one moved, delaying the moment when they would have to face the full implication of the officer's command. Although most of them came from Antwerp, few had known each other before. Yet how easily they had taken to each other! Now they set about making plans to return as a group, for to remain or even delay would add to their hardship.

The first problem was transport, and the men went out to find some, leaving the women and children behind. Brudi was pleased that he was allowed to join the men.

Victorious German troops strolled in the streets, their uniforms immaculate, their faces freshly shaven; they ignored the groups of tired and apprehensive Jews in their crumpled suits. Not quite sure what to do, the latter reached the Town Square just as the Germans were raising their flag on the pole which had for so long borne the symbol of a proud nation. The shattered window panes and crumbling masonry symbolized a power in decline. Soldiers were clearing the square and one threw his helmet into the air in jubilation. Here and there one could see French North African troops roaming the streets. The little band of Jews turned sadly away and walked down a side street towards the seafront, hoping to avoid the patrolling German soldiers.

"Here we are." Hershel Katz broke the gloomy silence. "Look at these abandoned British Army trucks!" These lined the roadside, blocking most exits, dirty but serviceable. The men walked along a row of vehicles.

"Who can drive?" asked Pappa.

"I can," said one eager young man. He tried the handle of the nearest truck — it opened easily. The next moment, he was behind the wheel. All the weariness of the past few days evaporated as he studied the array of knobs on the panel before him. Never before had he seen a truck such as this, let alone driven one, but here he was, in charge! He tried to start it. He understood that the black-topped lever on his left would control the gears, but did not know how to use it. The key was still in the ignition and he pressed the button, making the vehicle jump forward like a frightened kangaroo, and causing his admiring onlookers to jump aside. Flushed with excitement, the young man leaned out of the window to assure them that all was well and he would soon master the machine's working. After several more attempts, and many crashes in all directions, they felt it would be reasonably safe to pile in and let him drive them back to the waiting women and children. There they proceeded, but not without a few more scrapes along the way as the outsized lorry lurched crazily along the road away from the beach. Again they were ignored by the soldiers whom they passed. Triumphantly they alighted outside the damaged building that had been their home for two days, or longer. The sound of the truck stopping outside brought out some of the women with their children.

They quickly collected their few belongings and some, surprisingly, almost regretted leaving the cellar. They were now a close-knit group sharing a common fate.

Pappa looked around the two cellar rooms, which had served them so well. There was not much ventilation, the interior was rather damp, the two small windows gave very little light, but, as Pappa watched the last of the women packing their belongings, he realized that their safety was due to the smallness of the windows.

They climbed the stairs for the last time. No one spoke as they quietly piled into the truck, helping those who needed help, and arranging the few belongings of each family. There was frail Mrs. Adler, helping her husband, urging him to stretch his legs as he sank gratefully upon the narrow bench inside the crowded interior. His wife's fussing embarrassed him, but nevertheless, he was grateful for her concern. Mr. and Mrs. Adler had been the last to join the group in the cellar, having arrived only the previous day. How a couple of their advanced age had managed to survive the hardships of those last few days is difficult to imagine. Like many others, they had come as far as Ostend by train. They had been a pathetic sight when Mr. Greenberg and his son found them, wandering along the streets of La Panne.

For the children, excitedly jumping up and down in the truck, this was even better than the annual *Lag B'Omer* outing in school. No clean suit to worry about, hunger pangs forgotten, they were intent on enjoying every moment. Leon, the driver, was eager to start. Though unfamiliar with both the vehicle and the roads ahead, he promised to drive them safely back to Antwerp, with all the confidence of an inexperienced teenager accepting a challenge. If anyone noticed his lack of control as the lorry jerked forward, no one commented. Leon decided to keep to the main roads, but this was not always practical, for many were blocked with an assortment of vehicles traveling in all directions.

What was to become of the French, Belgian and even British soldiers roaming through the towns and countryside? Many would make their way to England via the hazardous routes through the French and Spanish Pyrenees. Others would spend the war years incarcerated in various prison camps. Yet others would join the Free French Army and melt into the background, while still others were destined to die in the infamous concentration camps. But all that was still to come . . .

❀ ❀ ❀

It was May 25, the third *Shabbos* of the war. The ship with Anneke, her parents, and their companion refugees was just sailing out of Calais as the lorry carrying Pappa, Brudi and their new friends was beginning its trip in the other direction, back to Antwerp. Leon was gaining confidence and better control of the truck with every mile covered. It was not long before they had left the coastal area behind them, their progress hampered by the battle-damaged state of the road which often needed clearing to avoid puncturing the tires, or because of having to wait for a convoy to pass.

They had almost reached the city of Ghent when their vehicle unceremoniously ground to a halt, and Leon had no idea what the problem could be. The men would have to walk to the nearest houses and seek help, while the women tried to soothe their hungry children. Three of the men were walking along the road when a German staff officer's car drew alongside. One of the occupants wound down the window and asked where the men were going. When they explained their predicament, the officer ordered his driver to return to the stalled vehicle. Fortunately they had not gone very far, so the three men soon joined the officers as they examined the truck. It only took a few moments to declare, "No gas!" Without further ado, one

German produced a heavy rope from the car, and tying it to the bumper of the truck, they towed the lorry full of Jews to the nearest gasoline station some miles away. It was closed and deserted. While one of the soldiers pumped gasoline into the empty tank, the officer who had first spoken to them asked where they were going. They explained that they were on their way back to Antwerp.

"It is unwise to travel any further today," the German said, for night was falling. "Do you have anywhere to spend the night?" They shook their heads. "Follow me," he commanded. They had no choice but, with mounting apprehension, to follow. Even the children were quiet as they drove behind the staff car, stopping outside an ancient village church. Reluctantly they alighted, one by one. When all had assembled, the officer told them to go inside. Then, extending his right arm in the Nazi salute, he marched back to the staff car. A few moments later the car sped away. Dare they disobey and risk being picked up a second time? It was getting late and the children were crying. Keeping together, they slowly walked towards the heavy double doors of the church hall. After a moment's hesitation, someone opened the door. What greeted their troubled eyes was like a fairy tale come true.

Long wooden tables and benches ran along both sides of the room, with almost every space filled. Young and old, fatigued and hungry, had been greeted with a welcoming smile by the kindly burghers. As soon as they were seated, each new arrival was given coffee, bread and cheese. How it came about that a German staff car was used to guide the hungry and homeless Jews to this haven remained for Brudi a tantalizing mystery forever after.

For the moment, cares were banished into the background as the group enjoyed their first meal in comparative peace and comfort. They sat or lay on the floor, recounting personal experiences and catching up with the rapidly changing turn of events. Victory was no longer spoken of. Soon, the peaceful sound of deep breathing lulled even the chronic insomniacs to sleep.

Next morning, Brudi opened his eyes as Pappa gently tapped his cheek. How pleasant it was to wake up in a brightly lit place, with the rays of the sun streaming through the open window and birds chirping cheerily as they perched on the branches of the elderberry tree! Brudi washed his hands and face, taking water from a large urn that their friendly hosts had placed in the courtyard for that purpose. Then he joined the line, patiently waiting for coffee. He made sure that he got some for Pappa too. There was bread only for the children.

It was time once again to pile into the truck and head for Antwerp. Everyone felt more cheerful after a good night's sleep. Leon whistled a popular tune as he eased the car into gear, noting with satisfaction the smoothness with which he accomplished this. The remainder of the journey took much longer than it should have. Some of the main roads were blocked, necessitating long detours over narrow congested roads, and they ran out of gasoline once again. There was nothing for it but to wait for an ever-present German patrol car to find them. Sure enough, some time later, one stopped to enquire if help was needed. On being told they had run out of fuel, the officer in charge issued an order; two soldiers jumped out, swiftly produced a rubber pipe and proceeded to siphon gasoline from their own tank into the truck. To get the roads cleared and everyone back to their homes was an overriding consideration, and they performed the task with the thoroughness inherent in their training.

Finally the party entered the once-proud city of Antwerp through the long tunnel under the river Scheldt. Home!

※ ※ ※

Sunday, May 26, would forever remain one of the proudest days in British history, when owners of small craft volunteered to ferry remnants of the army across the Channel, making the journey time and again, thereby saving thousands who would otherwise have perished. These would have been astonished had they known that their abandoned vehicles would be used to take people back to their homes!

Chapter Ten

The Belgian army had not yet surrendered, but for the citizens of Antwerp this last formality made no difference. It was six days since the German army had made their triumphant entry. Having been declared an 'open city,' Antwerp was spared the bomb damage inflicted on other towns, so physically nothing seemed to have changed. However, German soldiers were now patrolling the streets. Even the traffic police on duty were Germans.

The greatest change could be seen in the Jewish quarter. Gone were the people, some homes and shops had their shutters closed, while others were unlocked with no one to guard them. *Would the occupants ever return?* Pappa wondered, looking up and down the deserted street.

Reluctantly, he and Brudi entered their own building, their footsteps echoing through the corridor. Mounting the marble stairs, they hesitated outside their apartment. Brudi closed his eyes tight and prayed. "Please, *Hashem*, may all this be just a bad dream, and when Pappa opens the door, we shall find all the family awaiting us!" Alas! When the door opened, silence greeted them; the beds stood neatly made, the starched lace tablecloth on the dining room table with the bowl of artificial flowers in the center were just as Mamma had arranged them. Nothing had changed. In the kitchen hung the gleaming array of pots and pans so lovingly scrubbed and polished; there was the coffee mill with its ornate brass fittings, and the kettle in its usual place on the range.

"Come," Pappa called to Brudi, "let us go down to the shop and see what we can bring up to make a meal." The Ledermans' delicatessen was just as they had left it. Noticing some rotting apples in the fruit tray, they set about tidying the fruit and vegetable boxes, discarding the bad pieces and wiping the ones still edible. A middle-aged man came in. Pappa did not know his name, but had seen him in *shul* in happier days, so they greeted each other like brothers. The man bought a few provisions for the members of his family who still remained.

While the two men talked, Brudi went into the back room adjoining the storeroom, where the Lederman family used to have their snacks in-between serving customers. He lit the gas burner and put the coffee pot on to boil. There was no fresh milk, of course, so he opened a can of condensed milk and mixed some with water. Soon he carried steaming cups of coffee into the shop. Pappa smiled; this was better than eating upstairs in the empty apartment, where everything reminded him of his missing family. He could picture Mamma in the evenings, sitting in her favorite chair, busy sewing, making blouses for the girls or mending trousers for the boys, while quietly humming a familiar tune. Pappa could almost feel her presence as he dwelled on this cozy domestic scene.

No, far better to eat down here for the moment. Gratefully he accepted the freshly made coffee that Brudi gave him. Pappa watched him go again to the back room and return a few moments later holding a plate with Matjes herring. A packet of rusks completed the meal.

Pappa looked at his son as they ate in silence. It had taken only two short weeks to turn a shy youngster barely in his teens into the mature boy he was now.

As the days passed, more people returned. Very few families had remained intact. Since the onset of the German occupation, those Jewish families living in the provinces no longer felt safe, and preferred the security of a closely knit Jewish community, at least for the time being. Slowly a semblance of normalcy returned to the city.

It was decided to reopen the Jewish school — life had to go on, and children needed education. The Jewish school had few teachers, since not many came back, but there were enough for the few pupils who had returned. To everyone's surprise, one non-Jewish teacher had also returned, and taught secular classes for each age group in rotation.

✡ ✡ ✡

It was no fun playing marbles in the schoolyard anymore. In the old days you had to wait your turn to join the game, and competition was fierce. Brudi studied the brightly colored glass marbles in the palm of his hand.

Only four weeks had gone by since he had won these in this very same playground. His friends had formed a circle, with boys fighting to be in the front line with Brudi, who had challenged the champion. Excitement mounted as the spectators joined in their chanting of "putty, putty, putty." With only three minutes left of the lunch break, Brudi was declared the unbeaten champion. Accepting his opponent's prized marbles, as the rules demanded, he could feel the admiring looks of his younger brothers and heard them boasting to their friends. It was their brother, once again, who had been declared the winner . . .

The crushing crowds with their boisterous voices had disappeared. With practiced ease Brudi let the marbles roll in the palm of his hand. They were all he had left. His brothers were gone and so were his friends and most of the boys. Brudi walked up to a little boy playing a solitary game. "You can have these marbles," he said. They were of no more use to him.

※ ※ ※

Pappa had settled down to running the shop. It became a meeting place, where one could discuss events and opinions without the ever-present fear of being overheard by the wrong people. For the moment, the Jews of Antwerp were allowed to pick up their lives unmolested; this was an uneasy interlude which fooled no one.

As the weeks went by and spring gave way to the long lonely summer days, Pappa surveyed the slowly diminishing stock on the once crowded shelves, which he had no hope of replenishing. This was not the time for complacency, so he began to formulate a plan . . . So absorbed was he, that he did not notice when Brudi entered the shop.

"Pappa," called Brudi, excitedly. "You know that the Heide Yeshivah has moved to Antwerp?" This high-level religious school took its name from the area in which it was situated.

Pappa nodded. It was neither practical nor safe to keep a Jewish establishment outside the Jewish areas, so the school had moved into Antwerp. This once thriving yeshivah with its high standard of learning attracted students from many countries.

"Well," Brudi continued, "all the boys of my class are being transfered to the Heide Yeshivah." *All four of us*, he could have added. He longed to share this exciting news with Mamma and the rest of his family. He had always looked forward to his first day in the advanced yeshivah as the great event of his life, the day he would join the elite and no longer be referred to as a *chedder yingel*, a school child; the day that people would begin to call him a *yeshivah bachur*.

"That is wonderful," Pappa said encouragingly. It was not often lately that his son looked so happy; this was an unexpected bonus. He was well aware that the normal age of acceptance was fifteen, and then only upon passing a particularly difficult examination. But these were not normal times!

❈ ❈ ❈

Brudi crossed the road to join his friend Yossi. Together, they walked purposefully towards the main road, hardly noticing the policeman on traffic duty in German uniform. They stopped at the corner of Lange Kievitstraat and Pelikaanstraat, and listened to the impatient clanging of the tram cars. The owner of the tobacco shop on the corner continued to serve his customers with the same calm politeness that had helped him start his flourishing business, and if the customers were now fewer, so was his stock diminished. Crossing the road, the boys continued under the railway bridge, passing the tiny booth still selling coffee and rolls.

They turned into Stoomstraat on their right and, as the road curved, they reached the entrance to the courtyard of the building which was to be the new temporary home of the Heide Yeshivah. Over the next few days they happily adjusted to the strict discipline geared to the needs of much older boys. They were greatly helped by their *rebbe*, himself a comparatively young man, dedicated to instilling the love of Torah learning into his charges.

❈ ❈ ❈

An incident happened that would remain vividly in the minds of those boys who were fortunate enough to survive the war.

One Friday night they were absorbed in the evening prayers. As the students waited in silence for their *rebbe* to finish the *Amidah*, they became aware of a uniformed figure standing in the doorway. It was an SS officer. The solitary figure of the *rebbe* swayed gently as he finished murmuring the *Amidah*. Then, becoming aware that something was amiss, he turned slowly and confronted the officer, whose hand rested on the hilt of his saber. He pulled it out of its scabbard, and pointing it at the rabbi he shouted, *"Juden!* Who is in charge?"

"I am," answered the *rebbe*, with a faint trace of apprehension.

"Jew!" the officer continued. "What you are doing is illegal. You have no permission to be here and are therefore committing a crime! I am giving you until next Friday to vacate this building." He paused, savoring for a moment the effect of his words. Then, abruptly clicking his heels, he turned and was gone.

The *rebbe* looked at the pale trembling boys. *"Kinderlach,* we will continue to *daven* and learn Torah in these premises," he assured them, adding prophetically, "That Nazi will suffer greatly for the terror he has inflicted upon you. But not before he has returned to apologize."

They continued to learn and pray as before, some students sleeping in the building, others going home at night. The week dragged by. On the following Friday evening, the large room used for learning all week was once again the venue for the *Shabbos* evening prayer. A few boys had stayed away, their parents afraid of the consequences of disobeying the officer. Once again the door burst open and the same officer entered the hushed school.

Ignoring the terrified boys, he marched up to the *rebbe* and clicked his heels together. *"Herr Rabbiner,* I apologize for intruding! My enquiries have shown that you are indeed a legal registered house of study; you had applied and been granted permission to move your school from the Heide to Antwerp at this address, and therefore have the right to be in this building." Before the students had time to take in this extraordinary statement, the German clicked his heels, turned, and was gone.

❦ ❦ ❦

Life continued peacefully for a time.

"Pappa, it is a pity that all the people ran away from Antwerp when the war first started. We can see German soldiers everywhere, but they are polite and don't bother us at all," Brudi observed. "If

Mamma and the rest of the family could be with us, it would be so nice again."

"Do not be fooled," said Pappa. "They have their reason for their polite behavior, and it is not for our benefit."

(Indeed it was not; part of the Nazis' plan was to allay the mistrust of the Jewish population as much as possible, and in this they succeeded to a considerable degree. Had they not acted in such a peaceable manner at the outset, many thousands of Jewish families might not have returned to their home towns, but would instead have made every effort to reach Spain, or they might have acquired Aryan identity papers and blended with the rest of the refugee population. The Germans were so cunning! Jews actually believed themselves to be reasonably safe as long as they caused no trouble. After all, the Nazis were engaged in fighting against the British Empire. Surely they would not concern themselves with the Jews of Antwerp!)

Not everyone was fooled, and certainly not Pappa; he knew there was no time for complacency.

Chapter Eleven

The long hot summer was nearly over and there were still plans to be finalized. Although Brudi never asked, he knew Pappa was secretly making some arrangements which were fraught with danger, for Pappa, not easily alarmed, would often look startled when someone entered the shop as he tidied the shelves. Brudi would occasionally go with Pappa in the evening to a friend's house, ostensibly to join the man and his wife for supper. No meal would be served, however, and after settling Brudi with the wife in the kitchen, the two men would retire to another part of the house, leaving the kindly lady to talk and entertain the lonely teenager. Mostly they talked about Antwerp and school life before the occupation, and Mamma. Sometimes it would be hours before the men returned.

Brudi continued to attend the yeshivah by day. He began to dread the long evenings, for it was then that he remembered fondly the coziness of their kitchen . . .

The kitchen was always a hive of activity, with Mamma, dear Mamma, sitting in her favorite straight-backed chair, with an unending mountain of socks to be mended, keeping a watchful eye on her lively brood as they sat at the different tables in the large kitchen. Supper was a simple meal of hot buttered toast rubbed with garlic or raw onion. Often this would be supplemented with a few marinated herrings, smothered in a thick white sauce with lots of onion rings, and of course there was always the blue enamel coffee pot on the stove, filling the

> room with the delicious aroma of strong hot coffee made from freshly ground coffee beans and chicory.

How his heart ached with the memory, yet he clung to the vision of the homely scene ...

> Supper finished, the girls would clear the table and everyone would commence their homework. This was a most unpopular activity, with Mamma having to coax or occasionally resort to bribery in an effort to get the children to do it. Once started, the lessons tended to get finished quickly, so that a game of Lotto could still be played before bed.

Academic we were not! thought Brudi. *Ambitions we had in abundance, but these did not include being at the top of the class!* Brudi smiled to himself. *Perhaps I should have tried harder, for Mamma's sake ...*

❦ ❦ ❦

The walnuts ripening on the trees in the Stadspark were left to fall to the ground. *Gone were all the boisterous boys, vying with each other as to who could knock the most walnuts off the trees. How their fingers had turned a deep purple as they extracted the walnuts from their protective casings ...* Yes, autumn had chased the long, eventful summer away.

❦ ❦ ❦

Pappa and Brudi were sitting in the kitchen. It was evening; the last day of the fall *Yamim Tovim* had drawn to a close.

In normal times before the war, these four weeks, from *Rosh HaShanah* until *Simchas Torah*, would be a time of religious introspection and joyous celebration. This year's holiday season had been a nostalgic one, in which they remembered the past, compared it with the present, and worried about the future.

Brudi noticed that Pappa was unusually tense and preoccupied; he wondered whether Pappa was not feeling too well, for he did seem to act strangely and tended to jump at any unexpected noise.

When the time came to go to bed, Brudi stood up, but remained firmly resolved to keep an eye on Pappa. If Pappa was not better soon, Brudi would ask his *rebbe* for advice.

Hours later, Pappa studied the sleeping boy, then gently shook his shoulder. It was only 5 A.M. but there was no time to waste. He glanced at his pocket watch: it was important to be punctual. So much planning had gone into this scheme that he was about to put to the test. *I must stay calm and act casual*, he admonished himself. He knew too well that his and Brudi's lives depended on the success of his plans.

"Brudi, get dressed and *daven*." He waited while Brudi stretched, yawned, and then washed his hands. "Everything is ready. I have packed a bag with enough food to last us one week." Pausing, he reflected, "It should be more than we will need, but it is better to be well prepared." So this was the outcome of all those clandestine meetings, and the reason for Pappa's strange behavior!

Pappa had somehow managed to obtain authentic-looking documents to allow them to travel through Belgium, France, Spain, and finally Portugal, with their destination being South America. Excitement swelled inside Brudi; he was hardly able to contain it. Pappa put a finger to his lips to indicate the utmost secrecy. "We must not cause suspicion. No one must know. We will leave at exactly 6:45 A.M." Brudi realized how carefully Pappa had planned when he continued, "I have timed the distance to the station. We must walk at a normal pace, to arrive a few moments before the train leaves. We must not be seen standing about, or we may arouse suspicion."

"When will you buy the tickets?" Brudi asked.

"That's all taken care of."

Once again, with great trepidation, they closed the door to their apartment and turned their backs on the home that held so many memories. Down the marble staircase and into the street they strode; with great faith — and little baggage — they accepted the challenge of the unknown.

They caught the train without mishap, just as Pappa had planned. The train left on schedule. For the first time Pappa allowed himself to relax; he took out a precious cigarette he had saved. Being a heavy smoker, he relished this cigarette which would have to last him until evening, when he would light his last one. Hopefully by then he would be able to buy a few in Spain. Blissfully unaware of the ordeals ahead of them, he blew smoke rings into the air.

It was forty-eight hours later when they reached the French-Spanish border town of Bayonne, after a journey which was uneventful except for the frequent inspections by German soldiers who would board the train whenever it stopped, walk the length of the carriages, check identity cards and traveling documents, and thereby cause much delay.

Pappa waited with barely suppressed anxiety for each new inspection to end. At last they reached Bayonne, where they disembarked and waited for another train which would take them the short distance to the border town of Hendaye. This sleepy village was tantalizingly near to the Spanish town of Irún. A short walk from the station to the bridge, across that bridge and one was on Spanish soil! As they approached the barrier, which was manned by German guards, their hearts beat with excitement at the sight of the Spanish border patrol. They could see men and women crossing ahead of them.

"Halt!" the guard shouted. "Show me your papers."

Pappa tried to control the tremor in his hands as he handed his exit visa and traveling documents to his interrogator. Their hearts pounded as the German scrutinized the documents. Handing them back, he exclaimed, "Stupid *Juden*, why do you want to leave? Don't you know that nobody wants you? We in the German Reich are the only nation who allows the Jews to stay!"

Fear gripped them both. Pappa began pleading, begging him to allow them to cross over into Spain. "Are my papers then not in order?" he asked, but their tormentor had not yet finished.

"You still want to go, you stupid Jew?"

Pappa could only nod, his body shaking uncontrollably.

"Well, go then," he boomed. "But mark my words, you will be back, nobody wants you anywhere! Only we Germans take care of you Jews!" Saying that, he gave the command to have the barrier raised once again.

Over the bridge they walked, hardly able to believe that they had finally crossed the border and were truly standing on Spanish soil. A short walk from the bridge was the railway station. Brudi felt there was a festive air about the place, with its little round tables and chairs alongside the ticket office.

Pappa had hardly noticed the new surroundings, so absorbed was he in giving thanks to the Almighty for delivering them out of the clutches of the Germans. Now they joined the other travelers, who were drinking an assortment of soft drinks and local wines. The little café was doing a brisk trade among those awaiting their connections at this little station. How many thousands of hopeful refugees would remember Irún as the gateway to their dreams of freedom! They could not guess the many disappointments and heartaches still to come. Instinctively choosing seats that faced forward, towards Spain, with their backs to the French border, Pappa ordered cold mineral water for both of them, the cheapest beverage on the list. He knew he must be careful with his money — coming out of France was only the first stage of his plan. Where were they going? He could not really give an answer.

The waiter, obviously in high spirits, slapped their drinks onto the table, startling Pappa out of his reverie. He paid the man, who nevertheless still held his hand out! This gesture transcended all language barriers. Pappa tipped him. Satisfied, he tucked the battered tin serving tray under his arm and disappeared behind the beaded curtain of the café.

Laughter could be heard from the young Spanish border guards who were now relaxing in the cool interior of the building. Pappa surveyed the scene. Most of the passengers were Spaniards. The rest were possibly French men and women and among them were some who were certainly French Jews.

They waited patiently for the train which would take them over the border into Portugal. It was now only midday, but no one cared. The very air they breathed seemed to taste of freedom. Pappa closed his eyes and relaxed. He longed for a smoke as he watched some of the men at the next table puffing away at their strong Turkish cigarettes, but no! He strengthened his resolve as he touched the solitary cigarette in his breast pocket. He bought two a day and that was all he allowed himself. This was no mean feat for a man used to smoking forty or fifty cigarettes a day!

The sun was dipping behind a row of cottages on the horizon; the sunbeams, like golden arrows, playing on the tiled roofs. The whistle of an approaching train could be heard in the distance.

"Olé!" called the buxom lady sitting at a nearby table. Most of the waiting crowd had been dozing in the warm autumn sunshine, but now with true Latin exuberance they greeted the oncoming train. They hastily gathered their baskets, which were filled with personal belongings hidden from prying eyes by well-worn clothes. Boarding was fairly orderly, conducted under the watchful eyes of the Spanish gendarmes, who no doubt were relieved to get rid of their charges.

They settled down quite happily on the last part of the journey to their Portuguese destination, a town called Villa Formosa which lay on the frontier, linked to France by the direct railway line through the length of Spain. This trip, too, was accomplished uneventfully, and they arrived at the border on the following evening.

Once again there was a passport control, but this time the uniformed guards were Portuguese. Uneasiness began to creep into Pappa and Brudi. The gendarmes were obviously refusing entry to some unfortunate passengers, judging by the sobs and earnest pleading which could be heard in the quiet of the stationary train.

Now it was Pappa's turn to produce his documents. With trepidation he held out his papers — surely this was only a formality? It was not.

The official was a swarthy man in a well-cut uniform. He listened, his face impassive, while his assistant translated Pappa's plea that he only wanted a short-stay permit since he had the necessary documents to go on to South America. Pappa spoke to no avail; he and Brudi were ordered off the train and told they they would be put on the next train back to France. With hearts sinking and hopes fading, they heard the whistle blow and watched the train pull slowly out of the station ...

The sad truth soon manifested itself as Brudi and Pappa looked around the platform to see who else had been refused passage into the country. Only Jews had been ordered off the train. They stood shivering on the deserted platform, the solitary gaslight flickering in the evening breeze. With mounting apprehension they watched a group of armed soldiers who were assembling the stranded, frightened little group, each soldier taking charge of one person. Pappa held on to Brudi's hand indicating that they belonged together. The soldier assigned to them smiled reassuringly and beckoned them to follow him. To their immense relief and surprise, he marched them both a short distance across a courtyard, and into a friendly cottage. It transpired that this was the home which he shared with his family. He had to make sure his "guests" did not escape before they were safely deposited on the train that would take them back to France. Since there were no trains until the following day, Pappa and Brudi were welcomed into their home by his friendly parents. Not wishing to give offense, Pappa and Brudi accepted the offer to join the family around the large table, while the middle-aged lady busied herself preparing the evening meal.

Pappa and Brudi were surprised to feel a gentle heat coming from under the table, and on investigating, Brudi discovered a small charcoal oven. He was grateful for the warmth, as it became very cold once darkness fell.

Although the smell was tempting, they declined the non-kosher cooked food, but were glad to accept some delicious whole wheat bread with steaming black coffee. Shortly after eating, the soldier showed them into a room with two bunk beds.

Long after Brudi had gone to sleep, Pappa still sat on the edge of his bed contemplating the terrible prospect ahead of them. To have come only this far after all the months of planning and saving! His shoulders sagged and tears welled into his eyes as he watched his sleeping son. He had no illusions about the fate awaiting the Jews in occupied countries.

No, he would not be beaten! He still had some money and he would try again.

He lit his last, precious cigarette and inhaled its soothing smoke. It calmed him, as did the rhythmic breathing of the sleeping boy. Finally he, too, slept.

The following morning, the Portuguese Military Police escorted them back to the station to await the train which would transport them back to France. After another day, and another night, they sadly disembarked, still with their formal escort, in Irún. Gone was the exhilarating sense of freedom. With leaden feet and heavy hearts they walked the now-familiar path towards the bridge. Could it be that only two days had elapsed since they had crossed the same bridge with so much hopeful expectation — only to come back and be confronted by the smirking face of the same German officer, a man they had hoped never to meet again! He ordered the barriers to be lifted once again, and wagging his finger at them, said, "You stupid Jews, did I not tell you that nobody wants you?" Thus they were greeted on their return to Hendaye.

Pappa tried to cheer up Brudi as they boarded the train which would take them back to Bayonne. "Don't worry, perhaps our papers were not quite in order," he said reassuringly. "I shall go to the consul as soon as we get there. It should only be a formality, you will see." Brudi nodded. It pleased them both to pretend it was going to be easy.

In Bayonne, Pappa's spirits rose. Purposefully he sought out the Spanish and Portuguese consuls to obtain the necessary documents. One helpful official at the Spanish consulate volunteered the information that it would be easier to obtain a transit permit once they possessed a valid visa into Portugal. They thanked him and wasted no time, but hurried along the street to the imposing building which housed the Portuguese consul. With hearts pounding, they explained their request. The official behind the desk calmly filled in the lengthy questionnaire regarding their reasons for wanting to go to Portugal. This completed, he informed Pappa that he should call back in two months' time. Pappa gasped, repeating, "In two months' time?"

"Ah!" the attendant remarked, folding the money that Pappa had slipped into his hand. "Come back next week. Who knows, perhaps it will take less time." Bowing, he withdrew into the inner office, closing the door behind him.

Brudi looked at Pappa. To the young boy, suddenly life seemed wonderful again. "One more week!" he told Pappa, as they emerged into the bustle of the busy road. "In a week we will be able to board the train again, this time with the correct documents!" His imagination took flight at the thought of leaving the Germans behind them. Pappa too felt hopeful, although he realized that their release might well take a little longer. Still, it was with a sense of accomplishment that they boarded the train back to Hendaye. They had no idea at that time that the weeks would stretch into agonizing months.

The journey passed quickly as they planned the week ahead. It would have been more convenient to have remained in Bayonne, but they were advised against it, since the Germans were much stricter there and constantly stopped people in the street to check their papers. Pappa reckoned that they would be safer in the small but friendly garrison town. Although Hendaye is a French town, its inhabitants are predominantly Basque, and speak Spanish as their main language.

As Pappa and Brudi emerged from the station, they realized that they must find somewhere to stay. Nearby, a porter was loading boxes onto a pushcart. He was typical of the men in those regions, stocky and dark skinned with twinkling eyes, wearing a black beret pulled over one ear. He was concentrating on balancing the boxes which he had piled too high, and whistling a popular tune.

"*Excusez-moi*, could you direct us to a place where we could stay, maybe a week? Not too expensive?" asked Pappa. The little Frenchman stopped whistling, and scratched his head. Yes, their luck held.

"I have a spare room you can rent," and he mentioned a small fee, which Pappa readily agreed to. He lived across the road from the station. Full of gratitude, they were shown to their room, which was to become their temporary home for almost three months. It was heaven! Two metal beds, some blankets, a paraffin lamp (which needed filling), and a small table. Who could ask for more?

The shopkeeper nearby was very friendly and although most sympathetic, she was unable to supply them with bread without the necessary coupons. After four weeks of residence (this being the minimum time required to become eligible) their friendly host advised Pappa to apply for bread coupons. It was not without a measure of anxiety that Pappa presented himself at the municipal bureau, but all went well and Pappa emerged with the coupons. He gave a deep sigh of relief — he had become very concerned about the effects of their inadequate diet of fruits with occasional vegetables. Now he would be able to buy bread. They were accepted as part of this small community.

Pappa made frequent trips to Bayonne, hoping to collect his traveling documents. He no longer took Brudi with him, as he dared not spend money on two tickets. The days were long and uneventful. Brudi made friends among the rough, good-natured troops and was allowed at times into the barracks for a friendly chat, where he watched them as they cleaned their rifles. It was a welcome diversion, especially on days when Pappa went to Bayonne.

Twice daily, trains would arrive at this border town, and every arrival would be eagerly awaited by Pappa and Brudi.

They had both seen Mamma, Oma and the children at the railing of that beautiful French liner, and knowing nothing of the subsequent events, they had never lost the hope of being one day reunited with their family, who must surely be somewhere in France.

So they scanned the passengers as they emerged from each successive train, day in, day out, never missing a single one. Not one familiar face were they ever to encounter. As the weeks rolled by, the locals accepted this lonely Jewish man and his son, and they would be greeted wherever they went. Sometimes they would go to the barrier and watch the lucky ones walking across the bridge. Perhaps next week it would be their turn ...

One glorious day Pappa arrived at the office of the Portuguese consul, to be greeted with a smile. His heart missed a beat. "Monsieur," the clerk was saying, "we have your documents all ready, but there is an additional small fee to pay." Pappa eagerly handed over the money and waited while the official counted it. Then, with a flourish, he handed Pappa the precious documents. Pappa took them, thanked the official and bade him goodbye. The papers had to be stamped with a transit permit from the Spanish consul to enable the pair to travel through Spain, but this was a mere formality and was soon accomplished. How good it felt to board the Hendaye train for the last time . . .

Brudi was waiting at the station. He could see by the rare smile on Pappa's face that at last he had been successful. Buying a few provisions for the journey was almost an adventure.

As they walked towards the familiar barrier across the edge of the bridge, who should meet them but their old tormentor! Recognition was instant. "You again!" he said, making it sound like an accusation. "Why do you want to go again?" In answer, Pappa produced his papers and explained that having updated his papers he wished to continue on their journey to South America. Pappa and Brudi both recoiled as the soldier rocked with helpless laughter, joined by some of the off-duty guards. An eternity passed. Then once again the order to raise the barrier was given. Long after the guard had waved them on, his last words rang in their ears. "You will be back!"

Once again, they walked the short distance over the bridge. A few paces through no-man's-land, and they were once again on Spanish soil in Irún.

They sat down at the familiar little tables provided for travelers who were waiting to catch a train. The waiter came around. Someone produced an old mandolin and plucked at the strings, coaxing a medley of popular tunes from the battered instrument. The waiter hummed as he flitted from table to table, spreading an infectious mood of merriment.

A clatter of activity heralded the approaching train. The magical moment was over. After making sure it was going to Villa Formosa in Portugal, they boarded it. Once more, relief overwhelmed them as the train pulled out of the station. Neither spoke for the moment. Pappa unwrapped the sandwiches he had prepared, for neither of them had eaten that day. As the train took them past the towns and ancient villages, Pappa explained that ever since the Inquisition, when Spanish Jews were rounded up and burnt at the stake, a *cherem* (ban) had been imposed on the country; even traveling through it was to be avoided if possible. However, to save one's life in times of great danger, the *chachamim*, our wise sages, had decreed that it is permitted. "And so," Pappa concluded, "we are now in such a position, and it is to save our lives that we are here on this train." They both sat in silence thinking about that ancient tragedy, while swaying to the rhythm of the speeding train.

It was an uneventful journey. Their anticipation of freedom soared as they felt the train finally easing into the station at Villa Formosa. Freedom at last! Their hearts beat faster as they followed the other passengers off the train. For a moment they stood on the platform, watching those ahead moving slowly towards the customs-control point. Finally it was their turn. And there, with feet apart and hands on hips, stood the same guard! Looking Pappa straight in the face, while ignoring his outstretched hand holding the documents, he uttered just one word: "No!" No amount of pleading helped. He refused even to look at their travel documents.

Could it be possible that they would be refused entry? Indeed it could. Once again they were under arrest and taken to spend the night with a local family.

The following day five people sadly boarded the train that would take them back to France: Pappa, Brudi, and three other Jewish passengers who had also been refused entry.

Broken spirited, the motley group walked over the bridge to be greeted with these words: "Not only are you both back again — this time you have brought your friends with you!" How the guard enjoyed this joke! His fat belly spilled over his leather belt as he shook with laughter, while he went through the motions of examining their papers.

Pappa's heart sank as he watched the *Kommandant* fold the travel documents and then hand them to his underling. He still held the passport in his hand, as if undecided whom to give it to. The tension was almost too much for Brudi as he watched the troubled face of his father turn even paler. Abruptly, the officer handed Pappa the passport, saying, "I see you are a Hungarian. I have spent many a happy vacation in the beautiful city of Budapest. I myself am an Austrian," he continued. "Do you think I enjoy being here, away from my family?" Just as Pappa's hopes began to soar, they were crushed as the guard continued. "Of course I would like to be back in my native Salzburg, but my *Führer* has sent me here. Until we have conquered the whole of Europe and the English dogs have come to their senses, we all have to suffer."

Clicking his heels, he raised his hand in salute. *"Heil Hitler!"* Turning, he swaggered away, leaving the two hapless Jews to contemplate their worsening position. Having been deprived of their travel documents, they no longer had a legal right to be in France, so once again, Pappa took Brudi's hand and together they walked to the station and boarded the train to Bayonne. He must not succumb to despair; for the sake of his son, Pappa realized that he must pretend that all hope was not yet lost. Where was his faith? He must continue to do all in his power, he told himself, while watching the countryside flash by.

Soon they reached Bayonne. How many times before had Pappa made this very same journey? But always, in the past, he had been able to produce some documents on demand. Now even that was not possible.

Pappa did not waste time. They hurried to the Portuguese consulate, but the man shook his head. "So sorry, monsieur, but without your documents we cannot help you. Why not try the consulate at Bordeaux? It is a much larger town. Who knows? Someone there might be able to help."

Pappa decided to follow this advice, uncertain whether it had been given with a genuine wish to help, or just to get rid of them — two bedraggled Jews. So once more they made their way to the station and arrived at the ticket office. Pappa's heart missed a beat. How was he to obtain their tickets without the necessary travel permit? "Next," the man behind the grill called impatiently. On seeing Pappa's familiar face he asked, "Hendaye?"

"No, monsieur, Bordeaux," Pappa answered casually, holding his breath and sending a silent prayer heavenward. *"Voilà, monsieur!"* The clerk slapped the two tickets on the counter. They dared not relax until the train pulled out of the station, afraid that the clerk would remember that he had not checked their papers.

It was not without a tinge of sadness that they steamed out of Bayonne for the last time, leaving the last vestige of security behind them. Pappa mentally calculated the amount of his dwindling cash. What was to become of them? They had left Antwerp with such high hopes, and a fairly well-stocked purse. His intention had been to stay in Portugal until such time as he could discover the whereabouts of Mamma and the rest of the family. News had filtered through that the American Jewish Joint Distribution Committee (known simply as the "Joint"), with the aid of the International Red Cross, was attempting to serve as the invisible link between far-flung war refugees, and helping to reunite separated families.

(Pappa was deeply troubled, not knowing where we were. If only he could have known that we were living in London at that time, spending most nights in the comparative safety of an underground shelter in Victoria Park with hundreds of people who would all sing in unison, "Roll out the barrel..." We were still bewildered and in awe of the good humor of the British and their unshakable confidence in ultimate victory. We tried to join in the singing, while our minds dwelt on a devastated continent and we prayed for the safety of our loved ones...)

The train drew into the station at Bordeaux. Pappa stood up and opened the door. This was the largest city they had been to since leaving Antwerp. The multitude of people gave them a sense of security, and looking around, Pappa observed the indifference of people going about their business, a familiar trademark of any large town. The signs of occupation were more evident here; German military police were everywhere. Had it ever been otherwise? Brudi tried to imagine the tree-lined streets without the representatives of Hitler's Reich. Did the citizens not care? Or did they just pretend not to care?

They walked through the town center in search of the Portuguese consulate. "Here it is," called Brudi excitedly, pointing to a large building. Pappa sighed with relief, for they had been walking for some time and dusk was approaching; soon it would not be safe to remain outdoors. Pappa rightly assumed there would be a curfew at nightfall.

Tomorrow, when the office opened, Pappa would be there to beg for a permit, just one more time...

Pappa stopped outside a brightly lit drug store. "Tonight is the first night of Chanukah. Let us go and buy a small bottle of olive oil and some cotton wool. This is surely a *siman tov*, a good omen." Thus he provided himself with the essentials for making the Chanukah lights.

Shortly afterwards they found a small boardinghouse willing to take in two Jews. They remained three days in Bordeaux, engaged in a fruitless search for help. Their money was dwindling away, and since they no longer possessed food coupons, it was extremely difficult and expensive to obtain the barest necessities.

It was time to move on.

Pappa discussed the matter at length with Brudi, and explained that to remain in Bordeaux was pointless. They were in danger of being picked up by the Germans and sent to a labor camp. They had actually watched some unfortunates being apprehended and ordered into a closed van for not having identity papers and therefore being "undesirable aliens." Pappa did not doubt that he too would fit into that category if caught. In addition, their money was almost gone.

Paris, with its large Jewish community, seemed the most logical destination. They longed to be among other Jews and have a chance to blend in. Above all, Pappa reflected, money was needed for food, and perhaps in Paris he could find some work, any work, to help them to survive and remain free. (Ah! How ironic to think of anywhere in occupied France as free!) Well, it was all he could hope for at the moment.

For three days they had stayed in the small airless bedroom with paint peeling off the walls, and the pipes banging every time someone used the water. Pappa had hardly been able to sleep because of the noise, but nevertheless it had been "home" for three days. Reluctantly gathering their pitifully few possessions, they bade the room a silent farewell, and strode purposefully out into the street.

To be wary of the German police had become second nature; to avoid them, a way of life. Pappa and Brudi had both become quite expert at ducking into doorways or alleys to avoid being stopped and questioned. It was with great relief that they reached the station, which was only a short distance away.

How short lived their relief turned out to be! As they walked towards the ticket office, it dawned on them that they had no traveling permit. They hastily retreated and watched anxiously as other lucky travelers produced their magical papers. No pass, no tickets. Trapped! To remain standing in the station was to invite suspicion. They had to go, but where?

Walking across the forecourt of the station, they had no idea what to do. *Well, we must do something,* Pappa decided; he was never one to let a situation get him down for long. Almost at once, he whispered to Brudi. "Can you see that man in the center of the hall?" Brudi turned slightly to the left: there was no mistaking whom Pappa meant. Standing in splendid isolation, a tall, well-built, middle-aged man with an unmistakable air of authority surveyed the ever-shifting scenario of people arriving and departing. Brudi turned back, wondering why Pappa seemed so excited. How could that stranger possibly help them? Pappa had the answer ready. "You are a child," he said, "and your French is better than mine. Go up to him and ask him to help us obtain tickets to Paris."

"*Excusez-moi, monsieur,*" murmured Brudi, following the words with a little nervous cough. "Pardon me, sir." The man looked down at this thin-faced youngster who stared back at him with his large brown troubled eyes.

"What do you want?" he asked kindly.

"We wish to buy tickets for the train journey to Paris, but we have no traveling permit," Brudi replied in his best French, which was, in fact, a mixture of French and Flemish, since it was quite usual for children in Antwerp to mix the two languages. It seemed a long time to Brudi before the man answered. By then they had been joined by Pappa who had been anxiously watching, ready to be at hand when needed. Neither of them was prepared for the stranger's next question. "*Du redst mameloshen?*" ("Do you speak Yiddish?")

They looked at him in bewilderment. Then a grin spread over Brudi's face as he listened to Pappa explaining briefly how they had come to be in their present predicament. Taking the money from Pappa, the stranger asked them to remain where they stood. They watched in silence as he strode up to the ticket office. The large notice board in the center of the hall hid him from view. Neither spoke as they waited; the minutes ticked by, each one an eternity. Would he return only to tell them he was sorry but he could not help? What would become of them?

Mercifully the man reappeared before panic overwhelmed them. Still smiling, their benefactor handed Pappa the two precious tickets that would allow them onto the Paris-bound train. How could they thank him? "No, no," he waved the question away. "Do you have someone to stay with when you arrive in Paris?" he inquired.

Pappa shook his head "We have no one."

Writing a name and address on a piece of paper, the stranger handed it to Pappa, saying, "When you get to Paris, go straight to this family, the Schwartzes. They will help you." With this he bade them farewell, and moments later had merged with the new arrivals from the incoming train.

German soldiers were busy checking tickets among the new arrivals. How good it felt to be able to walk through the ticket barrier unhindered and board the train — the relief was overwhelming! For the moment they were safe; what did it matter if they had not eaten all day? The journey took many hours, giving Pappa ample time to reflect on their situation and marvel that Brudi could fall asleep so easily.

They arrived in Paris at 5:30 A.M., as dawn was breaking. German soldiers patrolled the station. For a moment they panicked — had it been a mistake to come to this city? But where else could they have gone? There was no choice. The sooner they got out of the station, the better. Squaring his shoulders, Pappa opened the door and, motioning to Brudi to follow, walked past the soldiers patrolling with rifles slung over their shoulders. Their helmets were pulled well down, giving them a fierce look that made Brudi shudder. Pappa took his hand and, looking straight ahead, walked with feigned confidence towards the main entrance. At any cost, they must not appear to be nervous.

Their luck still held as they emerged from the station; an old taxi was parked outside, the driver asleep at the wheel. Not waiting for him to wake up, they jumped in. How fortunate they were to have a destination! Pappa gave the address to the sleepy driver, who proceeded to coax life into his ancient engine. After numerous attempts, he grudgingly left his seat and, armed with a cranking handle, jerked the engine into life after a good many stops and starts. The car came to a halt outside an apartment house, they paid the fare and watched the taxi disappear into the grey damp dawn.

Now doubt came creeping in. What if this Monsieur Schwartz no longer lived at this address? Who had sent them? Pappa shook his head as if to dispel these thoughts. He walked to the nearest row of names set out on the doorpost with another row of electric bell buttons alongside. His heart raced as he scanned the list. Sure enough, there was the name, Monsieur Schwartz, clearly written alongside the second bell, marked first floor. They hesitated for a moment. Would it be wise to knock on the door of a total stranger at this early hour? But to remain outside was to draw attention to themselves. An intense weariness overtook them. Boldness born of a longing to find shelter overcame their reluctance to impose on others.

The entrance to the building being slightly open, they decided to go up the stairs and knock gently on the door. They waited for someone to respond. Nothing happened. *Perhaps they are sleeping and did not hear!* His heart pounding faster, Pappa knocked again, this time much louder. They could hear someone walking inside the apartment, but no one came to the door. Should he try one more time? Pappa looked at his tired homeless son; yes, he would knock again. He prayed that the occupant would open the door; again they waited. A child was crying somewhere inside. They heard a woman's gently reassuring voice as her footsteps came closer to the door.

"Who are you?" she called, with a note of unmistakable fear in her voice.

Dispensing with caution, Pappa answered, "We are *Yidden;* please may we come in?"

"What do you want?" she asked, her voice no longer fearful.

"We are strangers and have nowhere to go." In silence they waited, hope rising as the woman hesitated. Finally opening the door, she eyed the two travel-weary visitors. Instinctively they felt at ease with her. Closing the door behind them, she motioned them to follow her into the kitchen.

"I don't suppose you have had anything to eat yet," she commented, while busying herself with the coffee pot. "Who told you to come here?" She handed them steaming cups of coffee.

"A man in Bordeaux."

"I don't know anyone in Bordeaux," she remarked.

"Perhaps your husband does?" Pappa suggested.

"Perhaps." They drank their coffee in silence, relishing the delicious feeling as the hot liquid seemed to reach every part of their bodies.

Neither Pappa nor Brudi had eaten since leaving the boardinghouse the previous morning. Madame Schwartz did not need to be told that her guests were starving — she was all too familiar with the telltale signs. Hunger was no stranger in her house, as indeed in most Paris households since the German occupation. She would have loved to be able to serve some food, but she had none.

"My husband is the *gabbai* of the *shul* in the Rue des Rosiers," she explained. "He went there this morning as usual, and when the morning service is over he has to wait for everyone to leave so he can lock up. Then he goes to the bakery to buy a large loaf of bread before returning."

For the moment, Pappa and Brudi were content just to be allowed to remain in the kitchen while the young woman's attention was claimed by her children. One by one she brought them into the room. The youngest was a baby of six months, the next of eighteen months, then a three-year-old, and the eldest of the four boys was aged five. They were each given a mug of coffee to drink while the baby enjoyed his bottle, cradled in his mother's arms.

This homely scene was sheer bliss to Brudi, for it evoked his fondest memories. He grinned at the children as they stared at him with undisguised childish curiosity. It was little Mendy, age three, who was the first to accept a ride on Brudi's knee. His squeals of delight soon brought the others begging for their turn. Thus began a warm friendship that was to bring comfort to them all during the long, increasingly difficult months ahead. This tiny apartment was to become the haven to which Brudi would return whenever he could.

This, then, was the cozy scene that greeted the father of the children on his return. Brudi's aching knees were unceremoniously abandoned as the children ran to hug their father, who hardly had time to close the door behind him to shut out the hostile world. He handed his wife the precious loaf of bread, for which he had waited on line for almost an hour. He greeted his guests with a warm handclasp. Sitting around the table with coffee and bread, Pappa earnestly explained their plight as their host listened thoughtfully, absent-mindedly dipping his bread into the coffee in the traditional way.

"How remarkable," he said. "I have never been to Bordeaux, and cannot recall anyone who lives there. Your description of the man does not fit anyone I know. Perhaps," he said, searching for a rational explanation, "perhaps it is one of those businessmen from the provinces who travel frequently to Paris, and sometimes attend the services in our *shul*."

"Perhaps," Pappa murmured.

Being a practical man, their host applied himself to their most pressing need, a room of their own to sleep in. He would gladly share his home and his meager rations, but he could not accommodate guests in the tiny apartment for any length of time, and who knew how long they would be in Paris? Having been assured by Pappa that he could afford to pay a modest rent for a room, M. Schwartz delayed no longer.

The morning had been so pleasant that it was with some reluctance that Brudi rose to leave. He thanked the lady. He did not really want to leave their friendly home, and readily agreed to return the following day.

Leaving the apartment building, they were grateful for M. Schwartz's presence as they walked beside him. In spite of it, however, their hearts beat faster as they passed the ever watchful German patrols during the ten minutes' walk to their destination.

As they walked towards Rue de Rivoli, M. Schwartz told them a little about a remarkable Frenchman, the proprietor of a boarding-house called the "Hôtel de Sud." How wonderful to hear about a fellow human being who was prepared to let rooms to unfortunates who had no identity papers, even Jews! They quickened their steps. What if all his rooms were taken?

Crossing the road, they passed the entrance to the Métro St. Paul on Rue de Rivoli, and stopped at the corner of Rue Malher. Facing them was the Hôtel de Sud, the fading letters painted on the fascia. With some trepidation, Pappa and Brudi followed M. Schwartz, who boldly walked up to the reception desk.

"*Bonjour, monsieur*, I have brought two friends. Do you have a room available?"

The Frenchman checked his chart and stretched out his right arm to retrieve a key from the pegboard. He handed the key over the counter, saying, "Sleeping accommodations only; second floor, room twelve." Thanking him profusely, they hurried towards the staircase.

No questions were asked and the fee presented no problem for the moment. They unlocked the door and surveyed the room. It did not matter that they could not even boil water for a drink; such luxuries were not to be expected. Perhaps in bygone days the establishment had provided all the amenities associated with the title "hotel", but for the present, room accommodation was all it afforded its many grateful boarders. There were two beds, a small chipped dressing table and an aging wardrobe. And it was clean! Their possessions, all in a battered canvas bag, remained packed. It would take Mamma's touch to turn this bare room into a home!

Pappa looked at his son, whose shoulders drooped as he sat on the edge of the bed. "Perhaps you should get some sleep," Pappa suggested. "I will go out with M. Schwartz so he can help teach me to find my way around." Brudi readily agreed, and no sooner had the two men left the room than Brudi, sprawled across the bed fully dressed, was fast asleep. The faint rays of wintery sun streamed through the window.

❦ ❦ ❦

When they left the hotel, the two men turned right, into Rue Malher and then into Rue des Rosiers. They entered the Jewish quarter, known to generations as the *Pletzel*. "Look here!" called M. Schwartz, pointing to the building nearby. "This is our *shul*. It is known by the house number 'Twenty-five' Rue des Rosiers, and there," he said, pointing again, "is 'Number Fifteen.' Besides these two synagogues we have three others quite near, but let us enter Number Fifteen."

A quick look around was enough to reassure Pappa; it hardly differed from his own place of worship back in Antwerp. Nostalgia enveloped him, taking him back to the intimacy of the Terliststraat *Shul* ... *The hubbub of conversation as he and his friends waited for the morning service to commence* ...

His companion brought him back to the present. "Let's go now; evening service is at six o'clock. Let us go and meet some of my acquaintances on the Boulevard."

Thus Pappa was introduced to an altogether new way of life. The men would sit around at little tables on the pavement drinking hot black coffee while engaged in all types of business transactions — negotiating, bartering, advising — much as it was done at the Bourse in Antwerp, although there diamonds were the chief topic. Here one had a great variety of matters to discuss and debate in altogether more agreeable surroundings.

Since the occupation began, there were fewer elegant Parisiennes strolling past, to the regret of the old-timers. Nonetheless, the talks were still cheerful and lively in those early days of the occupation. The outdoor café was a meeting place of men from all walks of life. The newly arrived refugees eagerly looked for someone they might have known in the past: a face, perhaps a name ...

Pappa, having been introduced to the men sitting around the table, which was placed overlooking the crossroads, watched the policeman on traffic duty. The policeman had just been drafted from the German Army, and knew very little French. Shortly he would be replaced by a well-trained German Army policeman.

As time passed, Pappa seemed to accept the life in Paris, but he had only one aim, which was to seek out ways of escape. He never trusted the polite German occupation forces. Unaware that his beloved family were all safely settling down in England, he was restless and frustrated with worry.

A few weeks passed. Pappa made friends, and then came the first tentative inquiry ... Yes, for money one could be supplied with fresh documents and a guide who would take one over the Pyrenees. "A hazardous journey, monsieur," Pappa was warned by his contact. "No, no, it takes time ..." came the cautious reply to Pappa's plea for urgency. And so life went on.

Chapter Twelve

Brudi awoke as Pappa re-entered the room. "Wake-up, lazy bones, supper is being served," he called in mock reproach, and with a great flourish deposited a can of peas on the wobbly table. Just looking at the printed label displaying a dish with succulent peas, topped with a blob of glistening butter, made Brudi realize how hungry he was.

"Pappa, did you bring a can opener?"

"A what? Oh dear, no!" They looked regretfully at their longed-for meal.

"Ah!" said Pappa, quickly recovering from this minor irritation. "There is sure to be someone with a can opener in this house."

Now fully awake, Brudi jumped up. "I will go and ask," he said, hurrying to the door. Out in the dimly lit corridor, his enthusiasm evaporated. He walked slowly down the hallway, pausing at each numbered door, too shy to pluck up courage and knock. Feeling ashamed and miserable, he was about to turn back and confess to Pappa, when he heard the sound of subdued laughter coming from behind a closed door a little distance away. Not allowing himself time to think, he walked resolutely up to the door, and taking a deep breath, knocked gently. After a moment the door opened. The head that appeared was that of a middle-aged lady, with troubled eyes. These softened as she scrutinized the lonely boy standing in the hallway. She opened the door halfway; now he could see two more figures inside the room — a boy and a girl. A little sigh of relief escaped him. They were about his own age.

"Can I help you?" asked the lady, giving him an encouraging

smile — and so started a warm friendship with the kindhearted family Ostreicher.

Triumphantly, Brudi returned to their room where Pappa was waiting, holding a worn and dented can opener as if it were a newly found treasure. Pappa soon realized that it was the encounter with another Jewish family in similar circumstances, staying in the same guest house, that pleased his son so much. As he opened the can, taking care not to spill any of the liquid, he listened to Brudi telling him about his new friends. They were Austrians: a father, a mother, two daughters and a son. The children were teenagers, just a little older than himself. Now Brudi felt a little less lonely.

In thoughtful silence they ate the peas straight from the can. They were careful not to cut their lips on the jagged edge of the tin as they drank the liquid, their first drink since the coffee in Mme. Schwartz's kitchen in the early hours of that morning. Brudi noticed that Pappa gave him more than he took for himself, but his empty tummy would not let him protest.

Early the following morning they hurried out to be in time for morning prayers at "Number Twenty-five", eager to meet the men taking part. They gratefully clasped the hands held out in greeting, and replied to their *"Shalom aleichem''* with *"Aleichem shalom"*. At the far side of the *shul* hall, in a small alcove, was a table with a kettle boiling gently on a small gas burner. All around stood groups of men drinking tea. Pappa and Brudi were invited to make their own tea, and accepted readily. This certainly was an unexpected bonus! (The practice may have changed by now, but before and during the war it was customary in most of the French synagogues to provide tea leaves and constant boiling water for the men attending the daily *minyanim*. At times someone would bring a few lumps of sugar as a special treat.)

"Where have you come from?" someone asked Pappa.

"Antwerp."

"I have a brother living in Brussels; did you come direct?"

"Well, not quite," answered Pappa.

Just then the *shammash* called the congregation for the commencement of the morning prayers.

As they came out of the *shul*, Pappa told Brudi, "You go on to the family Schwartz, they are expecting you. You will be able to share breakfast with them."

"But what about you, Pappa?"

"Don't worry about me. The tea has refreshed me, and the sooner I make inquiries about obtaining new papers, the better it will be!"

Pappa had been given the addresses of a number of consulates in Paris and wanted to start immediately on his quest for an exit visa, be it to Portugal or Spain, Argentina or Uruguay — or any of the other distant places that would enable him to leave the country legally. He had no plan of action, just an ironcast determination to escape from occupied France. He was grateful to have found a family who welcomed his son, for this enabled him to devote all his energy to achieving his goal. They arranged to meet at their hotel in the early evening.

Pappa accompanied Brudi most of the way to the Schwartz apartment, leaving him when they reached the Rue de Rivoli. Brudi was warmly greeted by Mme. Schwartz, and by the children who all demanded to be given a ride on his knees again. He happily accepted the hot sweet coffee the lady handed to him, then they waited for M. Schwartz to come home with fresh bread from the bakery.

Breakfast over, Mme. Schwartz invited Brudi to accompany her and the children. First they took the eldest boy, Maurice, to school. From there they walked to various shops in the *Pletzel*, searching for some food that she could afford. Vegetables had become scarce and expensive, and were consequently beyond her means, but nevertheless, on most days she would manage to find something for an evening meal.

Marcel, the friendly shopkeeper, asked who was the boy with her. She glanced casually over her shoulder to where Brudi was standing, holding onto the stroller with the two little ones strapped inside, and grasping Pinny, the older one, by his hand.

"Oh, he is my nephew who's come to stay with me for a while."

It did not do to let strangers know the truth, and from that time on she was Tante Dena to him.

She was about to leave the shop, when Marcel beckoned. "Madame," he said, "would you like to earn a few francs?" She looked at him doubtfully, although there was nothing she would have liked more. Even before the outbreak of the war, her husband's meager salary had been barely enough to provide for their basic needs, but she would not leave her children to go to work. She was suspicious of work which a woman with small children might be asked to do.

As if reading her mind, he explained: "All you will be required to do is deliver small parcels that I will give you." Then, eyeing the children's stroller, he continued, "It is essential that you have the children with you on these errands, so that you will not be suspected."

She was horrified! It was unthinkable to use the children as a cover for smuggling.

Marcel held up his hand. "Please," he said, "I do not want an answer now. Go home and think about it." With that they left. As they walked along the busy road, Tante Dena discussed this strange proposition with Brudi. He listened respectfully, not quite grasping its significance. "I will see what Aaron, my husband, will make of this offer. It really is not for us," she observed thoughtfully.

Back at the apartment building, Brudi carried the stroller up the stairs. He declined when Mme. Schwartz suggested that he stay for the evening meal. He would go back to the boardinghouse and wait for Pappa.

Pappa had had an uneventful day, presenting himself at several of the consulates to register for a visa. The sullen clerks did nothing to bolster his confidence. Later he joined the group of men at the pavement café, and on his way back to the hotel, he again bought a can of peas. It was one of the few commodities left on the grocers' shelves still available without coupons, and cheap. Occasionally Pappa was able to buy a few fresh fruits or vegetables, and on some very rare occasions, bread.

As he thought over the day's events, he realized he must not be impatient. It was only his second day in Paris, too soon for anyone to divulge information. Also, he must not appear to be probing.

※ ※ ※

Pappa found Brudi engaged in animated conversation with the young Ostreichers, who were telling Brudi the story of their family's flight from Austria.

> They were well used to this way of life. In the early days of the Anschluss, when Hitler's thugs first made themselves felt in Austria, the early signs of their reign of terror included the indiscriminate rounding-up and transporting of Jewish men to the infamous Dachau concentration camp. It was only on the strength of a visa and passport to the U.S.A. that Herr Ostreicher was released, a broken man, after inhuman beatings

> at the hands of his jailers. Those were the days when not even the Jews were ready to believe the horrific stories told by those lucky enough to be released. It was only through his wife's selfless determination that he was let go; she stood on line for days and nights outside the American embassy, as did many other women, some with tiny babies in their arms. Then they came as far as Paris, intending to stay overnight before catching the train to Marseilles the following morning. It was not to be so. Subsequent events followed so quickly that they were forced to remain in Paris.

That was the story that Brudi later told Pappa as they shared their meal of canned peas. (They were becoming quite the experts regarding the different tastes and qualities of these vegetables. Those labeled *'Petits Pois'* were definitely superior, much sweeter, and therefore tastier than the rest.)

❦ ❦ ❦

The weeks went by. Brudi went for breakfast to Tante Dena and spent the rest of the day with her, helping with the children and accompanying her on her daily outings. He picked up Maurice from school so that she could go straight home with the younger children.

Pappa had formed a close friendship with an Austrian refugee of his own age, who was to bring a welcome diversion into their lives during the short time they were privileged to know him. This audacious and fearless man could find humor in most situations, and on his frequent evening visits, Uncle Menachem, as he liked to be called, would regale them with hair-raising stories. He would recall with great relish the time he was apprehended carrying a paper parcel containing a suit length.

> It was, of course, illegal to sell such items, which commanded high prices on the flourishing black market. After they opened his parcel, the two German SS men marched him to the nearest police station. His chances of ever walking the streets of Paris again were slim indeed, unless . . . His resilient mind leaped into action. As the charges were being read from the police commandant's desk — "Illegal immigrant carrying contraband" — he collapsed in a simulated seizure, rolling and twisting on the floor in apparent distress. The German

commandant and his men looked on with bored indifference, and the moment he 'recovered' they ordered him to leave, which he did in great haste.

As he was to recall with glee, "I would have liked to see their faces when they realized that I had tucked the parcel under my arm on the way out!" Brudi marveled; only Uncle Menachem could have pulled off such a feat!

❦ ❦ ❦

Almost three months had passed since Pappa and Brudi had first knocked at the door of the Schwartz's home. Brudi felt like part of their family as he gave a sharp, confident rap on their apartment door. At once the door opened to a chorus of "Brudi, Brudi!" from the children. Entering the dimly lit room, he instantly felt something was amiss. Tante Dena was reading a letter, which she must have read several times. She repeated the words by heart as she absentmindedly folded and unfolded the piece of paper with its official crest. "Aaron is to report tomorrow morning for work. There is no indication what work is involved," she said, looking at Brudi. "The only other information given is that he should bring an overnight bag."

This was the first organized roundup. Ironically, it was those foreigners or immigrants with valid identity cards, such as M. Schwartz, who were among the first batch to be picked from the registry. In fairness to the French authorities and the local police whose services were used, they believed that these foreigners were needed in Germany to replace the conscripted factory workers, and deporting them would have the advantage of leaving more jobs for the loyal French citizens. This ruse worked perfectly for the German overlords, allowing them to stay in the background, and since most of the deported foreigners were Jews, who would complain anyway! All around, life went on as usual; no eyebrows were raised, and the German Gestapo stayed well away, patrolling their allotted areas with the utmost courtesy and politeness.

❦ ❦ ❦

The following morning, the road sweepers cleaned the gutters, pushing their brooms in front of them. Cheeky sparrows hovered overhead, calling noisily to each other. A new dawn, a new day, nothing to mark it from any other day, except for the small group of people wending their way to the market square. Soon, maybe fifty to a hundred men — fathers and sons — had gathered, with their close families and friends to see them off. Children in high spirits shouted to each other as they playfully engaged in a game of hide-and-seek. An outsider watching them would have been forgiven for believing that the crowd was en route to an annual company outing. The men clutched their overnight hand luggage. What better proof that they would soon return? Who would have guessed, as the well-wishers waved goodbye while they watched their menfolk board the army trucks, that this was the beginning of a dreadful journey? I have no desire to inflict the details on my readers. Let it suffice that few came back.

❦ ❦ ❦

Morning prayers over, Pappa clasped M. Schwartz in an emotional farewell. It was not easy to part from this unassuming, kindhearted man. The only comfort Pappa could offer was the assurance that Brudi would continue to spend most of each day with M. Schwartz's wife and children and, along with Pappa, would help out however he could. "And may the Almighty speed your return," Pappa whispered, fighting back his tears. Then M. Schwartz was gone.

In silence, Brudi walked beside Tante Dena and the children, sensing her loneliness. Even the children seemed subdued. It would take weeks of frantic searching and pleading by the grieving families before the awful truth emerged about the fate of their loved ones.

It must be recorded that in spite of these deportations, life in Paris continued as before the occupation. It was essential to the Germans' orderly way of thinking that there should be no panic or even suspicion regarding their intentions. Panic creates chaos, and no self-respecting German officer would allow such a state of affairs. So they patrolled the streets and left the French to execute their commands. Three more transports had left since that fateful day.

Of course, not everyone was fooled by the deceptively polite attitude of the occupying forces ... And so the mysterious disappearances began, as those with known anti-German sentiments were arrested in the night by the dreaded SS and taken away, their protests muffled, their destinies as yet unknown ...

Chapter Thirteen

Mme. Schwartz considered her predicament. Her worst fears were coming true: who knew when her husband would be allowed to return? Her heart ached, but it was no use dwelling on her loss. The children needed to be fed and there was no money coming in. The *shul* sent her money occasionally, but she knew that sooner or later that too would stop, since so many of the members had been taken away. And no one knew when the others would be called ...

Her mind was made up. She looked at Brudi, who had just entered. How grateful she was for his company, for someone to talk to! She managed a wistful smile. "Let's get the children ready," she told him. "I have decided to apply for work."

"What kind of work?"

She chose not to answer.

Walking towards the *Pletzel*, Brudi felt quite excited. This was a welcome diversion, and he was eager to help.

Marcel beamed as they entered his shop; he did not ask why they had come. Fleetingly Mme. Schwartz wondered, *Did he have prior knowledge of the recent events? Did he know that she would be left to support herself and the children?* Irritated, she brushed the thought aside.

Marcel waited until the lone customer who had lingered near the box of newly arrived tomatoes selected some, paid for them, and left. Then, briefly, he explained what he wanted. Mme. Schwartz would be required to deliver certain goods or messages, and in return he would supply her with urgently needed food for herself and the children. She had no choice but to accept. The payment was not overly generous, but at least no one would go hungry. Brudi would probably even manage to take an occasional slice of bread back for Pappa.

One day Tante Dena asked Brudi if he would mind looking after the children until evening. She explained that Marcel had offered a modest payment in addition to the food she was getting, and for this they wanted her to travel on a bus or the métro to make deliveries. Since the round trip would take all day, her acceptance depended on Brudi's help. He readily agreed.

> *He was to tell me, years later, there were times when he wished he had not been so hasty.*
>
> *"It was bad enough having to cope with a teething cry-baby — but that was not the worst! Oh no!" he said, grinning. "By far the worst was having to change a dirty diaper." He winced at the mere recollection. "The first time it happened, I just pulled the awful soiled diaper off and sat the baby in his mother's bed. I let him crawl around there for a while until he managed to wipe himself clean enough for me to pick him up again and put a fresh diaper on him."*
>
> *"What did the poor mother say when she returned?"*
>
> *"Nothing, really; she just stripped the bedding off and soaked it in the tub."*
>
> *"Anyway," he continued, "the next time the baby soiled his diaper, I just sat him into the large sink. After the shock of the cold water wore off, he really enjoyed his little pool! I let him splash around and have a good time while the running water slowly cleaned his little bottom."*
>
> *No doubt Mme. Schwartz would have been horrified at this spectacle! She never saw it, however, and incredibly, the baby never slipped.*

❈ ❈ ❈

Tante Dena's homecoming was always greeted with delight by her young family, and Brudi too would sigh with relief, for he was never sure when she would arrive. He did not complain, but he liked to get back to Pappa as soon as Tante Dena came home.

One evening she looked very tired; the strain was taking its toll. She had traveled a long way, a fair part of it on foot, to a remote farmhouse. However, the farmer's wife had given her some freshly dug potatoes, which she quickly washed and set to boil in their jackets.

"Brudi, if you wait a little, I will give you some boiled potatoes." He gratefully agreed. He helped her settle the children and tidy the apartment, and afterwards hurried back to Pappa, carrying the hot potatoes tied in a clean handkerchief.

Pappa was always preoccupied those days, and he was deep in thought as they shared their unexpectedly grand meal. They no longer ate the peas from the can: Tante Dena had long since provided them with two plates, two spoons and a knife. Now Brudi eyed his plate of peas and potatoes — how good it looked! Pappa too was enjoying it, he could tell.

There was a knock on the door and in walked Uncle Menachem, who greeted Pappa with undisguised relief.

"You had me worried," he commented. "There was an *arrasier* this morning."

"I know," said Pappa. "I just managed to avoid it."

"Good," nodded his friend.

This dreaded menace, an *arrasier*, was conducted as follows: Suddenly, without warning, an army truck would arrive, closely followed by several large vans. A detachment of the Gestapo, fresh from a briefing, would instantly seal all exits leading to the side streets or into other buildings. Executed with military precision and thoroughness, the *arrasier* would last approximately two hours. Few, once ensnared, ever escaped. Ostensibly the soldiers were searching for contraband of any type and hidden weapons, but it was also a convenient way of rounding up Jews who had no valid papers or identity cards. One could hear the screams of the victims as they were loaded into the waiting vans.

Pappa and Uncle Menachem had both seen it happen from a safe distance, and Pappa realized he must intensify his inquiries regarding documents. He had not made nearly enough headway in that direction yet.

However, all was not gloom, not with Uncle Menachem. He looked at Brudi. "How would you like to come with me on a business trip?" Brudi thought he must be joking. He explained, "Brudi, I know you look after Mme. Schwartz's children twice a week. How about coming with me to visit the shops on the days she does not need you?"

Chapter Thirteen / 121

"I would love to, but what do we go to the shops for?"

"Why, to buy rubber balls. They are, of course, in short supply." He said this matter-of-factly, enjoying the look of puzzlement on their faces. Then he explained, "There seems to be a shortage of rubber balls, and I know someone who will pay me one franc over what it costs me for each one. So, for every ball I bring him, I earn one franc!" What an incredible man, finding someone who wanted to pay for rubber balls! Brudi's admiration was boundless.

"When do we start?"

"Tomorrow!"

And so it was. The following morning they set off together. Working according to a plan, they visited all the toy shops in as many streets as they could that day. They soon discovered that this would not be an easy assignment. There was indeed a shortage!

"Who would have guessed?" Brudi remarked.

"My dear boy, who would pay you money if you could just go and buy one?"

That day they managed to locate a grand total of three, which they duly delivered to an address a short distance from the *Pletzel*. Uncle Menachem knocked on the door and waited patiently until a short middle-aged man answered. Startled, Brudi realized the man was blind. Having recognized Uncle Menachem's voice, he beckoned them inside; they were taken into a small room with just a bed and a table. He did not seem to mind getting only three balls, and paid them. They left, promising to return with more. Three times a week they would visit the toy shops, in search of the ever-dwindling supply of rubber balls. On a good day they could muster five balls.

When Uncle Menachem mentioned that balls were getting too difficult to find, the blind man told them to look for small teddy bears! And so they did, starting with the first shops over again. When the supply was exhausted, they were told to bring toy cars.

One day, when they were ready to leave the blind man, Uncle Menachem asked him, "What do you do with all these toys? I have noticed that I am not the only one delivering to you."

"Don't you know?" he answered. "They are all sent to Germany and sold on the black market." The two stared at him in disbelief. "Well, what is wrong in making profit from the bastards?" he snapped. Then he explained. "This German officer in charge of transport is making himself a nice income by collecting small toys which he then dispatches to his contact in Germany, who sells the toys for him at a greatly inflated price to the toy-starved families with children."

"But surely this must be highly irregular and dangerous! And how come he trusts a Frenchman?"

"Why do you think he chose a blind man?"

And so their business venture came to an end. As Uncle Menachem explained to Brudi: "That same German officer could be organizing the deportation of Jews from Paris, and here I am doing business with him!" He shook his head as if to dispel this awful possibility.

※ ※ ※

The long winter months were slowly making way for spring. Sometimes Brudi would walk the length of the Rue de Rivoli. He would stroll around the Place de la Concorde, enjoying the warm rays of the sun and watching the ever-changing tableau of the sun-drenched square: young couples walking hand in hand; harassed mothers determined to share the delights of the early spring sunshine with their children. Then loneliness would overcome him and he would long for the intimacy of their bare room at the Hôtel de Sud.

One evening they were joined as usual by Uncle Menachem, who breezed in and within moments had banished the harsh world beyond. He could not stay long, he explained, as it was becoming increasingly risky to walk out at night.

"I had a special reason for wanting to see you tonight," he said to Pappa. "This morning, towards lunchtime, one of our friends sitting with us in the Boulevard Café remarked that you had not yet arrived. He called over to me, sitting at the next table, 'Do you know what is keeping M. Marcovits? He is such a punctual man!' Before I could answer, a gentleman sitting nearby came over and excused himself for imposing, but explained that he could not help hearing the name M. Marcovits being mentioned. 'Am I right in assuming that one of you is M. Marcovits?' he asked us. We looked at him in silence, not sure what to make of this Frenchman in his smart business suit. 'No, M. Marcovits is not here today,' we finally answered. 'Do forgive me,' he continued — he seemed embarrassed — 'but as it is an unusual name, I dared to hope it could possibly belong to a man my family and I are searching for.' He then asked, 'Do you know from which country he originates?' We all shook our heads, because we really did not know. After all, you don't pry into other people's affairs! He hesitated a moment, then said, 'I must go now, but I'll be here again tomorrow at the same time. Would you please ask your friend what country he comes from, and please, maybe you could ask him the name of his home town?' We listened in silence, for we did not want to commit ourselves."

In the safety of the hotel bedroom, Uncle Menachem warned Pappa. "I knew you had business to attend to, but you have to be extra cautious to avoid suspicion. Anyway," he concluded, grinning, "Where *do* you come from? How little we know about each other!"

Pappa shrugged indifferently, his mind occupied with a more urgent matter: How was he to raise the large sum of money demanded of him only that morning? His documents were ready, but his contacts demanded more money. Pappa tried to dispel the gloom that threatened to envelope him. Looking at Uncle Menachem, he said, in answer to his question, "I was born in Hungary, of course. That is obvious, I'm sure, from my accent. My birthplace is not a town, just a small village called Gibart." Then, leaning closer, he whispered, "I have made the necessary arrangements. As you predicted, I had to pay a substantial deposit. This has left me with very little, and I still have to pay the hotel proprietor, whom I owe two months' rent." His face was etched with strain and worry as he talked to this man whom he had come to trust and like immensely. "I am determined to go through with the plan on which I have worked all these months. My savings are gone and I still have the final payment to find. Also, I cannot leave this hotel before I settle my bill." For a moment they sat in gloomy silence, each with his own troubled thoughts.

"My dear friend," exclaimed Menachem, shattering the oppression. "Where is your *bitachon*? You must have faith! "Getting up, he looked at his watch. "Better be going, it's getting late." He bade them good night, and went home.

Chapter Fourteen

"Brudi, Brudi!"

Sleepily, the boy opened his eyes. Pappa was gently tapping him on the shoulder. Instantly he knew that something was amiss. It was not the usual time for Pappa to wake him; the room was still in semi-darkness and the slamming of doors along the corridor had not yet started. Pappa was already fully clothed. Wide awake now, Brudi jumped out of bed, cautioned by his father to be silent. His heart beat faster; clammy fingers of fear tightened around his chest. He dressed quickly, being careful to make no noise. How strange, one never notices how often one can knock into a piece of furniture while getting dressed! Quietly putting on his shoes, he wondered whether the other tenants of the building had also been alerted, especially the Ostreicher children.

Pappa beckoned him to come to the curtained window. Carefully he moved one curtain aside, so that they could look out into the street below. Brudi stretched out his hand to open the curtain a little wider, but Pappa gripped him. "Don't touch!" he whispered. "Just look out!"

What Brudi saw was enough to confirm his worst fears — they were surrounded by an *arrasier*. As the boardinghouse was a corner building, they could clearly see the main crossroads on their right, and a little further along, the Métro St. Paul. Although it was the main road, Rue de Rivoli remained open, and they could hear an occasional car passing. All the side streets had been blocked with military cars as well as vans manned by the Gestapo. With mounting tension they watched the victims being dragged out of the neighboring buildings and thrown into the vans, accompanied by the all-too-familiar wails of the victims' heartbroken families. As they soon discovered, the Hôtel de Sud had been requisitioned as the temporary headquarters, the usual procedure during these snap purges. Ostensibly the Nazis were looking for weapons and contraband, but their greatest success was in finding the unfortunate illegal immigrants.

As the tension mounted, Pappa tried to prepare himself for the inevitable. He prayed that they would spare his son, still a child. As Pappa and Brudi waited, they could hear the Germans moving systematically from room to room on the ground floor. They could only guess at what was actually taking place. Soon they could hear the jackboots tramping up the stairs.

With hearts pounding they waited ... Twenty minutes can seem like an eternity. Then came the knock on the door. (Oh yes, they always knocked before entering! Did they not pride themselves on being the most civilized people in the world?)

The two Jews were standing in the middle of the room, Pappa with his arm protectively around his son's shoulder, trying to reassure him as the Germans burst into the room.

"*Gut Morgen!*" said the officer in charge. "We have come to search for hidden weapons. Please move to one side."

Immediately they proceeded to take the room apart. Nothing escaped their probing bayonets; they slashed the mattress until the springs protruded, in their attempt to find hidden contraband. The wardrobe door was kicked in, because the key was missing. Pappa had never needed one, since they had no extra clothes to put away. The futile search completed, the Nazis frisked them both, emptying their pockets.

"*Jude*, where are your identity documents?"

"I have none," Pappa answered.

"You are under arrest," the officer informed them. "Please," he continued with the utmost politeness, "I request you not to leave your room. When we have finished our search, my soldiers will come to collect you."

He clicked his heels and strutted out, followed by his henchmen.

Once again they were alone. Pappa did not try to hide the tears streaming down his face. He put his arms around Brudi and kissed him on both cheeks. Brudi too was crying as he received his father's blessing. With head bowed, he listened to Pappa's instructions.

"I hope they will spare you," he heard Pappa say. "Once they have taken me from here, I want you to go straight to Mme. Schwartz and tell her what happened. I know she will care for you."

Brudi wanted to protest that he did not want to go. He wanted to accompany Pappa wherever he went, but knew the choice was not his. Numb with grief and fear, he watched Pappa prepare for his departure.

He put his *tefillin* in his inside pocket. His precious small *Tehillim* and *siddur* fitted easily into his jacket pockets. He was ready, nothing was left to do but wait ...

There was a gentle knock, and before they had time to respond, the door opened and the hotel proprietor entered, quietly closing the door behind him.

"Monsieur," he said, walking up to Pappa, "I have been informed that you are among those selected for deportation. Please trust me, you have nothing to fear. You and the others staying in my hotel will not be deported." He gave Pappa an encouraging nod. "I have negotiated with the Germans on behalf of my guests. Please do not leave your room under any circumstances. They will shortly be leaving this area, but you must remain in your room. I will come up and tell you myself when it will be safe for you to be seen." Then he left, closing the door softly behind him.

Pappa and Brudi looked at each other in disbelief. Was this true? Or had they been sharing the same incredible hallucination? The anguished cries of those caught in the net soon brought them back to reality — this dawn raid was obviously designed to catch people at home. The Germans' success could be measured by the tightly packed lorries now leaving the side streets. Soon the street and its inhabitants would return to the normal rhythm of life, and there would be nothing left to distinguish this dawn from any other morning. Nothing but the occasional little face at a window, anxiously looking out, waiting for a loving father who would never return.

Shortly afterwards the proprietor came to inform them that the danger was over. They thanked him as well as they could, but he shrugged their stammered words aside; he had to hurry to tell the others the good news.

Pappa extracted his *Tehillim* from his pocket, and his fervent prayer of thankfulness for their miraculous rescue was tinged with deep sadness for all those who had been taken away. He was deeply troubled, for he knew they could not go on relying on the protection of their host. His negotiating might not work the next time.

They sat together on the edge of the bed, shoulders touching, hardly daring to rejoice at such good fortune. It did not matter that the few creature comforts they had still possessed were now gone. The room was a shambles — but they never thought about how they were going to sleep that night. They had survived, and they were still together.

It was early afternoon when Uncle Menachem arrived. He stood transfixed in the doorway, taking in the spectacle of destruction.

"*Voilà*, my friends!" he boomed. "How did you manage to avoid being caught?" Clapping his hands together as if to dispel all gloom, he added, "You will have to tell me later. This explains why you did not come and join us on the Boulevard this morning. We waited for you." Seating himself next to Pappa, he said, "I have some interesting news for you, and since I feel sure that it is good news, I did not want to wait until this evening to come and tell you."

Pappa turned to him inquiringly. What possible good news could he be bringing? Might he dare to hope that the underground organization which arranged the routes and supplied the guides would possibly forgo the final payment he still owed them? No, he must banish such foolish thoughts from his mind! (As we were later to learn, these escape routes were set up for the benefit of the British Expeditionary Force soldiers and airmen known as "Avaders," and also for the occasional rich and influential Jew. That, Pappa was not!)

He was shaken out of his reverie by Uncle Menachem prodding him. "You recall the Frenchman I told you about, to whom the name Marcovits seemed to be significant? He had hoped to meet you today and was already seated at a little table when we arrived. I could see how disappointed he was when you did not show up. So I joined him at his table and told him that you were born in Hungary, although that is not the country you came from, and what do you think happened next?" He slapped Pappa's knee in a vain attempt to get him excited. "The little Frenchman jumped up from his seat, and grabbing me by my lapels, pleaded, '*Monsieur, s'il vous plaît*, do you know what town he comes from?'

"By now, my dear friends, I was seriously doubting his sanity, so in order to extricate myself from his grasp, I assured him that my friend could not be the one he is looking for, because you came from a village, not a town. Saying this, I must have touched some magical chord once again," continued Menachem, "for he grabbed my lapels as if they were the key to a hidden treasure. I begged him to let go — and would you believe it! I could not remember the name of the village! Not wanting to prolong his ordeal, I did tell him that I was sure the name ended with '...bart,' " said Uncle Menachem, stroking his beardless chin. He was beginning to enjoy himself as he saw that both Pappa and Brudi were at last giving him their full attention. Standing up for maximum effect, he declared, "Do you know what happened next? He grabbed my lapels for a third time!" His laughter was so infectious and he looked so comical trying to imitate the Frenchman, that even Pappa and Brudi burst out laughing. "Holding on to me excitedly, he asked, 'Is it Gibart? Tell me, is that what he said?' Well, of course, I had to agree, that was indeed the name you mentioned."

Uncle Menachem's rugged features creased into a broad grin of delight at the surprise he had in store, and he was pleased at having been able to make them laugh. He now produced a visiting card from his waistcoat pocket, which he presented to Pappa with an exaggerated bow. Pappa looked at the card, heavily embossed with gold. The name meant nothing to him, so he handed it back to Menachem, saying, "There must be some mistake. I do not know them and have never heard their name mentioned."

"Listen, my friend, all he wants you to do is call him, so you can confirm that you are the right Marcovits, which of course you are!" insisted this incorrigible optimist. "Look here," he went on, reading the address out loud, "this is a very exclusive residential area, a suburb of Paris, and he wants you to come to his house. He said something about meeting his mother. Come on, *mon ami*, let's go downstairs and phone him from the reception desk!"

Pappa greatly enjoyed the company of this exuberant extrovert, and was loath to stop him, but felt that on this occasion he would have to. "Menachem, don't be childish. The last thing I'd wish to do just now is have a telephone conversation with a perfect stranger, even assuming that we come from the same village."

"Very well," said Menachem. "I will go downstairs myself, telephone him and tell him that you will come to his house tomorrow. We will fix a time for you," he added, as an afterthought.

Pappa did not answer... Memories of Gibart were flooding his mind...

It was a beautiful, peaceful village where everybody knew each other; where the gentiles and Jews lived in perfect harmony; where the fields of corn, the poultry and cattle provided a comfortable living for the villagers. A place where one could pluck tomatoes in the summer, and watch the farm workers string the giant tobacco leaves to dry in the sun, while the children played hide-and-seek.

Nostalgia overwhelmed him for that faraway place, but most of all for his beloved parents who still lived there. What would become of them? Would the villagers take care of their Jewish neighbors, since laws had been instituted by the regime of Admiral Horthy prohibiting Jews from owning land or property — thereby robbing families such as the Marcovitses of their livelihood?

(Alas, they did not. Pappa was to learn of their fate from eyewitnesses after the war. The other villagers were only too eager to seize their possessions, leaving the defenseless Jewish families in abject poverty, to be transported to that hell on earth called Auschwitz, to join the other millions in Hitler's "Final Solution" . . .)

Suddenly he longed to talk to someone who would remember Gibart village as he remembered it, and the thought of hearing someone recall an incident connected with his dear parents dispelled his depression. He called to Menachem, who was just closing the door. "Wait, I am coming with you to make that phone call!"

They descended the staircase in search of the hotel proprietor. He was sitting in the tiny room which served as his office. Yes, he would let them use his telephone. Pappa dialed the number; he was surprised to feel his heart beating faster as he listened to the "bur, bur" on the line. Perhaps there was no one at home — should he replace the receiver?

Suddenly the ringing tone stopped. "Hello, Blanc residence." It was M. Blanc speaking. To be sure he was talking to the right Marcovits, he asked Pappa a few questions. Satisfied with the responses, he then invited Pappa to come and meet his elderly mother. A time was set for the following afternoon.

Although Pappa's natural caution went some way towards curbing Uncle Menachem's galloping fantasies, nevertheless the conversation had given them something to look forward to. A day that had started so ominously at dawn, when only his unshakable faith and the comfort from his prayers sustained him, had ended in joy and hope. Not only had they been spared untold misery, but Pappa was going to meet with a French family who were anxious to get to know him. His spirits soared. "Come," he said to Menachem and Brudi, "let us see what food we can buy today."

Pappa and Brudi had missed their early morning tea in *shul* before the morning service, and, of course, Brudi had also missed his breakfast at Tante Dena's. In fact, neither had eaten anything since sharing their usual can of peas the previous evening.

With renewed optimism they set out on the short distance to the *Pletzel*. Uncle Menachem kept them entertained with his lively tales of human ingenuity, when courage alone was not enough to outwit the enemy. He told them a story about a Jewish cripple, an incredibly brave man, who organized the printing of false documents for those in need of them, and provided shelter for these people until they could assume their new identities . . .

> Having bleached his hair to look more like an Aryan, and using the name Anton as his cover, for a while Avraham managed to deflect suspicion from his house.
>
> One day, however, a hubbub of excited voices could be heard in his room. Six men and two women were checking their freshly printed documents while their guide, a French partisan who would lead them over the border, concluded a discussion with Anton. Everything was ready, the money in a neat little parcel. Suddenly a young urchin, the cripple's trusted lookout, burst into the room. "Les Boches!" he called, then slipped away.
>
> The chair-bound hero took no chances. He snapped orders in an authoritative voice. "Please be quick — give me the documents and the money." He hid these on his person, then adjusted the blanket around his knees. "Now hurry, push my chair out the front door and go quickly — just follow your guide. If you are too late and they catch you, at least no incriminating documents will be found in your possession."
>
> "What about you?" someone pleaded, as they reluctantly complied with his orders.
>
> "Go!" he commanded. "I can look after myself."

The Gestapo found him outside, looking disheveled and distressed.

"Stay right there!" shouted the SS officer in charge. "Your house is surrounded! We know you have been harboring Jews!"

"You must be stupid if you believe that!" Anton shouted back. "Can't you see I am a cripple? They held me captive in my own home! The Jewish pigs fled when one of their cohorts came to warn them of your coming. They pushed me out into the cold, and ran!" By this time he was shaking with rage and indignation.

The officer ordered his men to search the house thoroughly, while he supervised the wheeling of the distressed man back into the house. The commandant and his underling remained with him as the search continued. Nothing was found to give rise to suspicion. At last the search was over. The commandant ordered their departure; this driveling Aryan cripple was making him feel uncomfortable. Clicking his heels and giving the hated salute, he marched out of the house.

Anton listened to the sound of their retreating footsteps, then covered his face with his hands, and sobbed uncontrollably.

"What do you say to that?" boomed Menachem, slapping Pappa on the shoulder.

They had reached the little cluster of shops. Pappa counted the small change in his pocket; he would have liked to treat his son to some extra food. Bread they could not buy — *Ah! A tomato will be nice*, he thought, as he paid for it.

Uncle Menachem walked back with them to the hotel, reluctant to leave, and the next few hours were spent in earnest discussion. Then it was time to go. To be outside any later would be dangerous. He considered staying the night — did he have a premonition? — but decided against it, as the room was almost uninhabitable. Pappa and Brudi finally walked him to the door, and Uncle Menachem departed.

Chapter Fifteen

The following morning Pappa and Brudi hurried to *shul*, happy to be among the fortunate ones still able to affirm their faith. Entering "Number Twenty-five," they sadly noted the dwindling congregation. The large kettle gently bubbling attracted the early worshippers as a honeypot attracts bees. A few pleasant moments of socializing followed as they sipped the life-sustaining liquid before the service commenced.

A short time later, Brudi made his way to Tante Dena's, where he was to spend the day. He planned to be back at the boardinghouse in time for Pappa's return, and was sure that Uncle Menachem would be there too.

❦ ❦ ❦

Pappa studied the map of Paris near the Métro St. Paul. He glanced at his pocket watch. That settled it: he was confident he could walk the distance quite easily and arrive at the appointed time. He had no other business to delay him, and the money saved would provide them with food for yet another day.

Two hours later he arrived at M. Blanc's gates. He had not expected anything so grand. He could not help noticing the contrast between the highly polished brass fittings, the shining surface of the heavy oak door, and his own shabby suit and dusty shoes. It was his only suit, the one he had worn when leaving Antwerp.

No, he could not expect people to receive him when he looked so shabby. Pappa thought. *Whatever had possessed him to agree to this meeting? These people had wanted to meet him because they were friends of his parents, and would naturally assume that he too was comfortably off.* Pappa heaved a deep sigh of resignation. *How foolish he had been to come all this way!*

As he turned to retrace his steps, the heavy double doors swung open. Someone inside the house must have been watching him from one of the windows. A dapper, middle-aged gentleman with a friendly, round, clean-shaven face and deep-set dark eyes raced out of the hall and down the flight of steps, leaving the bewildered butler still holding the door open. Pappa was not quite sure whether the man was coming to chase him away or to welcome him as he waved his arms excitedly while running towards Pappa.

"*Bonjour, Monsieur Marcovits!*" he exclaimed breathlessly, and, taking Pappa by the elbow, guided him into the house. The welcome of this man and the impact of the house overwhelmed him — rarely had he seen such grandeur! But he had no time to think: no sooner had he entered, than a large, ornately carved door was opened by the butler, and the man, still holding Pappa's elbow, ushered him into the room. M. Maurice Blanc withdrew his hand from Pappa's elbow, allowing him a few moments to glance around the exquisitely furnished drawing room. The walls were covered in a very pale grey silk damask, which exactly matched the heavy brocade upholstery of the many elegant armchairs and the two beautiful chaise longues scattered about the room in an apparently casual way. The mantelpiece was graced by an ormolu clock, ticking away the time. Large French windows with the curtain slightly parted revealed the delights of a well-kept garden. M. Blanc followed Pappa's gaze, and seemed to enjoy the impact the view had on Pappa. Then the butler came in, carrying a tray with two glasses of tea, a few slices of lemon and a bowl of lump sugar.

"My name is Maurice," Pappa's host said, extending his hand. "Please take a seat." He offered Pappa a glass of tea, which was gratefully accepted.

"Let me explain," M. Maurice Blanc continued. "We are four brothers and live here with our mother. Unfortunately, our dear father is no longer with us. It had always been his greatest wish to welcome a Marcovits of Gibart into his home. Alas, that was not to be, but we promised him long ago that we would continue to search for an opportunity such as this, to welcome a member of your family into our home. You cannot imagine how excited our mother is to meet you!" He rose. "I will find out if Mamma is ready to receive you."

Pappa finished his drink, and stroked his beard as he always did when something puzzled him. The whole affair was so mysterious! He was well aware of the many people whom his parents had helped. Their acts of *chessed* were legendary. But he felt like an imposter; how could he accept the hospitality of these people because of the kindness of his parents?

"Monsieur Marcovits!" It was his host calling, interrupting his thoughts. "My mother is ready to meet you, so let us not keep her waiting."

Did he detect Pappa's hesitation? He was too much of a gentleman to show it.

Pappa followed M. Maurice across the hall and up the wide sweeping staircase. A magnificent arrangement of freshly cut red roses stood on an oval table on the landing, filling the air with fragrance. *Did they buy the roses to match the priceless carpets?* Pappa wondered idly.

As they paused at the top of the stairs, Pappa noticed the intricate crystal chandelier hanging from the ceiling. A moment later, the doors were opened and he was ushered into the private sitting room of the grand old matriarch. A frail, elderly lady, her snow white hair parted in the middle with perfect waves framing her face, penetrating grey eyes her most dominant feature, she was sitting in an upright chair with her slippered feet resting on a *petit point* embroidered footstool. Around her hovered the three other brothers, waiting to be introduced.

Pappa marveled at their faultless manners; not once did they show any indication of having noticed his shabby clothing. He was acutely aware of his frayed cuffs as the sun streamed through the bay windows. He tried to move slightly to one side, but the soft deep pile of the carpet tangled with the nails protruding from his shoe where half the heel had come off. Gently he moved his leg until his foot was free.

Introductions were made, then the lady asked Pappa to sit beside her; it was obvious that she was pleased to meet him. She told her sons to sit down as well. Smiling, she turned to Pappa. "As you can perceive," she began, "we are no longer practicing Jews. Religion has no part in our lives, except for the High Festivals, which we acknowledge. But," she continued, waggling her bejeweled finger, "there is one commandment in the Scripture that my late husband and I vowed we would never forget, and that is the merit of..." here she paused, having obvious difficulty in pronouncing the unfamiliar Hebrew words, *"hakaras ha'tov"*. Pappa was able to help her once he understood the word she was groping for; he was surprised that she remembered it at all. She smiled again. "How could I forget? We had promised each other never to forget the gratitude we owe to your parents. But let me tell you about it. My sons have heard the story many times and I often despaired of ever being able to fulfill the *mitzvah* of returning a kindness. This is indeed a very happy event for me.

"The story begins before the turn of the century. Our surname was Weiss; we changed it to the French version, Blanc, some years after we settled in Paris. In Poland, where we lived, pogroms were rampant. Young Jewish men were plucked from their homes and conscripted into the army. Very few ever returned. We were newly married and expecting our first baby. My husband, Dovid, was a tall handsome young man, with a thick curly beard which made him look older than his twenty-eight years. I suppose it was inevitable that he should be caught in their net. One night there came the dreaded knock on the door: all pleading was in vain. They threw him in the back of the wagon and drove off as fast as the horses would take them. When they were a short distance out of the village it started raining. They had intended to drive through the night until they reached the army camp, but the bad weather forced them to seek shelter at a nearby inn until morning.

"The horses were given fresh hay and a dry stable." Here Mme. Blanc paused reflectively. "For their prisoner they provided some space in the stable, where they tied his leg to a post. After the soldiers retired to the warmth of the inn, Dovid could hear them laughing and carousing with the innkeeper. He looked around, hoping to find something sharp he could use to cut his fetter. On hands and knees he searched every inch of the floor accessible to him, and suddenly his hands closed on a metal object — a knife! It had been hidden in the darkness when they brought him in. He thanked the Almighty as he set about cutting the heavy leather strap. Beads of sweat collected on his forehead and trickled down his neck; at last he was free! He had to hurry — every moment was precious! He paused for an instant in the shadow of the inn, listening to the merriment, then ran as swiftly as his legs would take him, pausing only to ease the pain in his side. It took over two hours to reach his home. He knocked softly on the window, to avoid attracting the attention of his neighbor."

Old Mme. Blanc paused, her eyes clouded with memories ... She was no longer the grand matriarch — wealthy, cosseted, surrounded and protected by her grown sons — but Rivkah'le, the unsophisticated young Jewish wife, left to struggle on alone with her unborn child in a hostile country ...

> Rivkah'le looked up, startled; it was well past midnight. Unable to sleep, she had remained seated near the flickering oil lamp. With needle and thread she was embroidering exquisite little flowers onto a small pillowcase for the baby's crib. Her tear-stained face turned towards the window. Who could be knocking at this hour? Was it just her imagination tormenting her? If only Dovid were here to take care of her! But she must not panic, it might harm the baby. Again there came a gentle knock, and now she could see a face pressed against the windowpane.
> "Dovid!" she cried out, rushing to open the door. She threw back the bolt. "Dovid! You are soaking wet! What happened?" Not waiting for an explanation, she hurried to warm a pan of water, but he pulled her back.
> "Be quick and blow out the lamp so no one can see me," he whispered. He told her in a few short sentences of his escape. Their only hope was to flee and try to reach the Polish-Hungarian border before his captors could pursue him. She begged him to change into dry clothes, but to no avail — he knew only too well that such a delay might cost him his life.
> In the darkness of their home, she quickly gathered a few possessions. What food they had she tied into a cotton tablecloth; a change of clothing for each; and, as a last thought, she gathered up the feather quilts and pillows. Meanwhile, her husband harnessed their horse and cart, taking great care to be as quiet as possible. He guided the horse onto the dirt track, carefully avoiding the cobblestones in the small semi-circular courtyard in front of the cottages. Dovid helped his wife onto the seat beside him, and threw a blanket over her shoulders. The heavy rain eased off into a steady drizzle. Their meager possessions were protected by a tarpaulin thrown over the cart.

Neither dared to glance back at their neat little cottage with the crisp white curtains draped to one side and tied with a white silken ribbon. "Oh, Dovid!" she cried. "The candlesticks! How could I forget Mother's candlesticks!"

Shyly he squeezed her hand. "I knew how much they meant to you. I put them with the bedding." In the darkness of the moonless night, as they drove in silence away from their home, she marveled at her good fortune in having this wonderful caring man as her husband.

All the king's treasures could not have bought the kind of exquisite tenderness that flowed between them. Despair had no place in their minds as they faced the long hard trek into the unknown. Their trust in Hashem unshaken, they faced the future with optimism.

They traveled all night without stopping, mostly in silence, listening to the crunching of the wheels as they rolled over the uneven roads. It was only when the early morning sunrays began to warm her damp and chilled body that Rivkah'le fell asleep, her head resting on Dovid's arm. As the sun rose high in a cloudless blue sky, Dovid watched his sleeping wife, reluctant to wake her.

The cart carried them closer and closer to the Hungarian border. They approached the crossing point, marked by a wooden hut which was manned by two soldiers in colorful uniforms, whose main concern was to apprehend smugglers. Sitting on two upturned boxes, with a third box serving as a table, the guards were engrossed in a game of cards — a favorite pastime to while away the dreary hours on border duty.

Dovid woke his wife as they neared the outpost. His heart beat faster: what reason could he give for wanting to cross the border? He must make an effort to look unconcerned.

The soldiers were not too pleased at being interrupted. When he presented their identity papers, Dovid explained that they wished to visit relatives for a few days to celebrate a wedding. The soldiers examined the contents of the cart, which were hardly what a smuggler would carry. One poked his rifle into the feather bedding, and created a miniature snowstorm! Dovid winced. Irritated, and impatient to resume their card game, the guards waved them through.

Rivkah'le and Dovid could hardly believe their luck as they sped away, trying to put as much distance as possible between the Polish border and themselves.

Dovid's eyes were bloodshot from a sleepless night and the strain of constant vigilance. They stopped at the wayside to eat a hearty meal of delicious black bread and cheese.

"Two months later, in early summer, we arrived at the ever-open door of your parents' home."

Here Mme. Blanc paused, and her face softened as she looked at Pappa.

"I will not bore you with the details of the hardships and deprivations we suffered. I was by then heavily pregnant, in poor health, and mentally exhausted, but with your mother's help I soon regained my strength.

"We had been very fortunate to be directed to your parents' home. It was a large, white, single-story country house; the windowsills overflowed with boxes of bright red geraniums. A stream bubbled a short distance away. We were welcomed into this home by your wonderful mother, who made me feel instantly at ease. We talked as we watched her little ones playing on the floor of the kitchen. I had never seen such a large room before! One part of it was the working kitchen, and the other half was the living room. She inquired about my health, and asked when my baby was due. Then she invited us to join her and your father for dinner.

"After a hearty meal, we were taken across the courtyard to a small cottage, one in a row of similar ones, each simply furnished with comfortable beds and fresh linen. We were told to consider the cottage as our own for as long as we needed it. It was there that our baby was born. We lacked nothing: when my time came, your dear mother called the local midwife, and she herself stayed and held my hand. I felt as if I had a mother once again."

Madame Blanc looked out the window with unseeing eyes, remembering a faraway place of long ago . . .

> *They were happy in this peaceful village. Rivkah'le soon recovered her strength, and the baby thrived. Their host had provided a wonderful seudah for the baby's bris, and a second one for the pidyon haben, to which all the Jewish families in the village were invited. However, this idyllic way of life could not go on. Dovid did not want to take advantage of their host. Most*

of the other visitors who were put up in the adjoining cottages stayed for only a few days; the Weiss family's stay had already extended into many weeks. Having become a father, Dovid was eager to take on the responsibility of providing for his family. He had been helping out on the farm, where an extra pair of hands was always welcome, but he wanted to move on, perhaps to try life in a city or even in a different country.

Dovid went to discuss the situation with Mr. Marcovits, and to ask his advice. He explained that he had a cousin who had emigrated to France — he was not sure where — but based on the infrequent letters that arrived, this cousin seemed to be doing well. Mr. Marcovits, still a young man himself, turned the problem over in his mind as he drew deeply on his pipe. Dovid interrupted his thoughts. "If you could help me obtain the necessary documents, I would like to emigrate. I am not afraid of working hard and I feel that I can give my wife and baby son a better life. They say the French are very liberal with the Jews and allow them to live and work unhindered."

"That is so," Mr. Marcovits reflected; he had heard the same from other people who received letters from France.

"As you know," Dovid said, "I came to you with only the clothes on my back, so I cannot offer to pay you now. However, I promise you that if you help me, and the Almighty will grant me the chance to succeed, I will repay all the expenses I have incurred." Mr. Marcovits nodded his head; he would do his best. He was a prosperous landowner who provided most of the villagers with their means of earning a living. He also had influential friends in the government and did not hesitate to call for their assistance, paying generously whenever someone needed a passport or other vital documents.

The day came for them to leave. Passports, visas — all had been attended to — and now Mr. Marcovits handed Dovid a large sum of money. Dovid was aghast: how could he accept such generosity and hope to repay it?

"Do not worry about repaying me. The Almighty who provides for us all has plenty more. Just remember that when you will be in a position to help others, you can repay the chessed that Hashem has shown to you by helping those less fortunate."

"And we have never forgotten the assurance we gave," said the old lady, leaning forward in her chair, so she could be sure Pappa understood.

"With the help of the money your father gave us, we managed to settle here in Paris, in an apartment large enough for us to take in boarders, while Dovid looked for employment. It was not easy in those days, especially as we did not speak French. But we never starved as others did, and then, through a mutual friend, Dovid was offered a partnership in a small textile business. With the money we had managed to save — and we did not waste a *sou* — we rescued the business and it was soon thriving."

She leaned back in the chair and closed her eyes, suddenly exhausted. The hint of a smile played at the corners of her mouth.

She was about to fulfill their vow.

How she wished her beloved Dovid could be with her to share the moment! How strange it was to call him Dovid and how naturally it had come to her. It was a name they had soon discarded when they arrived in Paris; Dovid became Damien when they changed their surname to Blanc. Their desire to blend in with their new adoptive country was total.

Madame Blanc looked at her eldest son and signaled him to fetch something. The brothers had all been spellbound by their mother's tale, for she had never told it before in such detail. M. Maurice hurried away and soon returned with a large parcel. The old lady took the parcel and offered it to Pappa. "Please, Monsieur, do us the kindness of accepting this small token. No, no, Monsieur!" she exclaimed, as Pappa started protesting. "Allow me to fulfill our promise."

Not wishing to upset this frail old lady, and feeling acutely embarrassed, Pappa took the parcel and thanked them all profusely for their hospitality. As he was leaving, the Blancs made him promise to ask for their help at any time he needed it. He was deeply touched by their goodness.

❦ ❦ ❦

Not wishing to attract suspicion with his parcel, for there were Germans lurking everywhere, Pappa decided not to walk home, and reluctantly took a bus back to the hotel. Images from the past flitted through his mind during the ride home, and a persistent question kept nagging at him: *What had become of his parents?*

Chapter Sixteen

Brudi stood near the window, anxiously peering out at the streets below. He had a clear view of Rue de Rivoli on one side and Rue Malher on the other. There was no sign of either Pappa or Uncle Menachem, and soon it would not be safe for a Jew to be outdoors.

All day he had been excited, eagerly looking forward to Tante Dena's return, so that he could hurry back to the Hôtel de Sud. He played with the children and attended to their needs — the baby was teething and wanted to be cuddled all the time — but Brudi's thoughts occupied him, wondering what had happened to Pappa, as he absent-mindedly cradled the fretting baby in his arms. He prepared to leave as soon as Tante Dena returned. She did not ask him to stay, but gave him two slices of bread, for which he thanked her gratefully. It was not often that she could spare two slices.

He had been disappointed upon entering his room to find that Pappa had not yet returned, but not really worried. *Who would arrive first?* he wondered, as he took his place by the window. *Pappa or Uncle Menachem?* But that had been a long time ago, and now darkness was falling. He felt a heaviness creeping into his chest, making his heart beat faster. Suddenly it missed a beat: there, walking towards the entrance, was Pappa, carrying a parcel under his arm. Brudi raced down the stairs and out into the street. Relief shone in his face as he seized the parcel, and they hurried up to their room.

Pappa related all that had happened. He too had expected Menachem to be waiting for him; however, not yet alarmed, they discussed whether they should open the parcel. They decided against it, Pappa telling Brudi, "Let's wait a little longer; something must have delayed Menachem, but he is sure to come." He added, chuckling, "You know he would want to be here! He's not a man willing to miss a treat!"

They ate their supper — which should have been a joyful meal — in silence. Pappa had bought yet another can of *petits pois*. The tiny little peas, very sweet, with the unexpected bread which Tante Dena had given to Brudi, provided a very tasty meal, but all cheerfulness evaporated as darkness set in. They could not hide their misgivings from each other; if Uncle Menachem had not yet arrived, then something dreadful must have happened. He would not, by choice, have stayed away. They were only too well aware of the dangers lurking in every corner. With a sigh of resignation, Pappa slowly untied the brown paper parcel.

"Oh! Look at this beautiful suit!" Brudi exclaimed, lifting it out of the wrapping paper. "Please, Pappa, try it on," he begged, anxious to see how Pappa would look in this smart navy blue suit with the hand-stitched lapels. How shabby and threadbare Pappa's clothes appeared now!

Brudi held up the jacket, inviting Pappa to try it on, but Pappa shook his head. "No, Brudi, it is for you. I want you to have it." (They were about the same height then, though later Brudi grew to be much taller.)

"Look, Pappa," Brudi pleaded with perfect logic, "it makes little difference how I am dressed — after all, our clothes are reasonably clean — but you meet many strangers who don't know you and may judge you by your appearance."

Pappa could not but agree. He was very conscious that even among the refugees his clothes looked very worn and threadbare. They had traveled a long way since losing all their baggage at Ostend. If Mamma had been here, she would have transformed their old garments from shabbiness to respectability with a few skillful stitches. Well, Mamma wasn't here! And, he grudgingly had to admit, people did sometimes mistake him for a — well, it did not matter! He would try on the jacket. Taking off his shabby coat, he allowed Brudi to help him slip into the new one. What an improvement! Clothes do "make the man," he had to agree, admiring the perfect fit as he studied his reflection against the darkened window. The cloth felt soft and rich as he smoothed down the lapels.

Something seemed to crackle in the breast pocket. Pappa inserted his hand and extracted a large white envelope addressed to him in clear, bold letters; he read out loud, "Monsieur S. Marcovits et fils." They even had his initial correct! With Brudi standing wide eyed beside him, he slowly opened the bulging envelope. Carefully he counted the money enclosed. No, it could not be, no one would give away such a large sum of money! Dazed and bewildered, they stood gazing at the bank notes. The family Blanc/Weiss had waited forty years to fulfill their promise, and had made him the recipient of their gratitude.

What right had he to this money? Pappa wondered. *If only he could share it with his dear parents, the rightful beneficiaries of the Blanc family's generosity!*

Brudi was talking excitedly. "If only Uncle Menachem were here to share this moment with us!" he exclaimed.

As Pappa and Brudi prepared for the night, their hopes and prayers were for the safety of their friend, who had persuaded Pappa to visit their benefactors. Perhaps he would come tomorrow, and there would be a perfectly simple explanation for his absence ...

> *(Alas, there was none. By then, Menachem was probably, with his unshakable faith, trying to ease the oppressed spirits of the other prisoners packed into the airless cattle truck, speeding towards the German border. Faith and humor would be all he could offer ... His name was on the long list, issued after the war, of those deported to Auschwitz.)*

❈ ❈ ❈

The following morning, Pappa's and Brudi's worst fears were confirmed. The Germans had established a "transit" camp outside the city. When enough unfortunates had been collected to fill a freight train or wagon, it would be dispatched, making room for the victims of the next roundup. At the beginning of 1941, these transports were being increased. To the Nazi hierarchy this ranked equal in importance to their strategy of attacking the British Naval Forces in the Mediterranean, the planning of the invasion of Britain (code named "Operation Sea Lion"), and the imminent invasion of Russia.

Still hoping against hope, Pappa went to the Hôtel Rivoli where Menachem lodged. Perhaps there someone would be able to inform them of his whereabouts. What they were told did nothing to dispel their fears. Monsieur Menachem Maizels had not returned the previous evening. The manager was most obliging and allowed them to go up to his room.

If Pappa had hoped to find a clue to Menachem's disappearance, he was not successful. The room was as Menachem had left it that morning. There were no signs of a hasty departure, and Menachem surely would not willingly have left his neatly folded underwear in the drawer, and several pairs of good shoes at the bottom of the wardrobe, which also contained his suits. A few personal possessions on the dressing table were symbols of an affluent past. There, surrounded by the objects that his friend had cherished, undoubtedly salvaged from the home he left behind, Pappa felt close to Menachem. The room was as he had expected it to be, clean and orderly.

(Having come to France after Hitler had marched into Austria, Menachem had managed to pack most of his valuable furniture and other possessions into outsize cases called "lifts". Thousands of these valuable lifts must have been waiting unclaimed in some countries after the war.)

Pappa closed the wardrobe, taking care not to catch a coat sleeve in the door. He wanted to leave everything as his friend would like to find it on his return. One can but speculate how long the room remained undisturbed, waiting for its rightful occupant ...

Slowly, Pappa and Brudi walked down the stairs. Handing the keys back to the manager, they thanked him and walked out. What was there to talk about? They walked in silence, crossing at the intersection into Rue du Prévôt.

"Brudi, I want you to go to Tante Dena," Pappa said. "I have urgent matters to attend to. I will see you in our room later on. Please be careful." As he hurried away towards the métro, Brudi turned into Rue de Jouy.

The following days passed uneventfully. Brudi continued to help Tante Dena. Since Pappa had received a large sum of money from the family Blanc, he was able to meet the outstanding payment for the documents. There was nothing left to do but wait ...

By this time, Pappa was feeling the strain of meeting people in secret, never knowing whether he was being watched. It was frightening to hand over large sums of money to people whose identity he did not know, and to entrust his and Brudi's lives into their hands.

How he missed his friend Menachem, the only one he dared to confide in. Yet *Hashem* had surely ordained their escape for how else could he have come to be given such a large sum of money, if not with Divine help? The days dragged on ... Tension built up inside him, but he was acutely aware that he must show no signs of nervousness. It was almost three weeks since Menachem's disappearance when Pappa received the call for which he had been waiting.

❈ ❈ ❈

Pappa consulted his watch. The time had come to collect Brudi from Tante Dena's. The decision to take her into their confidence was not made lightly, but he felt he could not leave without her knowing. He intended to help her the only way he could, by placing some money in an envelope for her.

The Schwartz family was surprised to see Pappa enter the apartment, and even the children gathered around at this unusual event. Quietly Pappa explained that they were leaving and he had come to thank her for all her kindness. *Words are inadequate for what I am trying to say*, he thought, choking back the tears. He handed her the envelope as he waited for Brudi to take leave of the children. Even the baby knew something was wrong as Brudi held him tight, letting his tears flow unashamedly. Whether in sympathy or protest, the baby too burst into tears, setting up a loud wail, and thus Pappa and Brudi departed.

Back at the hotel, Pappa went to settle the outstanding bill. The proprietor met his eyes quizzically. "I am leaving to join some relatives who live outside Paris," Pappa said. The hotel keeper shook his head. He thought for a moment, then leaning across so his face was close to Pappa's, he whispered, "Please be careful. There are two routes being used at the moment. If they want to take you to Villefranche, don't go. The Germans know about it. Unfortunately, they have their informers. So avoid this route."

Pappa thanked him but said no more. He could do nothing about it: they were ready to leave and had a rendezvous to keep. As to their destination, Pappa had not been told what it was.

They were to remember the proprietor's warning, because it proved to be accurate.

It was midday when they walked towards the Métro St. Paul. Pappa had been given precise instructions: he was to take the métro to a certain station; from there he was to walk to the railway station and wait for the train due at ten minutes past the hour. They both shivered as they walked towards the entrance to the second station; a gust of wind almost lifted Pappa's hat. They hurried onto the platform, Pappa holding on to his hat, Brudi glad that he still wore the flat cap that all boys wore, fitting snugly over his head. Soon they could see the train approaching.

Will we ever return to Paris? Brudi wondered. Despite all the hardships and loneliness he had endured, he was sorry to leave. However, his youthful spirits did not let him dwell on the past; not as they were embarking on a most exciting and dangerous mission! When they were safely ensconced in one of the third-class compartments, Pappa entrusted details of their intended escape to Brudi. He had been told that there would be few passengers on this train, and he was to look for an unoccupied compartment. Pappa noted the time they had been traveling. Approximately two hours had passed since boarding this train.

"Brudi!" said Pappa, with growing excitement. "We should soon be approaching a small station near an old church with a high steeple. The engine driver will give three distinct blasts on the whistle as we pass the church."

His contact had told him that the train was not scheduled to stop at this station, but that a short stretch beyond it, as the road curved to the right, the train would slow down. At that moment they must be ready to jump off. Pappa tried to reassure both himself and Brudi that all would be well and *Hashem* was with them.

So far the journey had gone according to plan. Surely it was just excitement, not fear, that made his heart race faster than the wheels rolling under the carriage! Brudi searched Pappa's face, his eyes burning, pleading, *Do we really have to jump from a moving train?* Pappa understood, and squeezed Brudi's hand reassuringly. Brudi watched him take the small *Tehillim* from his pocket, and listened to him recite the comforting psalms, as he so often did.

Ah! Now they were approaching the unmistakable landmark. Pappa edged to the door, holding Brudi tightly, pushing him gently in front of him so he was touching the door. His hand was on the door lever. Suddenly, without warning, the train started slowing down — perhaps it always did so for safety as it approached the curve. There was no time to waste. With a swift movement of his hand Pappa wrenched the door open. *Don't think!* his brain told him, urging him into action. Almost simultaneously they tumbled out the door, and the next instant lay dazed on the grass verge. Neither moved as they listened to the sound of the train fading into the distance.

They were safe and unhurt. Bruises might appear the next morning, but that was unimportant. They rested for a few more moments. Pappa was the first to get up. "Are you all right?" he asked Brudi.

"Yes, Pappa. Are you?"

They looked around and saw, to their amazement, that they were not the only ones to have jumped off the moving train, but miraculously, no one was hurt. All were relieved not to be alone.

They heard a truck approaching, laboring over the uneven roads. All faces showed fear; they were expecting to be picked up, but how could they be sure it was not the Nazis? There was nothing to do but wait. The truck lumbered into view, and finally all sighed with relief as a young partisan jumped out.

It was a large truck, stacked high with wooden cases. The front of each box was made up of wire netting. These were typical chicken crates. Coming closer, Pappa and Brudi could see the chickens inside. Before they had time to wonder how all would fit into this truck, the young driver removed several boxes, revealing a large vacant area. He motioned to them to get in, whereupon he reloaded the crates of live chickens, hiding the people from view. They marveled at the ingenuity of their guide.

Very little was said for the next hour or so as they sat on the floor of the truck. The terrain was getting rougher. It was quite dark and they were unable to make out where they were being taken. Suddenly the lorry stopped. It must have reached an inspection point — they could hear someone giving an order in German! They hardly dared to breathe, as they listened to the driver descending from his seat. The German voice asked for his papers; a pause as he handed them over. Would he demand to inspect the lorry? Nobody moved. The Frenchman's documents must have satisfied the German, for the next moment their driver climbed back into the cab, turned on the engine and drove slowly away.

Finally the lorry came to a halt. Next followed a three-hour march, in darkness, through the woods. This brought the group to an isolated farm. There they were taken indoors and allowed to rest; they were given hot drinks and bread. They could hardly express their gratitude. As the night wore on, they were joined by other groups.

The following day was spent indoors. Someone arrived and explained that in the evening they would be split up into smaller parties, each with two guides. Everyone stretched out on the floor and tried to get some sleep.

At last, night descended. With relief they watched the lengthening shadows cast by the trees at the edge of the clearing.

More patient waiting ... then the first two guides arrived with their leader. Quietly the fugitives were marshaled into small parties. They listened with deep concentration to their final instructions.

"We are quite near the Vichy border, but, of course, we will guide you through the woods to a place which has, to date, remained safe for crossing. Let me remind you," the guide continued, watching the eager faces turned towards him, "this is not without danger. The utmost care has to be taken to avoid suspicion. The Germans will not hesitate to shoot if they discover someone fleeing. So listen carefully. Once you leave this farm, under no circumstances must you talk. Watch what we do. If we walk, you walk. If we suddenly disappear in the undergrowth, you do the same. Is that clear?" Heads nodded. They could not turn back now. The most dangerous part was still to come.

Pappa's party consisted of seven men, Brudi being by far the youngest. They walked, they crawled, and they walked some more. Their eyes were fixed constantly on their guide, who whispered that they were almost over the border, but motioned them not to make a noise.

Suddenly they were surrounded! "Halt!" shouted the German patrol. Everyone froze. They had walked into a trap! The German officer counted the people. "There are two missing!" he screamed. They all looked at each other, marveling at the speed with which the two guides had rolled down the ridge. So someone had betrayed them, just as the hotel keeper had warned.

"Where are your guides?" shouted the commandant, furious at being robbed of his prize quarry. Aiming his rifle at Brudi, he bellowed! "I will shoot this boy if you don't find them!" Then, assigning a soldier to each prisoner, they searched the undergrowth in an ever-widening circle. All this time the commandant held the rifle to Brudi's head. Two long hours passed in fruitless search. Those brave men who had led them so far had long experience in the art of blending into the background.

Brudi, although fearing for his life, hoped that their two guides would not be found. Time dragged as he stood, the rifle pointed at his head as he watched the search continue, wondering whether the officer would carry out his threat.

Suddenly the order was given to abandon the search. The captives were frog-marched to the nearest village and locked into the prison, which was part of the local police station. The following morning they were driven to a town which had a German caserne. Here they met many others who had been caught trying to cross the border. As the day wore on, more prisoners arrived. Two days later they were transferred in army trucks to a very large barracks in the city of Tours.

Chapter Seventeen

he barracks were divided into two distinct sections. One half was under French administration, and the other half was run by the Germans.

Their captors marched the prisoners into the German section, and halted in front of a row of stables. The captives waited while the horses were removed, and were then told to enter. German armed guards were posted outside to guard the thirty or forty men captured on the border over the last few days. No food had been given to them. The prisoners' intense hunger and thirst was hardly relieved by the occasional drink of water they were allowed. It must be stated that most of the prisoners there at that point were not Jewish.

The following day a German officer arrived and introduced himself as the commandant in charge of the caserne. "Therefore," he added, smiling, "I am in charge of your well-being!" Actually, he confided, he was not German, but Austrian. He asked whether they had received any food, and on being told that they had not eaten for a few days, he barked an order to his adjutant and left. A short while later a barrel was brought into the stable. Everyone gathered around, and willing hands quickly prized the lid off.

Wine! It was a barrel of wine. Thirty to forty starving people and they were given a barrel of wine!

Cupped hands eagerly dipped into the liquid.

Pappa stood by but would not touch it. "It is not kosher," he said, but permitted Brudi to drink a little. Late in the afternoon the same officer came back and asked whether they had enjoyed their meal. On being told that no food had been brought, only a barrel of wine, he laughed and said it must be a mistake, as he had given orders for food and wine to be sent!

Some time later a Frenchman came and explained that he was in charge of providing food, and later still, a small amount of food was distributed. It was not adequate, but at least everyone received a portion.

The prisoners asked for something to sleep on, for they had slept on the stable floor the previous night. This request was relayed to the commandant, who graciously provided half a dozen bales of straw. So for the next few days they slept in comparative comfort on straw beds, and food was provided twice daily.

Every day brought more prisoners, until there were over one hundred sharing the stables. When no more could be accommodated, the Germans made the adjoining stables available. The old prisoners willingly shared their straw with the newcomers. Within a few weeks after the first prisoners had arrived, two more stables had grudgingly been added for the swelling group of captives, but by then the straw was no more than a thinly spread covering on the three stable floors, for no additional straw had been provided. Not only did they have to share the straw, but the food portions too became smaller as more had to share the total amount.

Towards the end of their second week there, among a new batch of prisoners Pappa and Brudi recognized the two guides. They were, understandably, terrified of being identified. To destroy the underground network was a German priority as urgent as the extermination of the Jews. Those two Frenchmen knew they were among friends, but were worried that Brudi, due to his young age, might be less than reliable. So the following day, as they lined up for water at the pump, the guides approached Brudi and begged him not to tell anyone that he knew them. As Brudi was to tell the story years later, he just stared at them and said, "Who are you?"

❊ ❊ ❊

Six weeks passed. There was hardly room to move about, and the prisoners were only allowed out twice a day — to attend to their needs, line up for water and exercise their legs.

One day they were marched on foot through the town to a very large building, which they were to learn was the headquarters of the dreaded Gestapo. On entering, they were told to wait in a large room until called. They waited for many hours, as the prisoners were called one by one.

At last it was Pappa's turn. Brudi was allowed to stay with Pappa while he was interrogated and sentenced to remain in prison. Again they had to wait. Then, together with other prisoners, they were herded into a German military truck and driven away, arriving outside a large barrack surrounded by barbed wire and guarded on the outside by German soldiers.

Inside the camp, the Germans turned the truckload of prisoners over to the commandant of the camp, who was a Frenchman. He explained to the new arrivals that the camp was run exclusively by French personnel, but added that it was only a transit camp. It was well known that the Germans had chosen this camp as one of the centers from which they dispatched large convoys to the death camps of Germany and Poland.

The German guard departed, leaving the captives in the charge of this seemingly friendly French commandant. The camp consisted of approximately thirty barracks, all already occupied, and the newcomers were made to share the crammed quarters.

After talking to some other inmates, Pappa realized that they were no longer in a mixed camp. All present were Jews, some totally non-committed, but nevertheless Jews by birth. These innocent people were the victims of a mass transport of the entire Jewish population from the cities of Strasbourg, Metz, and others. Pappa and Brudi were told that upon his arrival, the rabbi of Strasbourg had immediately requested, and been granted, the facilities for setting up a makeshift synagogue with the help of his loyal *gabbai*. No sooner was Pappa told this, than he asked where he could contact the rabbi. All the others tried to dissuade him from such foolish action, pointing out that since Pappa and the rabbi were both conspicuously bearded, they would surely become a target of ridicule. Most of the Jews, even Orthodox ones, had shaved off their beards in a futile attempt to blend in with the general population.

But Pappa would have none of this! He was still as adamant on the subject of his beard as he had been (so long ago, it seemed!) in the Feldmans' boardinghouse in Ostend. He asked to see the commandant and pleaded with him that, as an Orthodox Jew, he would like to be housed near the rabbi. The commandant offered no objections and Pappa, with Brudi, was immediately transferred.

The rabbi had been allocated a barrack of which more than half was used as a *shul*, where they even had a Torah scroll; the rest served as living quarters for him and his wife, with another partition for the *gabbai*. A small curtained area was given to Pappa. It was quite luxurious in comparison to the accommodations of the other prisoners, crammed thirty to a room.

The rabbi and the *gabbai* welcomed Pappa, and they were soon immersed in earnest discourse, probing the magical depth of Holy Scripture that transcends all denominational barriers. One day, as they were sitting in the synagogue, the *gabbai* said to Pappa, "Are you not a Hungarian Jew, with a valid Hungarian passport?"

"That is so," Pappa answered.

"Well, I have been thinking, since you are a citizen of a country allied to Germany, why not ask to be released?"

Pappa looked at him in bewilderment. "How can it help me, a Jew?"

"It is worth trying!" urged the *gabbai*, adding, "We are French, and therefore the enemy. But you can plead that you are a citizen of an allied country, and therefore wish to be freed."

Pappa deliberated for a while. Dare he try it? He decided to ask the advice of the rabbi, who was sitting with his back to the wall, his head bent over the *Gemara* in deep concentration. Pappa explained the *gabbai's* suggestion and the rabbi's face lit up with delight. "Of course you should try it!" he encouraged him. "What have you to lose? Every day we see the trucks being loaded with our people and taken to Germany. It is only a matter of time before we will all be taken. So go and try it and may you be successful."

Pappa went outside, where Brudi was watching the French soldiers as they patrolled the compound. They were quite friendly and would often chat with him; occasionally he would be given an extra slice of bread, for they knew the rations distributed daily were insufficient.

Pappa called out to him, "We are going to see the commandant to ask for our release." Before Brudi could treat it as a joke, Pappa explained the situation. "I want you with me because your French is much better than mine," he said. They asked for, and were granted, a private meeting with the commandant.

Brudi and Pappa grew exceedingly nervous as they waited in the outer office. Pappa took out his *Tehillim*.

"Monsieur Marcovits, the commandant is ready to see you," called the sergeant, who had just come out of his office.

They both jumped up and advanced towards the door. Brudi's

heart was pounding and his feet seemed to have turned to lead. To have refused to act as interpreter was unthinkable; his confidence in Pappa's argument was total. He would translate what Pappa told him.

The commandant looked up as they entered. His handsome aristocratic face, with its high forehead and deep-set brown eyes that held the gaze of his listener, showed that he had great sympathy for these oppressed people, but, nevertheless, he had a duty to perform. The Germans had been victorious and they were now his masters. He did not like it, but he was duty bound to obey them. Speaking slowly and deliberately, he asked Pappa to explain the purpose of this meeting.

Brudi began, with a boldness that surprised them all. "My father has asked me to speak on his behalf since his command of the French language is not very good." Taking a deep breath, he continued, "We are Hungarian citizens with valid Hungarian passports. Hungary is not an enemy country. My country fought side by side with the Germans. I therefore demand that we be released forthwith!"

Both men turned towards Brudi in disbelief. Pappa felt horrified and astonished; he would never have used such strong words. What was to become of them now? As the seconds ticked by in utter silence, remorse overcame Brudi: he could not understand what had possessed him to speak like that! Frightened and bewildered, he let the tears flow unchecked down his cheeks. He and Pappa now stared at the commandant, who just looked from one to the other, not quite sure what to make of them. Suddenly he laughed out loud.

"I have never heard anything so audacious!" he gasped, rising to his feet. "What are you trying to do, pull a fast one? I'll tell you something — it might even work! But do you realize that if it does not, you are finished?"

He told Pappa to leave his passport and he would make the necessary inquiries. "Well," he remarked again, as they thanked him, "you never know, it just might work."

In great spirits they hastened to report to the rabbi and the *gabbai* who were anxiously waiting for news of the meeting. Pappa told them, "Do you know, it worked! Not only were we not arrested, but the commandant said he would try and get us released!"

The next few days were spent in a state of great expectation, but nothing happened. When two weeks had passed and they still had no word from the officer, they had to resign themselves to the inevitable. It had been a good idea, but it had not succeeded. They had hoped that the commandant would inform his German masters that he was holding two Hungarian citizens who were demanding to be released because there had surely been a mistake in jailing them, and would request permission to free them.

In fact, though they did not know it, this had happened. But so far no reply had been received.

It was now a few days before Passover. A list was being drawn up for the benefit of those inmates who would not eat bread on *Pesach*. There was, of course, no question of obtaining *matzah*, but at least the rabbi had successfully negotiated with the authorities to provide potatoes as a staple for those who would not eat bread during the eight-day holiday. The prisoners were also promised beans. Although beans are not normally eaten on Passover by Ashkenazic Jews, the rabbi of the camp gave permission for them to be eaten in order to supplement the meager rations.

On the day before Passover, the usual congregation of men was assembled in the *shul* for the morning service, when in walked a French soldier asking for Monsieur Marcovits to report to the commandant's office immediately.

Pappa hurriedly took off his *tallis* and *tefillin*, put them on the table, and quickly rushed to the commandant's office, followed closely by Brudi, who had also removed his *tefillin*.

As they entered, the officer was smiling broadly at them. His first words were, "It worked!" He seemed genuinely delighted, and explained, "I wrote to the German headquarters to explain that there must be a mistake. I told them I was holding two Hungarian citizens who are demanding to be released." Then he smiled again. "I did not enclose your passport. You know what would have happened had they seen your photograph! I kept it with me here in the office for their inspection. Well, I have just received a message. It states that there has indeed been a mistake. You are to be taken to my office and released. A car will call for you and you will receive an apology for wrongful imprisonment." He laughed again and continued, "I am to take good care of you and assure you that they will do all they can to help you!"

After a pause he continued. "You know what is going to happen if they come and see you! Not only will you be in trouble, I will as well. Now it says that I must look after you, but it does not say that I have to hold you against your will. I have no authority to hold you, should you want to leave. In fact, there is nothing to stop you from walking out at this moment, and when the Germans arrive I will tell them that you did not want to wait for them but insisted on leaving right away." He paused, his gaze resting on these two Jews, father and son, homeless, and unwanted. A more unlikely partnership was difficult to imagine. Here he was — of unimpeachable lineage, respected by his superiors and subordinates alike, with a beautiful, well-connected wife, and sons in the military academy — endangering his own position to help these two. The irony of it did not escape him.

"Hurry!" he said. "Go and collect your belongings and leave immediately. I expect the Germans to arrive within the hour."

They thanked him and ran back to the *shul*, where the rabbi and the *gabbai* were anxiously waiting. Pappa hurriedly explained what had happened. They all praised the Almighty for this miracle, then took a very tearful farewell of each other. Pappa and Brudi regretted parting from these two pious men to whom they owed their impending freedom. Pappa tried to thank the rabbi for his encouragement, and the *gabbai* for his original idea, but they brushed his thanks aside, not wanting to take the credit. "May *Hashem* be with you always," they said.

Pappa folded his *tallis* and *tefillin* into the faded blue bag; meanwhile Brudi, too, had collected his *tefillin*. Then they hurried back to the commandant's hut, where he was waiting for them. He handed Pappa his passport, and to their amazement, walked with them to the gate.

"You are on your own now," he told them. "If you get stopped, I'm sorry, I cannot help you. Just follow this road; approximately three miles up you will see a railway line. If you follow it you will come to a station. From there you can get a train to Paris. Good luck!"

Pappa thanked him, and followed his directions.

They came upon the railway lines, just as the commandant had told them, but had no idea which way to go, so they picked a direction and began to walk. They must have walked for at least three hours. No train passed during all this time; they were walking in open country with fields on either side. At last they came to a signal booth. At first, from afar, it looked deserted; but as they came nearer they noticed a man inside.

Pappa and Brudi approached with some caution, and asked him when the next train was due and where it was going.

He looked them up and down. They certainly did not look like two strollers enjoying the country air; he realized they were fugitives on the run. "I am expecting the express train to Paris; in fact, it is due in fifteen minutes. It does not stop here — my job is to signal it to pass through — but I'll tell you what I will do. As it approaches, I will make a mistake and throw the 'Stop' switch. Now you understand that as soon as it slows down to stop, I must realize my mistake and rectify it. More I cannot do," he said. "If you manage to jump on the train, good. If not, I cannot help you."

Pappa and Brudi thanked him and hid behind some bushes. Soon they heard a train approaching. Closer and closer — it came into view — it gave a whistle. Their hearts felt ready to burst; they heard a creaking sound as the guard threw the switch signaling the train to slow down. They dared not move as the engine passed the signal box. It was going too fast! Panic gripped them. Suddenly they heard the grinding of metal as the brakes gripped the wheels. As fast as they could, they ran the short distance to the nearest door, while the train with a sudden lurch started up again. Pappa could not reach the handle, but suddenly the door opened and hands stretched out to help them onto the train! With the help of people in the compartment they managed to get on, before the train picked up speed. Embarrassed and self-conscious, they thanked those present, then hurried out into the corridor and found an empty compartment where they settled down, exhausted but happy, for the journey to Paris.

A short time later they reached the station where the train stopped. Pappa and Brudi became terrified; they had no traveling papers, no tickets, no money, nothing. Two French soldiers entered their carriage and sat down opposite each other. They propped their rifles up between themselves and Pappa and Brudi. They did no more than glance at their fellow passengers, and spent their time in animated conversation as the train sped towards its destination. All of a sudden, from the far end of the corridor, the unmistakable guttural sound of Germans asking people for their traveling documents could be heard. In cold terror the two Jews listened as the Germans noisily progressed towards their compartment.

The German party consisted of three civilians and two uniformed men. The civilians were members of the Gestapo. They opened the door and asked the two French soldiers to produce their documents, which they did. Handing the papers back to the soldiers, the Germans called out to Pappa for his. Unconcerned, the two soldiers turned to Pappa and Brudi. Pappa's face had turned ashen, Brudi's eyes were full of terror. In an instant, the two French soldiers took up their rifles and crossed them in front of the terrified fugitives. Turning to the Germans, one soldier snapped, "These are our prisoners; we are taking them to Paris. Now please leave the compartment." The Germans saluted and left.

The sliding doors closed, and they were alone. Pappa could not speak; he was overcome with gratitude.

"Think nothing of it," one of the soldiers said. He was a well-built, dark-haired youth with the ruddy complexion of a farmer more at ease with a pitchfork than a rifle. His companion, slightly built, with a pale face and blue eyes, nodded his head in agreement as the former continued. "We will guard you for the rest of the journey," he promised.

Having somewhat recovered, Pappa and Brudi tried to convey their thanks as they approached their destination. The two soldiers were debating how to avoid the next hazard as the train steamed into Paris. Getting up from their seats, they slung their rifles over their shoulders, and one said to Pappa, "You both follow me, and my pal will walk behind you, so you look as if you are prisoners. When we get off the train, stand still and we will take up our positions on either side of you. Then, when we start marching, you do the same. Now remember, once we are outside the station, we will walk away. Good luck!"

People were being stopped by military police as they disembarked, and asked to produce their traveling permits once again. No one took any notice of the two French soldiers escorting their prisoners out the front entrance. How did they ever hope to have succeeded unaided?

And then they were alone, watching their benefactors marching down the boulevard and out of their lives ...

❦ ❦ ❦

This eventful day had drained what little energy they still possessed. They had missed their breakfast rations that morning, and what food they had eaten the previous day was hardly enough to sustain them for another day.

It was *erev Pesach*, the eve of Passover. Pappa and Brudi walked towards the *Pletzel*, no longer as strangers. It was important to buy some food and find a place to stay before nightfall, so they decided to go back to the Hôtel de Sud. If the landlord was surprised to see them, he did not show it; he just nodded as he greeted them and handed over the key. So they had a room, but no food yet, and very little time.

They hurried down the stairs and out into the street. Soon the Jewish shops would be closing for *Yom Tov*. The first place they went to was the Jewish bakery in the *Pletzel*, hoping to be able to buy some *matzah*. To their dismay, they found bread and *matzos* stacked together on the counter. Pappa would not buy *matzos* from a bakery which produced both leavened and unleavened doughs. They walked sadly out of the shop. Where could they buy some food which they might eat on *Pesach*?

"Let's go to the *shul*," Pappa said. "Perhaps we will find someone to help us." Brudi longed to visit Tante Dena, but they had decided not to go until after *Pesach*, knowing that she would have insisted on sharing her meager *Pesach* rations with them.

It was wonderful to walk up the large winding staircase of the "Number Twenty-five" *shul*. They were welcomed by two of the old members who were busy preparing the long table in the *beis hamedrash* for a communal *seder* to be held that evening, and their invitation to join was gratefully accepted. The dwindling congregation had still found the time and resources to provide for those less fortunate, the many refugees who would otherwise have had no means of making their own *seder*.

Twelve months had gone by since they last celebrated this joyous holiday; a single year separated them from a life which seemed like a fairy tale in retrospect. But Brudi remembered it so well . . .

> *Pappa, resplendent in his dazzling white kittel, the collar edged with lace, looked every inch the king of his domain. He presided at the head of the table, so lovingly prepared by Mamma and the girls, now dressed in their beautiful new clothes. They had spent all afternoon in a flurry of activity preparing the table for the seder. Silver candlesticks were polished to perfection, the candles' flickering light reflected on the silver tray. Gleaming cutlery shone against the snowy white damask tablecloth; each place setting had its own silver cup and saucer. The table designed to seat twelve in comfort would accommodate many more on these occasions. Mamma sat at Pappa's right while all the male guests were seated at his left. Tired after weeks of intense preparation, Mamma would beam*

happily at all those assembled, listening to the excited, endless questions of the younger children as Pappa prepared the seder plate, a beautiful, two-tiered platter with a white satin covering. Pappa would give the little ones slices of apple and walnuts, as he cut up the remaining apple with nuts, cinnamon and wine to make the charoses. Mamma cautioned the children not to spill wine on the crisp white tablecloth . . .

The vision faded abruptly. Brudi turned away, and walked down the stairs — it would not do to dwell on the past. He was fortunate to be free — unlike his friends left behind in prison that very morning — free to walk the streets, if only by day; free to participate in the time-honored ritual of this holiday.

✼ ✼ ✼

The festival was celebrated in the traditional way. *Kiddush* was followed by the reading of the *Haggadah* and lively discussions of the miracles performed, which had culminated in the redemption of the Jewish people. *Matzos* were served instead of bread, to commemorate the flight of the Israelites from Egypt, which they left with their unbaked dough carried in sheets slung over their shoulders.

An air of solemnity prevailed as those assembled continued with their prayers. Every place was occupied at the large table; a few small tables had been hastily assembled to enable the few families present to conduct their separate *sedarim*. People of many diverse backgrounds and lifestyles were there, bound together by a common unshakable faith.

Chapter Eighteen

Pesach passed uneventfully, and Brudi hurried to visit Tante Dena and the children. He had missed them, and looked forward to seeing their happy faces at their reunion. He was also looking forward to the food he would be given, for hunger was his constant companion.

However, he found it difficult to settle down to the old routine. During his absence, Tante Dena had paid a neighbor to mind the children while she continued with her errands; now the Schwartz children were delighted to have Brudi back. The evenings, however, without Uncle Menachem, no longer held their magic moments. The family Ostreicher was no longer in the boardinghouse. It was not until the war was over that Brudi met them again.

Pappa tried hard to re-establish a connection with the underground, but without his contact, Uncle Menachem, he had little success.

One day, deep in thought, Pappa halted outside the Jewish school, École Lucien de Hirsch, Avenue Secrétan, attracted by the laughter and shrieks of the children enjoying their lunchtime break. *How much longer will those innocent children be able to enjoy such carefree diversion?* he wondered. Pappa shook his head as if to dispel a sense of foreboding — he must not allow a mood of dejection to overpower him.

Pappa's premonition came to pass. As the children and their teachers were absorbed in their lessons one day, the Gestapo encircled the building, herded the terrified children and their teachers into trucks and drove them away to Germany — fresh fodder for the hungry furnaces. An entire school was completely wiped out. The heartache and deprivation suffered during that infamous journey is part of the darkest chapter of Jewish history.

※ ※ ※

Spring turned into summer, 1941. The freedom of the fun-loving Parisians was being eroded by the patrolling Nazi soldiers. Most commodities were in short supply, as they were increasingly being confiscated for the benefit of the conquering armies, so the black market flourished. A calculated indifference towards the Germans gradually developed into open defiance, which unfortunately would sometimes lead to the arrest of a dear one in the middle of the night by members of the Gestapo.

Resentment and defiance surfaced in the most extraordinary places. Brudi was sitting in the railway carriage on the métro, when he noticed the Frenchman sitting beside him idly cutting pieces out of his railway ticket. He quickly covered the ticket with his free hand whenever the German soldier standing in the aisle looked his way. Intrigued, Brudi watched and soon discovered that most of the other passengers also seemed to be fidgeting with their hands. The Frenchman, having noticed Brudi's puzzled look, winked at him and stealthily handed him his torn ticket. Brudi glanced at it and immediately understood. By cutting out a few oblong pieces the man had produced the emblem of the *Croix de Lorraine*, the symbol of the Free French resistance movement. Looking down at the floor, Brudi noticed that the majority of discarded métro tickets had been transformed to symbolize freedom. Brudi looked at the German soldier, who must surely have been aware of the hostility emanating from the riders in the compartment. He was very young, and Brudi wondered if he was just a little bit intimidated.

※ ※ ※

One day Brudi was waiting for Tante Dena to return, when there was a knock on the door. To his surprise, it was Pappa who entered. The children were delighted with their unexpected visitor. Watching Brudi marshaling the children back into the kitchen, Pappa marveled at his patience. Shortly after that Tante Dena came home. Pappa explained that they would soon be leaving Paris. "I hope to reach

Marseilles; I have heard that there are still ships leaving from the port. So I am hoping to cross safely over the Vichy border and then make our way to the harbor."

"I have a sister living in Marseilles. I will give you her address," said Tante Dena.

Pappa thanked her, carefully folded the paper with the address, and placed it in his wallet. He was grateful for it; one never knew. He had been extremely fortunate to re-establish contact with the people who arranged the escape routes. The price was high; Pappa had to part with nearly all the money which he had received from Mme. Blanc, but now they were ready to embark on their next attempt to reach freedom.

Pappa and Brudi traveled by train to their first secret meeting place, greatly relieved to find their contact there ahead of them, as promised. They jumped into a waiting truck and were driven along an unmarked road away from the village, until they reached a lonely farmhouse, which seemed to be on the edge of a forest. It was ideal for use as an illicit meeting point. They were not the first fugitives to enter the large, comfortable living room: five men were already present. Each new arrival was offered hot coffee, which was gratefully accepted. Pappa and Brudi were soon followed by three more new arrivals. A nervous tension prevailed as they waited, each engrossed in his own thoughts, fears, and perhaps doubts — the fear of the unknown.

Brudi moved closer to Pappa as a shudder went through his body; he was frightened. He tried hard not to think of what lay ahead. Would they succeed this time? How could they be sure that they had not already been betrayed, that there was no traitor lurking somewhere outside?

Mercifully his thoughts were interrupted by the arrival of their guides. They introduced themselves and gave a brief outline of the journey ahead. This helped to dispel some misgivings.

The last leg of their journey was about to begin. Divided into small groups, they left the safety of the farmhouse. The guide knew every inch of the forest, and would signal for them to take cover by lying down in the undergrowth, or a ditch, whenever his trained ears picked up the slightest unusual movement. The hours dragged by. Sometimes they would pause to rest for a few moments. Suddenly the two guides indicated that all should come closer together, then whispered, "We are now over the border and in Vichy France. We must warn you: if you are caught they will deal harshly with you. Do not venture further in a group. We advise you to split up into groups of no more than two or three. You will find a railway station nearby for those of you who wish to travel onwards. Good luck!"

The next moment they were gone.

The sun was shining brightly as Pappa and Brudi walked towards the railway station. Delighted to be free, yet mindful not to attract attention, they proceeded with the utmost caution. Ever watchful, and wary of anyone they met, they approached the station, hoping to be able to travel to Marseilles from there. Pappa decided to wait outside while Brudi went in and bought two tickets. He soon emerged, beaming as he handed them to Pappa; then they sat at the foot of an old sycamore, the spreading branches providing a welcome shade, as they waited for the train to arrive. Chatting excitedly, they made plans for the future, hardly noticing the passing of time. They hastened into the station as soon as they heard the train screeching to a halt.

They were tired and hungry, but grateful for their good fortune — they had succeeded! Pappa leaned back and closed his eyes. Brudi looked out the window and watched the countryside flash by, every moment taking them further away from the dreaded Nazis. Maybe that evening they would sleep in the apartment of Tante Dena's sister and maybe she would give them some food — ah, food! The very thought made his stomach growl.

Arriving in Marseilles, they cautiously alighted. The station was nearly deserted as they walked towards the exit, and Brudi was startled as he almost collided with a man hurrying towards the waiting train. Brudi apologized and Pappa inquired whether the stranger knew Marseilles, taking the paper with the address from his pocket. The stranger read it, then handing it back to Pappa, he asked, "Are you from the occupied side of France?"

Pappa nodded.

"Can you produce documents if apprehended?"

"No," Pappa replied.

"My dear fellow Jews," he said, "don't go into Marseilles — the gendarmes do not deal kindly with anyone caught. They will escort you right back over the border. Take my advice and go to Nice. The police are much more lenient and do not bother the illegal refugees. It also has a very large Jewish community. Take my advice," he repeated, as he hastened to catch the train.

As they watched the departing train, Pappa turned to Brudi, saying, "This is an omen, and we must heed it. We must not stay here. Let us take the next train to Nice. It is not far from here."

An hour later they were on their way.

※ ※ ※

Nice was an altogether delightful place. The palm trees, the wide elegant roads, the friendly policemen dressed in crisp white uniforms and tropical helmets — all were an incredible contrast to anything they had experienced in the last eighteen months. Unsure in which direction they would find the Jewish quarter, if indeed one existed, they walked towards the sea front, enjoying the last mellow rays of the sun as it slowly dipped beyond the horizon.

Pappa observed everyone they passed, until an elderly Jewish-looking man approached.

"Please, could you direct us to a synagogue, and also a place where we can get cheap accommodations?"

"Certainly," said the man kindly. "But you have quite a long way to walk." They did not mind, and at last entered a much poorer district where the *shul* was, near the apartment building which the man had recommended. The concierge was pleased to give them a single-room apartment on the second floor. The rent was cheap and the room had a small gas burner for cooking. The concierge told them where to find a food shop and they went out, first to *shul*, to *daven* and meet the congregation, then to buy some provisions, after which they eagerly returned to their apartment.

It had been a very long and difficult day. After they had eaten their first meal in freedom, it did not take long before they were both fast asleep.

Chapter Nineteen

The sun was streaming through the windows of the little room. Pappa gently shook Brudi to rouse him. "Wake up," he urged. "I want to catch the early *minyan*." Brudi stretched and opened his eyes. He looked for a moment around the unfamiliar room; then he remembered. They had arrived the previous night and they were free! He quickly got up to wash and dress.

Soon they were out in the street, walking towards the building which, as they were to discover, was not only the *shul*, but also included a community center, and two separate rooms used as *batei midrash* for the different segments of the Jewish community. The Sephardic Jews and the Ashkenazic Jews lived together as one close-knit community, yet each group proudly retained its individual *minhagim*, traditions, in its own synagogue services.

They were warmly welcomed by those present. After the service, no one seemed to be in a hurry to leave: life was lived at a leisurely pace. Few had jobs to go to, so a holiday mood prevailed. Some of the regulars had formed a study group which met twice daily. Pappa joined them and enjoyed those hours spent learning in the *shul*.

The authorities accepted the unseasonal influx of people good-naturedly. They caused no problems and so were left unmolested.

During the short week before the Jewish New Year, Pappa made friends with a few of the regular *shul* members, and on their second day there, someone told him that the Red Cross had an office in Nice. Maybe they would be able to trace his family! He immediately went to see them; they listened sympathetically and wrote down details. Pappa described how he had last seen his family amid the chaos following the bombing of Ostend, when the harbor was being evacuated. He had seen them boarding a ship; which one would be impossible to say. The officials promised to make enquiries, and he left his present address with them, not daring to hope too much. Life went on peacefully.

Pappa was very careful with his money, and had become skilled at producing nourishing and satisfying meals with the minimum of cost. Food was not in short supply. Pappa's favorite recipe was to cut up a few slices of toast, fry them in butter until golden brown, add caraway seeds and let them roast, then add boiling water and a pinch of salt. This made a most satisfying and tasty bowl of hot soup, which they both enjoyed.

On *Yom Kippur* night, right after the fast ended, Pappa and Brudi were sitting at the table enjoying their plates of hot caraway soup, when there came a knock on the door. It was a middle-aged lady, a refugee from Holland, tall and stately with her greying hair tied back in a bun. She reminded Brudi of Mamma. Mme. de Lang, a lonely figure resigned to spending the war years separated from her family, had the room across the landing. She too was hoping to hear good news through the efforts of the International Red Cross.

She was holding two plates in her hand. "I made some extra *gefilte fish* and I wondered if you would like some," she said.

Brudi could not believe his eyes! *Gefilte fish* balls, like Mamma used to make! They had not had any since the war started. "We must have *davened* well today," Brudi remarked happily, bringing his plate to the table. The food tasted delicious. He soaked up every drop of the jelly with his bread, glad that he still had a slice of bread left to wipe the plate clean.

The meal over, the plates were carefully washed and dried, and Brudi hastened to return them to their kind neighbor. Pappa went along to thank her once again. "Where did you buy fish?" he asked. "All the time we have been here, I have never seen fish being sold."

She laughingly said, "Fish? Oh, no, it would be much too expensive even if it were available! No, I just make it look like chopped fish. I boil onions and mix them with bread soaked in water, add a generous dash of salt and pepper, and there you have delicious *gefilte fish* balls!"

❈ ❈ ❈

One day the Red Cross informed Pappa that his family was safe and sound, somewhere in England! "Thank You, *Hashem!*" Pappa kept repeating, letting the tears flow down his cheeks, oblivious to those present. Now he knew it was time for them to move on; there was no point to staying in Nice for the duration of the war, for he had no faith in the assurance of neutrality.

Friends tried to dissuade him from going to Marseilles. "Why do you want to leave?" they asked. "We are safe here: we walk the streets unhindered, the shopkeepers treat us courteously, the policemen are helpful!"

Pappa would shake his head. "You are deluding yourselves," he would answer. "I do not trust the Germans, and Nice is also too close to the Italian border."

No one understood the strange reasoning of M. Marcovits.

Mme. de Lang was incredulous. "Marseilles!" she exclaimed. "You are leaving Nice to go to Marseilles? Please don't do it, stay here with your son. The air is so beneficial, the people are friendly and you have a comfortable apartment. You will find Marseilles very different."

Pappa felt a sadness for these Jewish people. They clung to their belief that the Germans had nothing to gain by marching into southern France. Alas! Events were to prove them wrong. And as in all the occupied territories, among the first priorities of the Germans was the rounding up of the Jews.

❀ ❀ ❀

Late in the evening they knocked on the door of Madame Furst, Tante Dena's sister, who welcomed them to her home in Marseilles. "I received a letter from Dena telling me you were coming. But that was some months ago, and I have been concerned. Thank *Hashem* you are both safe."

It was a modest apartment. Her husband had been employed in a factory and was at the moment out of work, but managed to do some odd jobs in the community to eke out a living. Pappa and Brudi had not eaten that day, but did not ask for food, thankful to have somewhere to stay overnight. Madame Furst apologized for only being able to offer a hot drink: food was in short supply even if one had money, she explained. "I do have some cooked spinach left. You are welcome to that," she said, going into the tiny kitchen, and coming back with the pan and two plates.

"No, thank you," Pappa said, "I don't eat it, but I'm sure Brudi will enjoy some." Brudi ate the delicious spinach as fast as he could. A short time later his tummy rumbled in protest at this sudden overloading, but the fullness itself was comforting even if it did mean indigestion! He wondered whether Pappa had deliberately pretended to dislike spinach so that he, Brudi, could have his fill...

They spent the evening discussing events of mutual interest. Brudi found Mme. Furst easy to talk to, as he watched her bathing her two young children, Sendor, five, and Sheah'le, aged six. She felt his loneliness and instinctively knew how to make him feel at home.

"Here is a *siddur*," she said, handing Brudi a worn book. "Would you be kind enough to read a few passages with the older boy? It would give me time to tidy the room and leave my husband in conversation with your father."

Brudi readily obliged. He had been in the habit of teaching Tante Dena's children while he waited for their mother to come home. It helped to pass the time much more quickly.

Brudi enjoyed teaching Sheah'le; he was a bright boy who could read Hebrew quite fluently and was eager to learn the translation. Brudi happily accepted the offer of teaching the boy every day for as long as they remained in Marseilles.

Weeks went by. Brudi missed the bright, clean, tree-lined streets of Nice. Although it was November, it had been quite warm and he had enjoyed taking long walks through the busy town center and watching the traffic pass by.

Marseilles, in contrast, was cold and wet. The streets were narrow, the houses in the Jewish neighborhood were drab and in poor repair. Brudi had not ventured beyond the Jewish quarter, its population swelled by the influx of refugees.

He was grateful for having been offered teaching jobs, for not only Mme. Furst but also two other families close by had asked him to teach their sons.

With the help of M. Furst, Pappa had drawn up a list of consulates still in Marseilles, and lost no time in visiting their offices in an attempt to find a way to leave France. Naturally he preferred to leave by legitimate means. He was well aware of the consequences should they be caught again trying to cross illegally! So, day after day he would 'do the rounds'. It was generally thought that the Venezuelan and the Argentinian consuls were more sympathetic and issued more visas than any of the others. In consequence, the lines there were longer, but this did not deter Pappa. He would spend hours in one line just to register his name, than move on to the next, and the next. Then he would return the following day. Few ships ever left — hence the long waiting lists. But what else was there to do?

This routine continued for almost four weeks. At last Pappa received a visa for Venezuela, stamped into his passport. "Tomorrow we will try for the Spanish border," Pappa declared. "We have nothing to lose."

Pappa invested part of their meager savings in two tickets to the nearest border town, where they arrived at midday. Hungry and tired, Pappa and Brudi walked directly from the railway station to the border. The appearance of wandering Jews hoping to cross into Spain was no unusual event of late. The guards eyed these two bedraggled Jews with derisive merriment, ready to rebuff them. It was a delightful game of cat and mouse with the odds stacked just as conclusively.

How singular a race of people we must appear to them, reflected Brudi. *Hated, unwanted, yet we maintain our traditional garb, our side curls and black hats, even though they cause us to be so easily picked out in a crowd . . .*

Pappa boldly approached the guard near the barrier.

"Halt!" commanded the sentry, aiming his rifle at them. Pappa tried to steady his shaking hand as he handed over his passport for inspection. The soldier did no more than glance at it, then called to his superior, "Here's a Jew with a false visa!"

Pappa and Brudi were terrified as they watched the commandant coming towards them. Pappa insisted that the visa was valid, meanwhile praying inwardly that the officer would not notice that the Hungarian passport, his only document of identity, had expired.

At long last, the commandant handed the passport back to Pappa. His eyes seemed to soften as he declared, "You are a Jew, therefore you cannot have a valid visa. They no longer issue visas to Jews. So don't let me see you again."

Dejectedly they walked away. An ordinary-looking, very young man approached them; he was of medium height and extremely thin, with brown wavy hair and dark brown eyes. He introduced himself — "My name is Yonah; I'm an Orthodox Jew" — and went on to explain that he had lived in this border town for the last four weeks. "Every day I present myself at the barrier and plead to be allowed to go through. As a Frenchman with valid identity papers they let me go through, and every day I am turned back on reaching the Spanish barrier. One day I will succeed, perhaps!" he concluded hopefully. He strongly cautioned Pappa against trying the same.

"Once you cross the French barrier, assuming that they might let you through one day," he said, "they would arrest you on re-entry, and prisons in Vichy France are reputedly just as harsh as in Germany, if you are a Jew."

Pappa listened earnestly. There must be a way around this dilemma: his faith in the Almighty was unshaken. "Do you know a cheap place where we can stay overnight?" Pappa asked.

"Please come and share my room; you can sleep on my bed and we two boys will sleep on the floor."

The young Frenchman was obviously delighted when they accepted — to give up his bed was a small price to pay for the company of fellow Jews. He had found the loneliness difficult to endure.

That night they said evening prayers together, including a special plea for an early deliverance — to be allowed a safe crossing over the border. They all slept soundly. Pappa was the first to rise the following morning. He quietly took out his small battered *Tehillim* and recited the familiar lines, finishing just as the youths awoke.

"What shall we do today?" asked Yonah, when they had finished their prayers.

"We will go once again to the barrier and hope that with the help of *Hashem* we will succeed."

Yonah was incredulous. "You know what will happen!" he pleaded, unwilling to lose his new-found friends so soon.

Pappa's mind was made up. "Come, let us go," he told Brudi.

"I'm coming with you," called Yonah.

At the barrier they were stopped by the familiar shout, "Halt!" It was the same commandant from the day before. "Did I not tell you that you cannot pass?"

Pappa was about to plead, when the officer suddenly began to laugh. "Do you know what day it is today? Well, I will tell you," he told the frightened trio. "It is New Year's day, 1942, and as a New Year's present, I will let you go through! But I warn you, you will not be allowed into Spain. The borders are closed to foreigners, and once you leave French soil, you cannot come back. I would have to arrest you on your return to France." Stepping back, he gave orders for the barrier to be lifted.

Yonah, greatly distressed, was pleading with Pappa and Brudi not to step over the demarcation line. "You have no chance of being allowed into Spain. This is a trap!" he exclaimed.

"Nonsense!" said Pappa, brushing his argument aside. "Come, we have to do our share and *Hashem* will do his!"

Saying this, he took Brudi's hand and walked resolutely into the no man's land, closely followed by Yonah.

They had overcome one hurdle; *Hashem* would be with them at the next — of that Pappa was sure. They traversed the short distance separating them from the Spanish barrier, the mocking laughter of the French soldiers echoing across the wasteland.

They walked in a daze, halting only upon reaching the Spanish barrier. Two guards came out of the guard room, curious to see who could be disturbing their celebrations. With mounting jollity, holding a carafe of wine, they scrutinized the three bedraggled humans. A third soldier, their spokesman, emerged from the hut, and walking up to the barrier he called, "Show me your papers!"

"We have none!"

"You have none?" they repeated in unison. The audacity almost sobered them, but not quite. They stood eyeing the three hapless Jews for what seemed an eternity.

"I'll tell you what," said their leader. "It is the first day of the New Year. To celebrate, I will let you through!" It was sheer magic! They had made it! They were standing on Spanish soil, and were free!

Chapter Twenty

There was no time for celebration. They were directed to the railway station, and while waiting for the train to arrive, Pappa changed all his francs into pesetas at the *Bureau de Change*, a tiny office next to the ticket booth. They boarded a train to Barcelona, arriving late in the evening. Yonah did not leave the train; possibly he traveled on to Madrid. They were not to meet again.

It was quite dark as they emerged from the station. Barcelona, having a fair-sized population, was sure to have its own Jewish community, Pappa reasoned, so they walked up to a waiting taxi and asked to be taken to the synagogue. The driver shook his head. Though skilled at interpreting tourists' gestures, he was now totally baffled. These two did not look like tourists, but he was willing to try to understand them. Brudi repeated, "*la synagogue;*" as this drew a blank, he added, "*shool, shul, shill,*" clasping his hands together for good measure, but it just did not register with the driver. He tried to understand, but never had he heard of such a strange-sounding place.

"*Olé!*" He had found a solution! Waving his arms and beaming broadly, he indicated that he would take them somewhere. With a sigh of relief, Pappa and Brudi entered the taxi. They were somewhat alarmed as they stopped outside the police station, but were soon reassured by the friendly manner of the taxi driver, who tried his best to make them understand.

"I think he wants the police to act as interpreters. Come, Brudi, you will have to help me," Pappa said. "Your French is much better than mine." Brudi was not sure how that would help with the Spanish-speaking police. With mounting apprehension, they entered the police station, to be greeted with unaccustomed friendliness. No one asked them to produce their identity papers; the officials listened patiently as the driver spoke. To him it had become a challenge to deliver his charges to their desired destination. Someone remembered that their superior could speak French. He soon emerged, and Brudi explained that they would like to be taken to a synagogue. The same blank expression spread over his face.

Pappa decided to state the obvious. "We are Jews," he said in French, but made no impression. Brudi added, "*Joden, Yidden, Juifs.*" This exhausted his vocabulary, but there was still no response. Pappa racked his brains, there must be a word to make them understand. Yes, of course! "*Yehudi,*" he said. "We are *Yehudis.*"

"*Yehudis?*" answered the policeman who spoke French. He was a man of the world, and understood before his colleagues did.

He explained the word to the others, and Brudi, encouraged, asked, "Could you direct the driver to take us to the place where the *Yehudis* pray?"

"We don't have a prayer house for Jews in Barcelona; we only have one Jewish family. I will give the taxi driver the address."

The driver looked them up and down with interest. This must have been the first time that he had encountered Jewish people. He would probably go home that evening and tell his family all about his experience...

They climbed back into the car, and away he drove. Soon the taxi stopped outside an apartment building in the residential area, and the driver told them to wait while he rang the bell. Someone dressed in a somber, well-cut business suit opened the door, and listened to the driver's explanation. The man walked towards the car. He was in his early thirties, with jet black hair held in neat large waves with a generous application of pomade, so fashionable in those days. To Pappa's immense relief, he welcomed them to his house.

His wife greeted them also and offered a meal, which they eagerly accepted. After washing themselves and brushing their clothes they were able to relax, while their host enquired as to their reason for coming to Barcelona. Briefly Pappa explained the events of the last few months, adding, "My reason for choosing a harbor town is because I feel it is the only way I may find passage on a ship."

"Well, that seems logical enough," his host remarked, "but let me advise you. No passenger ships leave from Barcelona. You should really go to Bilbao."

So it was arranged that they would spend the night with the couple, and the following morning their host would drive them to the station.

In the morning Pappa and Brudi awoke early, eager to leave. After breakfast, they thanked the lady for her hospitality; the food they had eaten for breakfast would sustain them for the rest of the day. Their host drove them to the station. "Please do not thank me," he said. "It is not often that we have the opportunity to welcome fellow Jews into our house."

They boarded the train that was to take them to Bilbao. If Pappa had any misgivings as to the outcome of the tedious journey, he never showed them. The train stopped at every station, and it was late in the evening when they finally steamed into Bilbao. Tired and hungry, but with fresh enthusiasm, Pappa set about finding accommodations for the night. "We must find the poorer quarters in this city," he commented, "if we are to find a place that we can afford."

Soon they reached a small, unpretentious square, where most of the buildings had the magic word *Pensión* painted on the front. Pappa decided to try one. The owner spoke a little French and gave them a key to a small room with two beds; he told them that breakfast would be served beginning at six o'clock. Breakfast! They would just have to wait until morning.

In the privacy of their room Pappa counted his money. He had been extremely careful, only buying the bare necessities. This room, though very small, was clean and cheap and it included breakfast! He counted and recounted the pesetas. Even if they made do with the one meal a day which was provided with the room, his sum total was four days' rental. His faith was firm, but he was nevertheless concerned.

※ ※ ※

In the morning they went to the dining room for breakfast. The tantalizing smell of freshly baked rolls had wafted up to their bedroom as they concluded their prayers. Some of the guests were already seated. Pappa and Brudi chose an unoccupied table, and using great restraint, each unhurriedly cut the roll which was already at his place setting. A waiter brought hot coffee. How good it was to wash down the bread with the steaming brew!

Suddenly Brudi stiffened. "Pappa," he said, "have you noticed that we are alone?" Pappa looked around the room — it was true. The unfinished food left on the adjoining tables confirmed their unspoken fear — the other guests were deliberately avoiding them. The bread that Brudi had so relished only a few moments ago now stuck in his throat. They could hear the men in animated discussion just outside the dining room door, then all was quiet.

A few minutes later, one by one, the men re-entered the room — each with a hat on his head — sat back down at the tables, and resumed eating breakfast. Only then did it dawn on Pappa and Brudi what had happened. On seeing that Pappa and Brudi, who were obvious strangers, ate with their hats on, they had all walked out and, with impeccable good manners, put on their hats, rather than embarrass the new guests.

Pappa and Brudi spent the whole day walking through the streets of Bilbao. First they strolled along the harbor, vainly searching for a Jewish-looking face. They saw Spanish sailors loading heavy bales into the hold of an ancient freighter, and passed some peaceful and agreeable time observing them. The timeless fascination of watching a ship being fitted for an unknown destination has a magic all its own.

Pappa and Brudi walked away from the harbor towards the busy town center, noting the location of various consulates. "Tomorrow," Pappa declared, "we will visit the English and American consulates. For today, let us continue to look; maybe we will find even one single Jew who could give us some information."

At the end of the day, Brudi remarked wryly, "I noticed that food is in short supply in this town. The windows of the bakeries have no bread on display; it must be almost as scarce as Jews!" At that moment they passed a grocery. Impulsively, Pappa entered and searched for something they could eat which would not make too great a dent in his savings. He selected two fair-sized onions, the cheapest commodity available.

Back in the hotel room, they each peeled an onion, removing the outer layers of golden brown skin. Brudi watched Pappa patiently cutting his onion into perfect rings of equal thickness, then, handing his son the only knife they had, he sprinkled salt over the rings. The blue and pinkish veins running through the onions provided an unexpected splash of color on Pappa's plate. As Brudi worked laboriously to make his plate as attractive as Pappa's, he marveled at the many hues in an onion. It had never occurred to him that an onion was anything but colorless. Brudi made the tears running down his cheeks flow more copiously by unwittingly rubbing his eyes, so Pappa helped him cut the last few rings.

The onions not only looked nice, they also tasted good — quite sweet. It was amazing how much Brudi had learned about an onion. Never again would he treat one with disdain! (To this day, his favorite meal when on vacation is a chunk of whole wheat bread, butter, and raw Spanish onions.)

✽ ✽ ✽

The following day, as they walked down the broad, tree-lined road, they were attracted by the sound of a brass band playing. It was coming from the city square, the Place de Franco. Pappa was in no mood for frivolity: after paying the rent for that day, he would not have enough for another day. By this time they had reached the square, where a large crowd had gathered around the military band. Pappa and Brudi circled aimlessly around the bandstand, idly staring at the crowd.

"*Shalom!*" someone called, startling Pappa out of his gloom. Instantly they both turned to face a young man who looked no different than any other Spaniard, wearing a dark suit with the black beret worn by most men. Perhaps they had heard wrong! As if to reassure them, he held out his hand and repeated, "*Shalom!*" Immense relief overwhelmed them. *Hashem* be praised, they had spent two days looking for a Jew without success and now one had found them!

"What are you doing here, and where are you staying?" he asked. Eagerly, Pappa poured out his heart. He would willingly do any work for a roof over his head and a little food!

"No, no, you must not mention work. The Spaniards are short of jobs for their own people. It is true, we do not have a Jewish community," the young man said, "but you need no longer worry. We have a representative of the American Jewish Joint Distribution Committee which was specifically set up to help Jewish refugees. Come, let's collect your belongings from the boardinghouse and I will take you directly to the Hotel Angleterre where all the other Jewish refugees are staying. You will also be given a small amount of pocket money."

Pierre, as their new-found friend was called, was a Frenchman by birth, who had lived for many years in Bilbao with his wife and son. He made his living as a street photographer.

Delighted to have someone ready to help them, Pappa readily accepted his offer to act as their interpreter. They settled their bill in the hotel, and as they walked out beside Pierre they felt as if they had known each other a long time.

The initial attraction for Pierre had been Brudi's *payos* — the traditional side curls — and Pappa's beard. (Although Frenchmen too wore beards, they generally kept their heads uncovered.) He had encountered many Jewish refugees since the start of the war, but none who had clung to their old traditions. He was fascinated by Pappa's concern to find kosher food and a synagogue, both of which were non-existent in this town and everywhere else in Spain, Pierre declared. These two Jews reminded him of his own parents, whom he had not heard about for a long time.

Reaching the fashionable section of the city, with Pappa and Brudi trailing behind, he entered one of the most expensive-looking hotels. The Hotel Angleterre was a large and luxurious place, making Brudi feel ill at ease in his shabby outgrown suit. After booking a room for two with full board, Pierre took them upstairs. Pappa thanked him for his assistance, but Pierre had not yet finished. "I am sure you are hungry," he declared. "Come, let us go down. I will explain that you have only just arrived and would like something to eat."

Over a welcome cup of coffee and a buttered roll, Pierre explained that there was a great shortage of food and most things were rationed; in the hotel the food was also strictly rationed per guest. Brudi would have loved another roll but one was all he could have. However, they were grateful for this unexpected meal and could not quite believe that from then on they would be served three meals each day.

"Now I will take you to the police station for registration." Pierre had to laugh when he saw the alarm in Pappa's eyes. "Do not worry," he said reassuringly. "You have to register to make your stay legal. Leave it to me." He completed the arrangements, and by the time they walked out of the police station, they were duly recorded as residing at the Hotel Angleterre Pierre had done all the talking, no objections had been raised, and Pappa was not asked for his documents.

On the way back to the hotel, Pierre explained that the headquarters for the Joint Distribution Committee was in Madrid.

"They send a representative here once a week. He settles the bill at the hotel and attends to all other matters concerning the refugees. He is due tomorrow, so make sure to be in the hotel when he arrives," Pierre told Pappa as he left, promising to keep in touch.

How fortunate they were to have met Pierre! Their entire situation had changed: they were no longer destitute, but had comfortable lodgings, were assured of food and had a good friend to call upon. It had been a most encouraging day.

It was tempting to consider staying in comfort in Bilbao, but Pappa thought of Brudi's interrupted education. In his bag, besides his *siddur* and *Tehillim*, he had only a *chumash*, a copy of the Pentateuch. Pappa need not have worried, however. What Brudi learned from his father during those turbulent years — lessons about the strength of the human spirit when tested — he never forgot.

The hotel was owned by a fiercely patriotic German named Mr. Loefler. He and his English wife, who came from Southampton and was affectionately referred to as "La Doña," looked after their many Jewish guests with the utmost courtesy. Nevertheless, Pappa asked the Joint's representative to provide him and his son with cheaper hotel accommodations, explaining that he would like to save the difference so that he would eventually be able to afford passage on a ship leaving Bilbao.

"That is out of the question," said the man with the purse. Money set aside for hotel bills had to be used for just that. Pappa could have a weekly allowance, as did all the other refugees.

Weeks passed. Pappa had been to the British consul to ask for a visa for travel to England.

"No one can come to England," he was told. The International Red Cross also had an office in Bilbao and Pappa never tired of going to enquire for news of his family in England. Finally the day came when, on his usual visit, Pappa was informed that his family had been traced to an address in Manchester, and if he wished to write to them, the Red Cross would be happy to forward his letter.

Communication at last! What did it matter that a letter would take two months to arrive! Pappa and Brudi hurriedly wrote their first letter, feeling a closeness to their distant loved ones that had for so long been eluding them. It was to be many months before they finally received a letter in reply, assuring them that all was well, but that they were greatly missed.

❁ ❁ ❁

I well remember the excitement and happiness when we received our first letter from Pappa via the International Red Cross!

From Crystal Palace we had been sent to a family in Catford, South London. A wonderful old couple, they had a beautiful house with seven bedrooms, and made us all feel welcome. Although Mamma was very grateful for the kindness shown, she explained to our hosts (who spoke a little French) that we would like to be relocated to an area where other Orthodox Jewish people lived.

The man agreed to act as our interpreter with the authorities, but warned Mamma that we might have difficulty finding alternative accommodations for so many under one roof.

The total lack of prejudice towards Jews, and the kindness of our hosts and everyone with whom we came into contact, was very strange to us — a wonderful new experience which needed getting used to. How we longed to share it with Pappa and Brudi!

After spending the late spring and summer months billeted with different families, Mamma was granted permission to set up her home in a furnished apartment in the borough of Clapton, overlooking Victoria Park. An uneasy peace prevailed in those early days. The war was far away, across the sea. It was not uncommon to meet soldiers, sons and brothers of neighbors who had survived Dunkirk, who liked to tell us of the places they had been, and to describe their experiences. Our command of English still being very limited, we never really understood those brave soldiers.

It was in July that Esti and I decided to look for a job. We were thrilled to be offered work with a hat manufacturer in the city. Esti was taught to sew on an electric sewing machine, and I became a pattern cutter. I was given a pair of shears so large and heavy that I could only use them by supporting the lower blade on the cutting table. I did not learn a word of English there since, for reasons only known to himself, my boss treated me as if I were deaf and dumb and explained what he wanted me to do by gesticulating. This often made me have fits of giggling which I tried hard to suppress, although not very successfully.

As the beautiful warm summer days came to an end, a new era started. Early in September the peace was shattered by the air attacks on London, which continued unabated. By early October, daytime raids had stopped, but night attacks intensified.

Thus, like millions of other Londoners, we went to work by day and spent the nights in the air-raid shelters of Victoria Park. It was clean and comfortable compared to some other public air-raid shelters. We had room to stretch out and sleep. As we emerged each morning, we surveyed the devastation around us and felt thankful to have been spared. Eventually it came to pass that a few refugee families who shared the same shelter with us decided that, since none of us had roots in London, it would be better if we all moved up north, to a safer place. After some deliberation, the necessary permission was applied for, arrangements were made, and in December we were ready to wander once again.

Mamma agreed to join a group who wanted to settle in the northwest of England. Manchester was the obvious choice; it was known to have an Orthodox Jewish community and was also a thriving industrial and commercial center. The cold damp climate stood in stark contrast to the warm and friendly Mancunians. For generations, Manchester had been a haven for the persecuted Jews from Eastern Europe. It offered the opportunity of earning a livelihood in those days (long before the emergence of the "Welfare State") when earning a living was of paramount concern.

So that is how we came to be in Manchester when Pappa's letter reached us.

Pappa took his letter to the British consul as proof that his family were living in England, and requested permission to join them. His application was duly recorded and he was warned that the possibility of his succeeding was very remote, but he could wait and see. Pappa presented himself at the office at regular intervals.

Pesach was drawing near, and Pappa was concerned about food. He and Brudi had managed quite well so far to avoid the cooked food provided by the hotel. Although Spain was not at war, food was not plentiful and bread was strictly rationed. Fruits and vegetables were their mainstay, and they were also allowed a generous supply of boiled eggs. Even so, Pappa decided that their present diet could be improved.

With *Pesach* just a week away, he decided on a bold plan. Why not approach the proprietor, Mr. Loefler, and explain that he would like to buy a pan, since both he and Brudi felt the need for cooked food? Mr. Loefler listened patiently as Pappa explained, as best he could, the reason why he was unable to partake of the food provided for the guests. To Pappa's immense relief, the man agreed to his request. That same afternoon Mr. Loefler gave Pappa a brand new pan and some cutlery. For the first time since they arrived, Pappa could once again practice his culinary skills. The kitchen staff were good natured as they allowed Pappa to prepare his own meals. Even Brudi became an expert with fried onions and eggs, using pure olive oil to produce delicious omelettes. From that time on they kept the pan and cooked all their own meals for the rest of their stay.

Mr. Loefler and his family were most helpful and friendly to their Jewish guests, taking a special interest in Brudi. Often he would be invited to join them when Mr. Loefler took his sons on Sunday outings. This provided Brudi with a welcome diversion. It seemed odd that they liked Brudi, who was so obviously a Jew.

The two Loefler boys were proud to be members of the Bilbao *Hitler Jugend* (Hitler Youth Club). They enjoyed going to meetings in their uniforms, which were the same as those the German youths wore. Like all children in Spain, they had been brought up to consider the Jew as a figure of ridicule, always the bad guy. Brudi was to become familiar with the many comic magazines showing the Jew as having horns on his forehead, and a tail. In fact, most Spaniards were convinced that all Jews had horns, if not a tail. In spite of their obvious anti-Semitic indoctrination, the proprietor, along with his family and his staff, treated the Jewish hotel guests with kindness at all times. Mr. Loefler let it be known that although he was a patriotic German, he did not share his *Führer's* hatred of the Jews, and this was reflected by his behavior towards the Jewish refugees staying in his hotel.

Brudi would often be invited by the sons for an early morning swim, together with the young waiters of the hotel. One morning, as they watched Brudi undress and fold his *tallis kattan*, the traditional fringed garment, one of the young waiters asked how come he did not have horns. The question hardly surprised Brudi, and he assured them that the Jew with horns was a myth perpetrated by Jew-haters. "But it can't be," they protested. "Everybody knows that Jews have horns!"

"I know what," said one, brighter than the others. "Brudi is too young to have horns, perhaps. They only grow when you get old!" They all looked at Brudi for confirmation.

"No," he said. "Look at my father — he is old and has no horns!"

"Indeed he has not," they all agreed.

There is a sequel to this story. A few days later one of the young waiters asked Brudi if he would be kind enough to come with him to visit his grandmother, whom he often visited on his day off from work.

"Why do you want me to come?" asked Brudi.

"I told my grandmother that I have a friend, a Jew. She has never seen a Jew and would like to meet you. She asked if you have horns!" the other replied ...

❦ ❦ ❦

Summer followed spring and then it was autumn once again. Almost a year had gone by since Pappa and Brudi had arrived in Bilbao. During that time they had received two letters from Mamma and they longed to be reunited. Sometimes, on his frequent visits to the English or Portuguese consuls, Pappa would come away with hope renewed, only to have it dashed at a subsequent meeting. He did get an offer for passage to Venezuela, but declined. The rest of his family was in England, and he only wanted to join them.

The other guests in the hotel could not understand Pappa's restlessness, or his frequent visits to the English consulate. "Why don't you just settle down like the rest of us?" he was asked. "You will not succeed in going to England! Consider yourself lucky to be here, and enjoy yourself."

Passive acceptance was alien to Pappa. "*Hashem* helps those who help themselves," was one of his favorite sayings.

❦ ❦ ❦

Early one morning in December 1942, they boarded a train which would take them to the small harbor town of Vigo. Pappa again chose a town with a port in the hope of finding a ship going to England. Vigo's being almost on the border with Portugal presented a twofold attraction.

Having checked into the only hotel they could find, Pappa lost no time in enquiring where to locate the office of the Portuguese consul. To his dismay he learnt that Vigo was not important enough to have a resident consul. The office was purely "honorary" and carried no authority.

There must be some other way. Border towns by their very nature have always been an attraction to peddlers and merchants looking for an opportunity to make money, not necessarily legally. Deep in thought, Pappa re-entered the hotel. He was surprised to find Brudi in animated conversation with two other guests whom he had noticed earlier as he was leaving. Brudi was happy to introduce them, delighted to have found two men able to speak Yiddish. They had arrived the previous evening, hoping to find a way across the border, and now were no longer alone.

Soon the talk turned to ways of discovering the hideouts of possible smugglers. All this was fascinating to Brudi; it sounded like one of the stories he had read back home in Antwerp, something to do with a desert island. But this was much more exciting — this was real!

The men explained to Pappa that they had been spending their time walking around the small town, dropping hints in the obvious places, hoping this would eventually lead them to a contact. Finally it worked! The following day, they told Pappa that he was to introduce himself to a man he would meet in a small café just outside the town. The man would be wearing a black beret pulled over his left ear, and sitting at a table on which rested a basket of eggs.

Pappa did as he was told. Money changed hands and arrangements were made for Pappa and Brudi to be picked up the following day. "If all goes well," Pappa confided in Brudi, "this will be our last evening in Spain."

Elated at their forthcoming venture, they pushed aside any doubts that crossed their minds. Pappa decided they would do well to make it an early night, in readiness for the morning; but if he hoped to sleep peacefully, he was disappointed.

※ ※ ※

Restlessly Pappa turned in his sleep. Distances melted away, as he felt himself transported back to his childhood in Gibart... *He could see his beloved parents in the forecourt of their large, white-painted country house. His father sat in the shade near the entrance, engrossed in the sefer which was always in his hand, and Mamma, his dear Mamma, tended the masses of geraniums growing in the window boxes along the length of the house. He wanted to call out to them, when suddenly he heard the sound of jackboots along the gravel path. Turning, he saw men in the dreaded uniform of the SS coming to collect his parents. He cried out to warn them... and woke up distressed, drenched in perspiration. Groggy with sleep, Pappa groped for the light but could not find the switch. He got out of bed and walked to the window, where he could just make out the time by the faint light of the moon. It was ten minutes past two o'clock. What was he to make of that terrible dream? He opened the pages of his Tehillim, trying to find solace in the familiar words.*

❈ ❈ ❈

It was not until the war was over that Pappa learned the fate of his parents. They, in common with many thousands of Hungarian Jews, had indeed been rounded up for transportation to Bergen Belsen.

(The assembling of Hungarian Jewry began in the late spring of 1944. The towns and villages were "cleansed" of their Jewish inhabitants who were herded together in abandoned, desolate brickyards, known as *"tégla-gyár,"* which served as transit camps. The weeks passed. An air of ill-boding prevailed, heightened with each cartload of new arrivals. They came from such diverse places as Pécs, Szeged, Györ Miskolcz, Eger, and many more, dots on the map, names that have earned their places in Jewish history due to the great sages who lived there.)

❈ ❈ ❈

It was one Shabbos day in June when the cattle trucks rolled to a halt outside the compound of one such tégla-gyár. The inmates were herded into the waiting trucks which were packed to capacity and then sealed shut. "You are being transferred to labor camps" — the old and frail together with the children and their parents. "The journey will take two days," they were told.

Malkah and her sister Edie had come from Eger, together with their mother. They had tried very hard to stay together, for the picture of their father being forcibly taken away was still fresh in their minds. Slowly Edie relaxed, as the lorry started on its journey. To move freely was not possible. The heat was unbearable as the sun beat down from a cloudless sky. The days wore on; the driver and the armed guards alighted periodically to eat and rest. At each stop, the unfortunate innocents cried out for water, and to be allowed out — but no one came. The convoy of sealed cattle trucks waited to move on. Did anyone pass and hear their anguished cries? Did anyone care?

On the following Shabbos they finally reached their destination. Too weak to care, someone remarked as he peered through the narrow slit, "Look, we are being brought to an asylum! Just look at the inmates!" Through the barbed wire surrounding the camp, they saw shaven-headed men and women all dressed in coarse grey garments, staring with blank expressions, with unseeing eyes as if they were blind.

The doors of the trucks were opened and out stumbled the victims, falling into a heap on the ground. Even those who were the healthiest among them at the start of the journey were barely able to stand. They were weak from lack of food and water, and the sudden exposure to sunlight hurt their eyes. Many had succumbed and many more were dying. Malkah and her sister supported an old couple, helping them into the compound, prodded by the rifle-wielding guards.

Hardly had they entered when the infamous selection began. Right: the old people, the mothers with young children; and left: the able-bodied for slave labor. The old lady blessed Malkah before being led away.

The following day, Malkah was standing by the barbed wire looking out with unseeing eyes, just like the others, with the blank stare of the deeply shocked on her face. She was to survive the horrors of Bergen Belsen, and was destined to be Brudi's wife.

There are those who would wish to deny the truth of these monstrous events!

Chapter Twenty-One

The following morning, as Pappa and Brudi were having breakfast in the dining room, a waiter came to their table. "Excuse me, there is a gentleman who wishes to see you. Would you please step outside?" Puzzled as to who it might be, Pappa rose from the table, closely followed by Brudi. The visitor was a police officer, who politely asked them to accompany him to the station. Unable to refuse, they walked across the square to the police station on the opposite side, and were told to wait. No explanation was given. Soon they were joined by the other two Jewish men from their hotel, and a short time later, two women were brought in.

With mounting uneasiness they tried to make light-hearted conversation. Finally an officer informed them that they were under arrest. Asked on what charge, the officer shrugged his shoulders: he did not know, and since it was Sunday, he could not find out because all the government bureaus were closed. Their combined pleadings and protestations were to no avail. He marched them to the prison cells and the door clanged shut behind them.

The cells, designed to hold two prisoners each, now held four. Pappa and Brudi found their roommates to be old-timers, two locals who had been caught at petty thieving. Cheerfully they informed Pappa that his crime was far worse: the authorities did not deal kindly with people who were caught trying to illegally cross the border into Portugal!

"You will be taken to one of the prisons near Madrid," they informed Pappa and Brudi. "It has a terrible reputation. Here at least we are treated well and do get three meals a day."

Each morning, and also at midday, they were given a bread roll made of a mixture of corn and wheat flour, with a mug of coffee; and in the evening they were handed a tin plate of bean soup with potatoes.

It was useless to protest to the warders, and they were not allowed to see the governor of the prison. Two weeks passed without any indication as to their fate. Then suddenly, and without any explanation, they were marched back to the police station. With mounting apprehension they waited once again in the anteroom as the other prisoners from their original group were brought in. Then the officer in charge informed those assembled that there had been a mistake, and they were now free to leave! He could give no more information because, as he said, "It is Sunday and all government offices are closed." Then, casting a sympathetic glance at their relieved faces, he added, "I advise you not to stay in Vigo!"

They walked back to the hotel, where the owner had kept their few possessions in his office. Pappa had thought of a plan, so he asked the hotel keeper to keep their small parcel a little longer, as he had business to arrange. The man nodded his head understandingly.

Pappa wasted no time in seeking out his contact, who was still sitting where Pappa had last seen him. No wonder in a small village such as this everybody knew what went on!

"Ten o'clock tonight," he said, as if the last two weeks had never happened.

Elated, Pappa went back to the hotel. He and Brudi had something to eat, paid their bill, and then waited for the time to tick by. "Tonight is the first night of Chanukah," Pappa told Brudi, trying to be cheerful. "That is a good omen, and a propitious time for us, *Hashem* willing." Pappa prayed fervently for a safe crossing, aware of the dangers they would have to face. Finally ten o'clock came. As the village clock struck the hour, a car drew up alongside the two lonely figures, sitting at a table in the deserted café, prey to doubts and fears.

Pappa and Brudi could hardly squeeze into the car, as it was almost full with the other two men from the hotel, the two women they had met at the police station, and one newcomer, an old lady.

Two hours later the car stopped outside an apparently deserted wooden shack in a forest clearing. A man came out and joined the driver, and together they led the fugitives up a steep slope. Higher and higher they climbed, occasionally stopping to let the old lady catch up. Everyone took it in turn to help her make progress, for she was beginning to have difficulty with her breathing, but she would not permit them to slow down. A few moments' rest, and she would resume the difficult climb over the unseen terrain as the heavy clouds hid the light from the moon, giving them the protection they needed. Suddenly they came to a halt. They could hear a river flowing. They had reached the edge of a cliff, a sheer drop to the torrent below.

As they wondered what would happen next, they watched the two men busying themselves with some rope. Leaning over the cliff edge, the men fastened the rope to a wheel hidden inside a crevice. One of the men cupped his hands over his mouth and called out; from the opposite side someone replied, and instantly the rope tightened across the ravine; they could hear the wheels of the pulley squeaking and could only guess at the distance separating them from the other side.

Their two guides produced a heavy rope, similar to the one strung across the ravine, but theirs had the ends knotted together, forming a circle. Looped over the line, the rope hung down, resembling a crude swing. This, they intimated — pointing to the swinging rope — was now ready to take them across. Everyone looked aghast! Surely these two burly Spaniards could not possibly be serious! People in their right senses would never risk their lives dangling underneath what was no more than a glorified clothesline! A heated argument ensued. They had not come this far to be dashed against the shadowy rocks looming in the darkness, to be washed away by the rushing waters below! No one was prepared to be the first.

One of the guides took the initiative. In a soothing voice he said, pointing at Brudi, "Take this lad; he weighs the least of you all. He will go first and you can all see how safe and easy it is."

Brudi was terrified, but nevertheless he agreed to be the first. Once the decision was made, he felt impatient to proceed. Two strong arms held him as he lowered himself into the swaying rope; he tried to sit down as the voices now coming from above urged him to hold on tightly to the rope with both hands. The instant they let go of him, Brudi's weight caused him to plummet into a seemingly bottomless abyss. He screamed out in terror, *"Shema Yisrael!"* — convinced that he would be smashed against the rocks below. After what seemed like an eternity, the left side of his head banged against the opposite cliff. Dazed and bleeding, he felt strong arms lifting him, urging him to let go of the ropes. The next moment he was lying on the ground, and could hear the sound of the rope being pulled back for the next passenger.

Scarcely able to believe that he was still alive, he watched anxiously as one of the younger women was hauled over to his side. As soon as the rope slackened, the men on the other side winched it across. The next one to arrive was the old lady. Brudi marveled at her courage as she sank uncomplainingly to the ground. She had her eyes closed, her head resting against a clump of earth. He could not quite make out her features in the greyness of early dawn. What had compelled such an old lady to undertake this arduous escape?

At last Pappa was helped over to Brudi's side. Like everyone else, he too needed a few moments of rest on the firm ground to reassure himself that all was well.

A few moments later Pappa unbuttoned his jacket to retrieve his worn velvet pouch with his *tallis* and *tefillin*. Against all odds, he had managed to preserve them intact. Brudi felt his right-hand pocket; he too had carried his *tefillin* in his pocket since leaving Antwerp, but it was not as bulky as Pappa's *tallis* bag.

Their new guides indicated that it was time to move on. It was heartening to hear them talking in an unfamiliar language, proof that they were in Portugal at last. Slowly, following their leader, the Jews descended into the valley, where they were told to wait. The guides left them. An hour passed; they were tired and hungry and above all afraid of being detected, and by now were beginning to suspect that no one would come to help them. Maybe the guides had been caught themselves, or had simply left them to their own devices.

The bedraggled group never did find out, for suddenly in the distance dogs could be heard barking. Perhaps it was a border patrol looking for illegal refugees? They made a quick decision to move on to a village which was just becoming visible as daylight broke through the clouds.

It was still very early as they approached the village: only one house had lights on. Quietly they walked up to the shuttered windows. One man lifted Brudi onto his shoulders and told him to look through the gap in the shutters; Brudi reported seeing three men sitting around a table. After a short consultation in muffled voices, it was decided to take the risk and knock on the door. To their relief and delight, they had come to the village bakery! The bread was in the oven and the men were waiting for it to bake.

With sign language and imagination, they explained their plight and begged, "Please, no police!" The baker nodded in agreement. With more gesticulations they requested transport, producing Spanish money to help the men understand. They understood.

By now the bread was baked and each fugitive was given a piping hot bun. Never had bread tasted quite so delicious.

After they had eaten, they paid for their promised transport, and the baker seemed quite happy to change their pesetas into local currency. Grateful for his wonderful hospitality and help, they thanked him warmly as they hurried out to look for the car waiting outside. However, instead of a car they found a hearse! The driver alighted from his carriage, patting the horse reassuringly. The carriage itself was built not unlike a large four-poster, the coffin in the middle with benches at its head and foot. It had a rail with black velvet curtains around the outside of the four pillars, presumably to allow the mourners to grieve in privacy. The three ladies were helped into the carriage and were seated at the head, the three men were seated facing the women, with the coffin between them. The curtains were drawn. Brudi was invited to sit next to the driver, and away they went.

The horse's hooves could be heard clip-clopping down the road at a respectful pace. As they passed through another, larger, village an hour later, a policeman on duty in the village square held up his hand to stop all other traffic and allow the hearse to continue on its way unhindered. People along the way greeted the passing hearse, raising their hats, as it slowly wended its way towards the cemetery.

Brudi enjoyed his brief moment of importance as he sat perched on his elevated seat beside the tobacco-chewing coachman. Once out of the town they picked up speed, arriving at the cemetery only half an hour later.

"That's it!" announced the driver, getting down from his seat and pulling aside the curtains. "You will have to continue on your own from here." All their protests were to no avail.

"You must understand," he said, "that if I were to drive on, I would invite suspicion. This is as far as I can take you."

"Don't leave us stranded, not knowing which way to go! We are sure to be picked up and sent back over the border! You can't do that to us!" they pleaded. But he could, and he did.

"You walk in that direction," he said, pointing south, "and you will soon come across a railway line, no more than a mile or two from here. Follow the tracks, and you will arrive at the next railway station."

Dismayed by this turn of events, they started walking in the direction they were given, and eventually reached the station. After some deliberation it was decided that the safest plan would be for them to go to Lisbon, and were told a suitable train was due in at midday. After buying their tickets they sat down to wait. Lisbon would not be too bad; it was a capital city, a long way from the border, and known to have a Jewish community and many refugees.

"The American Jewish Joint Distribution Committee has its headquarters in Lisbon," the old lady said. "They are very good, providing hundreds of families with their basic needs and assisting them to travel on." Brudi wondered if she was Jewish.

Everyone jumped to their feet as soon as the train came into view, boarded it, and dispersed throughout the open carriage, as they did not want to draw attention to themselves. Pappa sighed with relief; he did not care if the train did stop at all stations on the way. For the moment he was content to reflect on their incredible escape, a great stride nearer to his ultimate goal. He looked at Brudi, blissfully watching the landscape flashing by. The lad was in his teens, but now mature far beyond his years. Perhaps they would soon be free...

The train jolted to a stop at the next station. Pappa stiffened as he saw two policemen standing on the platform, waiting for a few passengers to alight. They boarded the train and slowly, deliberately, scrutinized the faces of the passengers. Pappa and Brudi watched with mounting fear as they picked out one by one the men and women from their original party, only ignoring the old woman, who had been sitting halfway down the compartment. They approached Pappa and Brudi and demanded to see their papers. They had none, so once again they were under arrest and marched off the train. They were driven in a convoy to the nearest city, Oporto, which is, as its name suggests, a harbor.

At the police station they were treated well, given food to eat, and politely listened to. They spent that night at the station. To their immense relief, the powers-that-be chose not to send them back over the border; however, still under arrest, they heard they were to be split up and placed in a number of different prisons around the Lisbon area. No one cared where they were taken as long as they could remain in this land with its friendly people. An almost light-hearted mood prevailed as they once again climbed into the cars waiting to take them to their destination.

Sometime around midday they stopped outside a somber-looking prison facade, and Pappa and Brudi were handed over to the care of the prison warden. Once they had reached the inner office, the police escort was permitted to leave and the two prisoners waited to be taken to their cells, believing this to be just a formality which would eventually lead to their freedom.

A prison officer came into the room and issued an order. The guard standing at attention came over to Pappa and Brudi and indicated that they were to empty their pockets. Pappa did so, hesitating for a moment when asked to place the *tallis* bag which he still held onto the table with the rest of his belongings. They were led out into a long corridor. Facing the room they had just vacated, against the opposite wall, were three large metal cages stretching along the length of the wall, each holding approximately fifteen prisoners. The door of the middle one was opened, and Pappa and Brudi were told to step inside. The heavy iron door was closed behind them.

They watched, dazed, as the guard locked the heavy padlock. There was a constant clanging and squeaking of rusty hinges as the doors were opened to receive a new recruit or let someone out. These three cages were not used for prolonged incarceration, but only to house prisoners in transit. "Most stay no longer than a few hours," they were told by a French-speaking inmate. "The only ones to stay longer are the vagabonds picked up during the night and not released until the morning."

Brudi noticed a bucket in the far corner. *I could not possibly use that! I am sure that I will be able to wait until we are transferred*, he thought, reassuring himself. Hours passed and night descended. Prisoners were taken away and new ones arrived. Guards were changed, and still they were not called. Pappa called to the guard pacing up and down. He stopped and listened to Pappa's appeal, went away, then came back and resumed his vigil outside the cages.

Two guards arrived, wheeling a large black metal pot. It was the only meal served during the whole day, for those unfortunates who had to stay over until the following morning, and it was now becoming clear to Pappa and Brudi that they were among those chosen ones. They were desperately thirsty as well as hungry, for they had last eaten at the police station in Vigo early that morning.

Each prisoner was handed a tin plate. It was difficult to see what was in the large pan so they waited with patient expectation for the inmates of the first cage to be served. At last it was their turn. The bars of the cages were too close together to allow the ladle with the hot food through; the gap from the floor to the bottom of the door was just high enough to allow the guard to push the ladle in and pour its contents into the plate placed just inside the iron gate. Horrified, they looked at the gruel on their plates. Never during all their experiences had they been offered such revolting food — it looked and smelled vile! Starving though they were, neither would even taste it, but preferred to wait until the following morning. Dejected, they lay down on the floor, hoping that sleep and oblivion would soon overtake them.

With the new dawn came renewed hope. Surely someone would remember, and release them from their present incarceration! They were weak from the lack of food. If only they could be taken out into the fresh air to relieve themselves — but their pleadings fell on deaf ears. Could the guards be really unaware that two of the inmates had been there since the previous day? Thus the second day passed, with the now-familiar clanging and banging of the cage doors.

Once again it was evening and the meal of the day was being served through the gap between the floor and the cage. This time Pappa and Brudi took their turns holding out their plates. The grey mess on the plate looked and smelled no less obnoxious than before, but they ate it. The prisoners who had only recently been brought in refused to touch the food... Another night began. Pappa let the tears flow freely as he fervently prayed for *Hashem* to deliver them from this prison. Brudi too found relief in a flood of tears.

Time had lost all meaning. Brudi guessed it must be late morning when he heard someone calling to him in Yiddish. "Psst! Come over here. What are Jews like you doing in a third-class prison?"

Brudi looked up in the direction from which he had heard the voice. High up in the brick wall near the cage, he could just make out a face at a barred open window. Poor fellow, thought Brudi, no wonder his mind is unhinged. He wondered sadly how long it would be before he too became deranged.

"Psst!" The man beckoned. Not wanting to upset him, Brudi moved further to the back of the cage so he could almost touch the wall. "What do you want?" Brudi asked kindly.

"Don't be silly," came the impatient reply. "What are you doing in this third-class prison? You should demand immediately to be transferred into the first-class section."

Brudi just stared in disbelief. The poor man!

"Boy!" the man almost shouted. "Who is the Jew with the beard?"

"My father."

"Well, go and fetch him."

Brudi went to call Pappa, who was at that moment trying unsuccessfully to get the attention of the guard. He tried to explain the situation to Pappa and asked him to go to the back of the cage and maybe calm the poor Jew behind those barred windows.

Pappa listened to the man patiently, and asked him a few questions. Returning to Brudi, he said, "I know it sounds unbelievable, but I do think he is telling the truth. He is trying to help us, so what have we to lose?" Pappa thanked their new friend, then told Brudi to call out to the guard in Spanish (which Brudi spoke quite well), demand to be taken to the first-class section, and say that they had money to pay for it. There was no reaction from the guard, who continued to pace up and down.

"Did you say you had money to pay for first-class?" It was one of the prisoners in their cage! He was a Spaniard, and a petty thief.

"We have," answered Brudi.

"*Allo!*" called their interpreter to the guard, and in Portuguese continued, "these two want to pay for first-class!" The guard stopped in front of them and asked a question; presumably whether the information was correct. They nodded. At that, the guard marched into the office. A short time later he re-emerged and resumed his pacing. "That did not work," Brudi remarked, hardly surprised, though he felt disappointed. Within half an hour, however, an officer came to the cage and asked, "Have you really got money to pay for first-class?"

"Sure," said Brudi, almost convincing himself.

"Get these prisoners out of here and take them to the first-class section," the officer commanded.

So it really was true! They were taken along a narrow corridor and up the stairs; hence the high barred window. The first-class prison cells were on the first floor. *Who would believe it*, Brudi marveled, *such luxury!* The floor was divided into approximately twelve individual cells, most of which were occupied, each having its own bed and blanket.

But the greatest luxury of all: water! There was water to drink and water for washing — and a toilet!

"Psst!" called a familiar voice as they passed the locked door of one of the cells. "I told you!"

"But we have no money!" Pappa replied, hoping the guard did not understand.

"None of us have," the man answered. "A representative from the Joint Distribution Committee calls daily, and he will pay for you. We also have our food brought in. You will see."

The following day a representative did come. He wrote down Pappa's and Brudi's names, ages, and country of origin, and asked many other questions. He assured Pappa of their unceasing efforts on behalf of the many illegal Jewish refugees constantly streaming into the country. Meanwhile he would provide them with the few comforts that they were allowed. After his visit, days stretched into weeks while they waited for news.

It must have been in the middle of the night when Brudi was awakened. The jailer had unexpectedly switched on the lights in the corridor, illuminating the little cells. *What's going on?* he wondered. The prison governor himself was talking and laughing with his assistant. The prisoners, startled by the unusual commotion, were watching the warden pacing up and down the corridor, peeping into the cells. Having established that all were awake, he declared, "Gentlemen, do you know what day this is? It is the first day of January, 1943! A Happy New Year to you all! To celebrate, it is our tradition to pardon one prisoner. As your governor, it is my prerogative to choose whom to pardon."

Every prisoner held his breath, willing the warden to look his way. The tension was palpable as he scrutinized each face, enjoying the drama he was creating. Abruptly stopping in front of one cell, he called to the guard, "Open this door, I have made my choice!" Then stopping in front of Brudi's cell, he chuckled. "You know what? I have decided to pardon not one, but two. Release the boy at once!" he commanded. Then he walked away.

Brudi argued that he was not going to leave without Pappa. "You must go," Pappa urged. "We have been given the address of the Joint in Lisbon; go and see them, and beg them to obtain our release. You can be of far greater service to us in that way than if you refuse to go."

Reluctantly Brudi allowed himself to be propelled down the stairs and ushered out the prison gate by a janitor impatient to rejoin his mates in their New Year's revelry. The gate slammed shut behind Brudi and the other pardoned man, leaving two lonely figures stranded outside the prison gates, hardly able to communicate. They peered out into the darkness, as the street lights were out, and wondered where to go: the streets were deserted. They were just about to walk away, when they heard footsteps approaching. Soon, the figure of a man appeared; he had the black hair and dark complexion of the natives. The man with Brudi approached him, and he stopped. Brudi listened, catching an odd word here or there as the ex-prisoner explained their predicament. "Could you please direct us to a place where we can spend the night?"

"Come with me," said the stranger. They followed him to his apartment, and gratefully accepted a cup of freshly brewed black coffee. This did not stop Brudi from sleeping soundly, bedded down on the floor.

Next morning they thanked their benefactor and went out into the street, where they parted company. Brudi could not help reflecting that if it were not for this man, he would no doubt have spent the night somewhere out in the open.

He must not waste time, he decided — he had a mission to fulfill at a destination he first must reach. Every town had a taxi service, but it was not always easy to differentiate their cars from the private ones. Brudi finally hailed a taxi as it was cruising past, then handed the driver the piece of paper with the address.

"Ah, Lisbon," said the driver, pleased to have picked up a long-distance fare. An hour later they arrived outside the office of the American Jewish Joint Distribution Committee, a veritable haven for the tattered remnants of European Jewry. (The whole-hearted dedication of this organization towards helping penniless Jews is worth noting. Its representatives are remembered fondly by thousands of their once-hunted fellow Jews who were treated with kindness and sympathy upon their arrival from war-torn Europe.)

While someone paid the taxi driver, Brudi was welcomed and given some food to eat. He listened to the hum of activity while munching his roll and sipping coffee. An efficient-looking young woman approached, holding a questionnaire; she sat down next to him and patiently extracted the information needed to complete her dossier. "I know your father is still in prison; we have someone working very hard for his release and for that of many other refugees, too. Come, we will take you to one of the most prominent men in the Jewish community here. Although in business himself, he has well-placed influential friends who have promised to help. He knows about you, and wants to meet you," she said, getting up.

A car arrived to take Brudi, accompanied by a representative, to meet this man, and drove them to the smartest district of Lisbon. Stopping outside a most imposing apartment building, Brudi was very conscious of his shabby crumpled suit, so out of place in the spacious, gleaming portal. His companion knocked on the door of the first-floor apartment. It was opened by a stately middle-aged man, Mr. Ricardo, wearing an exquisite dressing robe of shimmering, deep-blue embossed silk. Brudi, with an involuntary movement, shrank back; then the next moment he was welcomed into the luxurious study. The heavy blue velvet curtains perfectly matched the padded seats of the comfortable high-backed chairs. The carpet, too, matched the prevailing colors.

Brudi blushed as he felt the kindly gaze of his host resting on him. To his relief, this man whose looks were so typical of the Latin population asked him questions in fluent Yiddish. This had the desired effect of putting Brudi at ease: he found it easy to talk to this gracious man. Mr. Ricardo explained to Brudi that, within a matter of days, he hoped to finalize the release of all the Jewish refugees from the prison.

"I understand your deep concern for your father. Let me assure you that it will not be for long. Arrangements have almost been completed to transfer the refugees. Two seaside holiday resorts are at this very moment preparing to absorb the many homeless Jewish families."

Arrangements were made for Brudi's temporary shelter, and when they drove back to the Joint office, someone offered to take Brudi to visit Pappa. Brudi told Pappa all that had happened, assuring him that in a few days he too would be free, along with all the other innocent victims.

As it transpired, events moved faster than expected, and by the following afternoon all Jewish refugees were being collected from the prison detention camps.

The Portuguese philanthropist came personally to collect Brudi from his lodgings. "Come, my boy, this is a great day for us Jews and a proud day in the history of this democratic country. I want you to come with me in my car." Brudi protested shyly. "Do not worry," laughed his benefactor. "I have a surprise for you. You will meet your father in much happier circumstances. Come on, let's go."

With this he ushered Brudi out of the house and into his waiting car. He drove to a large square in the town, where Brudi saw four big coaches full of people. The philanthropist, in high spirits, explained that these buses were full of people just released from detention who would now be given a decent place to live, and would also receive financial help. Forestalling Brudi's question, he chuckled. "Don't worry! Your father is in one of those coaches and you will meet him at our destination."

Their arrival in the square seemed to be the signal for the buses to start their journey. Brudi's car appeared to lead the way, with the coaches following. It all seemed like a fairy tale to Brudi; he did not dare to speak lest he break the spell, but peered behind him at the following coach, hoping to glimpse Pappa. The journey would have been so much more enjoyable if he could have been absolutely sure that Pappa was with them. "Don't you believe me?" asked Mr. Ricardo. "You will soon be reunited. Look!" he said, pointing ahead. They had driven into the seaside town of Ericeira, and were heading towards the town square, with the imposing Town Hall ahead of them. On the sweeping stairs in front of the building stood the mayor in full regalia, the local dignitaries around him. In the center of the square stood the standard-bearer, accompanied by the local band. They struck up a tune as soon as the convoy approached.

Someone stepped forward to open the car door as they came to a halt right in front of the mayor's party. Totally bewildered, Brudi did not know where to look first. The town's population had turned out for the occasion. The local and national press was well represented, positioned at a respectful distance just behind and to the left of the mayor. To his right Brudi noticed with alarm what appeared to be press and newsreel cameras, which came to life with bulbs flashing as soon as he and Mr. Ricardo stepped out of their car. Meanwhile, the coaches had stopped, the refugees started streaming out, and the band escorted the bewildered groups towards the reception party. Brudi sprinted towards Pappa as soon as he spotted him in the crowd. This was the cue Mr. Ricardo had been waiting for; he signaled the film crew to train their lenses on the tearful reunion. Then the reception committee with their guests moved into the Town Hall. More formalities followed, with the camera crew busily recording this momentous occasion. Finally they were taken in groups to the three large hotels where accommodations had been prepared for them.

What a day it had been! A day which had started out with the prisoners being collected with no indication as to their destination, and fearful of being deported. They had been driven first to Lisbon, and it was not until they had witnessed the incredible reception prepared for them in Ericeira that it finally sank in that this time, not only had they been freed, but given official recognition.

Chapter Twenty-Two

Never, since Hitler had come to power, had the refugees been made to feel welcome before. They lacked nothing in their luxurious hotel: comfortable rooms, hot and cold water, service, and all the food they wished — all these were provided for them. The air was full of light-hearted chatter as the refugees enjoyed their first meal in freedom.

Pappa and Brudi shared a table with an elderly couple from Paris who had also spent the last few weeks in prison. They were puzzled when Pappa and Brudi only ordered uncooked food, refusing the many tempting dishes offered. Pappa tried to explain the dietary laws to these totally uncommitted Jews.

Brudi reflected on the irony of this situation. He wondered how many more Jewish people there were in Europe who had lost touch with their Jewish heritage, but had, nonetheless, suffered the same fate as the observant Jews. Brudi watched the old lady as she listened with total concentration to Pappa's explanation. He could not help but pity her: to have to suffer, so late in life, such indignities, deprivations and hardships, without the inner strength of faith to sustain her.

The following morning, as everyone came into the dining room for breakfast, Pappa approached each table asking whether the other guests were willing to form a delegation for the purpose of requesting permission to rent apartments. He pointed out the advantages of such a request.

"Surely," he explained, misreading their hesitation, "the Joint

Distribution Committee would agree to our request since it must be very costly to keep us in such luxury."

But his suggestion was met with ridicule: nobody was prepared to leave the pampered security of this four-star hotel. However, that same day Pappa contacted the Joint office. To his great relief, no objections were raised, and Pappa received assistance in finding an apartment which suited his needs.

Pappa and Brudi spent the next few days looking at rental accommodations. Less then a week after their arrival in Ericeira, they were happily installed in their own comfortable rooms.

While Brudi set about familiarizing himself with his new surroundings, Pappa did not allow himself this luxury; he still had work to accomplish. A Jew must have a place of worship where a quorum of men, a *minyan*, could assemble for prayers. So, once again, he went with a request to the Joint office.

To their credit, no objections were raised. In addition, their representative told Pappa that they had decided to open a branch office in Ericeira. It would be more practical than sending their representative daily from Lisbon. This news was welcomed by the members of the large Jewish community, most of whom seemed likely to stay in Ericeira for the duration of the war.

The following day the Joint's new representative, Mr. Eduardo, introduced himself and announced that he would need an assistant. Brudi eagerly applied for the job, and to his delight and surprise was accepted and immediately given his first assignment.

"Your first job is to find a vacant house which is large enough to serve as the branch office for the Joint Distribution Committee and my living quarters. It should also have sufficient rooms left for use as a synagogue." As an afterthought, Mr. Eduardo added, "When I get back to Lisbon, I will arrange a salary for you."

Brudi was elated. They were going to pay him too! He was the youngest of all the refugees and the first to get a job. He immediately applied himself to the task of finding a suitable building.

Ericeira is a small seaside village perched high above sea level, the temperate climate making it an ideal holiday resort. The town square was its focal point, and this was surrounded by shops and restaurants, with two drug stores to cater to the seasonal influx of visitors.

Brudi found an ideal house just off the square, and waited with mounting excitement for his boss's approval. It was a large old house.

Mr. Eduardo liked the spacious rooms and told Brudi, "I will use the rooms on the right for my private residence and the room facing the stairs will be the office where people can come to see me. This will leave the larger rooms on the left for use as a *shul*." Patting Brudi on the shoulder, he added, "Now run along and organize some furnishings for use in the synagogue. You will need a carpenter to make the *shtenders* (lecterns), and so on. And I will attend to the lease of the building."

Having obtained the name of the local carpenter from the hotel proprietor, and arranged for his services, Pappa, helped by Brudi, drafted the layout for the interior of the synagogue. The carpenter made the Ark to hold the Torah scroll which they had been promised by the Joint Committee in Lisbon. He also carved two beautiful, ornate candlesticks out of wood.

It was a proud moment for Brudi when, four weeks later, he put the final touches to his handiwork. So much effort had gone into producing the large signs with the bold Hebrew letters, which he now carefully nailed to the walls.

Pappa felt immense pride in his son as he watched Brudi admiring his work. "This evening we will conduct our first service," Pappa said happily.

It was not long before the other Jewish refugees came to admire the new synagogue, and to Pappa's delight he had no difficulty arranging regular services twice daily.

Soon people tired of being served their meals in the hotel and having nothing to do. They gradually followed Pappa's example and set up homes for themselves. The old couple moved into a pleasant little villa where Pappa and Brudi became frequent visitors.

Though resigned to remaining in Ericeira for the duration of the war, the favorite topic of conversation was about the future, once the Germans were defeated — no matter how long it would take. Most of the younger members of their group hoped to settle in what was then Palestine, the ancient Jewish homeland. Consequently, a committee was formed and representations made to the local authorities with a view to acquiring land for farming. These young idealists wanted to utilize their time constructively, and learn about farming in a practical way, until such time as they would be allowed into Palestine.

Once again the Joint Committee stepped in and was instrumental in acquiring a sizable plot of land which had not been farmed.

Thus a *hachsharah* program was established. A lorry would arrive at 4:30 A.M. every morning to collect the volunteers. Work would commence at 5:00 A.M. They spent the first few months just digging the earth. Brudi, too, had joined the group, not out of any idealistic sentiments, but just as a welcome diversion. Although it was still only February, the weather was warm and dry, and ideal for outdoor work.

Brudi only worked until 8:00 A.M. and was always back for morning prayers. His job with the Joint office did not start until ten o'clock, and he finished there at one P.M.

Next the newly formed committee set their sights on forming a social club for the benefit of the refugees. Soccer was the most popular sport voted for, with an amateur dramatic society for the less active. A soccer match was arranged between the local club versus the refugee club. This proved so successful that the theater group wanted the locals to see their show too. Since the players had come from many different parts of Europe, and spoke different languages, all the plays were performed in Yiddish, the one common language. What the locals made of this performance in a totally foreign tongue can only be guessed at; let it suffice that they did not attend any subsequent shows!

❀ ❀ ❀

Meanwhile, Pappa had requested permission to travel to Lisbon. There he contacted the British consul and applied for a visa to England. This became a regular journey. He would take the bus in the morning, and return the same evening with renewed hope. Meanwhile, the days stretched into weeks and months.

One joyous evening Pappa returned to Ericeira with two visas — one for himself and one for Brudi. Now came the next hurdle: to book seats on a flight to England.

"Impossible," he was told by the booking clerk. "We cannot book you in advance; we have to keep the seats for important people."

One day, as Pappa presented himself at the booking office, the ticket clerk confided to Pappa, "You son is still a minor. If he were to present himself alone, he would have a much better chance of getting a flight. Let him stay here in Lisbon so he can come over twice a day; that way I may get him on a plane."

Pappa was overjoyed. At last they had been given hope! He did not hesitate to let Brudi go. Before returning to Ericeira, he visited the

Joint office. They promised to arrange accommodations for Brudi with a Jewish family in Lisbon while he awaited a flight.

Brudi was reluctant to leave Pappa behind but was finally persuaded to go to Lisbon. A hasty farewell party was arranged, for he had become a popular member of this close-knit community. It was now the end of September, 1943; they had lived in this village for the last nine months. It had never really been home, yet parting was an emotional event.

He settled in nicely with the friendly family chosen for him; they originated from Poland but had lived for many years in Portugal. The weeks went by uneventfully. Brudi would present himself twice daily at the airport booking office, to no avail. He kept in touch with Pappa through the Joint office. They allowed him the use of their telephone and Pappa would go to the local branch at a prearranged time. Brudi spent *Rosh HaShanah* and *Yom Kippur* with the family in Lisbon.

One day, upon arriving at the airport, he was told to come back that afternoon with his belongings. Brudi sprinted to the Joint office to tell them the news, then phone Pappa. They said a tearful goodbye. Brudi arrived at the airport at the given time and was told to wait. Hours passed until, as the night closed in, he was told that no flight was available — all seats had been taken. Sadly he returned to his lodgings. From then on he spent every day at the airport with his meager belongings. It was a difficult, nerve-racking time; not all flights leaving Lisbon would arrive safely at their destination; many were shot down by enemy planes.

Then one day, when Brudi presented himself, he was told that there was a seat available. There was no time even to notify Pappa. Someone from the Joint Committee would have to tell him.

Hardly comprehending what was happening, Brudi let himself be taken onto a plane. The doors were shut, and they were airborne! He soon struck up a conversation with the man seated next to him. His name was Mr. Schwartz, and he was the head of the Joint Distribution Committee. He told Brudi that he frequently traveled with a diplomatic passport; this enabled him to continue to carry on the organization's vital work.

The flight took many hours. Finally they arrived at an unmarked British airfield. Brudi spent the next two weeks in a military barracks, where he was the youngest and the only civilian.

He was interrogated by a succession of officers, first in French and then in Yiddish. It was clear that they were hoping that he would be able to supply them with fresh information. Brudi readily answered all their questions, but never discovered whether he managed to be of use.

At the end of the second week he was taken by car to Stamford Hill, London. Brudi was able to give them the address of Esti, who had gotten married the previous year and moved back to London with her husband.

❧ ❧ ❧

Four weeks later, Pappa too was flown to England. At long last, after three and a half years of separation, we — one of the very few Jewish families to survive the war intact — were joyfully reunited.